DANCING
WITH THE
DOCTOR

'Lorna Jowett's indispensable *Dancing with the Doctor* offers a fascinating look at how gender is represented on-screen in the series (and its spin-offs) ... offering detailed but accessible discussion of key characters, episodes and staff, together with analysis of the series' fandom, the book will be vital to all those interested in a new perspective on the worlds of *Doctor Who.*'

Rebecca Williams, University of South Wales,
author of *Fast-Object Fandom*

DANCING
WITH THE
DOCTOR

Dimensions of Gender
in the *Doctor Who* Universe

LORNA JOWETT

I.B. TAURIS

LONDON · NEW YORK

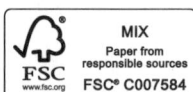

MIX
Paper from
responsible sources
FSC
www.fsc.org
FSC® C007584

Published in 2017 by
I.B.Tauris & Co. Ltd
London • New York
www.ibtauris.com

Who Watching

ISBN: 978 1 78453 374 8
eISBN: 978 1 78672 146 4
ePDF: 978 1 78673 146 3

A full CIP record for this book is available from the British Library
A full CIP record is available from the Library of Congress

Library of Congress Catalog Card Number: available

Text design and typesetting by Tetragon, London
Printed and bound in Sweden by ScandBook AB

CONTENTS

ACKNOWLEDGEMENTS

This book would never have been written were it not for Kim Akass inviting me to speak on gender and *Doctor Who*, initially at a one-day symposium and then as a keynote speaker at the academic 50th anniversary conference Walking in Eternity in 2013 at the University of Hertfordshire. Following my keynote speech, Philippa Brewster from I.B.Tauris persuaded me that there should be a book on gender and *Who*, and the project evolved from there. Thanks, Kim and Philippa, for encouraging me to stir things up.

The supportive and perceptive comments of the anonymous reviewer appointed by I.B.Tauris were incredibly helpful, both in reassuring me that this book was worth writing, and in pointing out some areas for improvement.

Thanks are also due to members of the Summer and Autumn Writing Clubs, whose Facebook sharing of just how hard it is to write a book was incredibly supportive. In addition, as any full-time academic knows, the book would not have been completed without the support (verbal, practical and emotional) of my immediate work colleagues. Thanks, Kate, for allowing me the flexibility to fit this in, and my gratitude goes out to all the MY14ers at the University of Northampton.

Stacey Abbott and Bronwen Calvert deserve special mention – our mutual friendship, debate, commentary and sometimes just plain silliness is the definition of academic community. Long live The Trio.

My sister, Fiona, and her three daughters, Eilidh, Ciorstan and Iona, have all contributed to my thinking on the *Who* series and to the material in this book, not least by forcibly persuading me to watch *The Sarah Jane Adventures*. Thanks, girls.

And finally, I am indebted to Verity Lambert, Elisabeth Sladen, Julie Gardner, and all the women who helped make *Doctor Who* the global success it still is, more than 50 years after its debut.

INTRODUCTION

'I make it up as I go along. But trust me, I've got history.'
The Tenth Doctor, 'The Runaway Bride'
Doctor Who 2006 Christmas special

As one of the longest running science fiction television series ever, *Doctor Who* has proved its adaptability and its success in terms of longevity: in 2013 it celebrated its 50th year. Like other British franchises featuring male heroes, various actors have played the lead role while striving to retain a core sense of the character and the stories he functions within. Certainly there have been many changes to perceptions and representations of gender since the 1960s. This book, then, gathers together and develops discussion around gender representation in the franchise, looking specifically at how *Doctor Who* has 'rebooted' its gender representation for a twenty-first-century audience since 2005.

The series set a precedent for reinventing itself when the premise of Time Lord regeneration was introduced in 1966 because William Hartnell could not continue in the central role. Like both *Star Trek* on television, and the *James Bond* film series, *Doctor Who* adopts particular strategies for updating and refreshing its formula. The spin-off series *Torchwood* (2006–11) and *The Sarah Jane Adventures* (2007–11) also provide new opportunities for renegotiation of gender representation in programmes that are less constrained by a long history and established conventions. Aspects of gender as presented in a range of *Doctor Who* texts (from the series itself, to its spin-offs, *Torchwood* and *The Sarah Jane Adventures*, to 'minisodes', narrative extensions and other paratexts) are explored in the book, and a variety of perspectives on television cultures, narratives and the TV industry are used to illuminate them.

I am acutely aware that debates about gender, especially in *Doctor Who* itself, have raged and will doubtless continue to rage, with viewers and commentators offering widely differing interpretations of gender roles in the programmes and their paratexts, of the duty and responsibility involved in creating popular television drama, and of the mission of public service broadcasting.

Ever since the reboot of *Doctor Who* in 2005, the series, and its expanding franchise, has come under scrutiny for its representations (of race, ethnicity, nationality and sexuality, as well as gender), as might be expected of a flagship BBC production. One headline in a news article covering the publication of Lindy Orthia's edited collection of essays, *Doctor Who and Race*, blared 'Doctor Who "Thunderously Racist"' (*Telegraph* 2013), presumably in an effort to stir up opinion. Yet a decade after the reboot proved that *Doctor Who* could still engage a contemporary audience, diversity and representation seem to be high on the agenda, attracting comment and debate in mainstream news outlets, as well as on social media and the blogosphere, especially when the focus is a major franchise. Marvel's superhero films have come in for criticism, and speculation about how *Star Wars: The Force Awakens* (2015) would negotiate such issues, given its casting of a young white female and a young black male in lead roles, was succeeded by debates about how effective the characters were. Its huge success on opening weekend suggests that either these things attract audiences or, perhaps, that they do not actively discourage them. When the trailer for the next *Star Wars* film, *Rogue One* – clearly featuring another female lead – was released in April 2016, further debate ensued.

In terms of *Doctor Who*, now the only continuing television series in the *Who* stable, things have also been shaken up, perhaps in response to such criticism. With the announcement that actor Matt Smith was giving up playing the Doctor in 2013, speculation erupted about whether a female or a non-white actor might finally be cast. When Peter Capaldi, at 55 an actor much older than previous post-2005 Doctors, was announced as the Twelfth Doctor it seemed an opportunity had been missed. However, his age changed the dynamic, particularly between the Doctor and his female companion, and at the end of the same season, the Doctor's arch-enemy and fellow Time Lord, the Master, was revealed to have transformed into a woman, now calling herself Missy. As Catherine Johnson notes, this 'raised a number of interesting debates around sexuality and gender' (2014), and the range of responses to Missy are discussed at more length in Chapter 6.

At this point, the series was also attracting criticism for not employing more women behind the scenes: there had been a dearth of female writers and directors since Steven Moffat took over as head writer/showrunner in 2010. Whether or not this could be directly attributed to Moffat or, as he argued when challenged about it, that it was partly the nature of the industry, the criticism seemed to bring about some change. Season 9 was heralded with announcements that two female writers were already signed up, as well as two female directors, including some who were returning after having previously directed successful episodes across the franchise. This suggests that the BBC and the *Doctor Who* team are aware of its public position and realise that they need to be seen to be addressing issues of diversity. Moffat is now leaving the series and will be succeeded as showrunner by Chris Chibnall. It seems, then, an appropriate time for this book to take stock of how the series, and its two spin-offs, have negotiated gender.

Like many Britons, I grew up with *Doctor Who*, watching it on television (or hiding my eyes from it), reading the Target novels and occasionally the *Doctor Who* annual. And again, like many others, I stopped watching it before it was cancelled, giving up around the time Peter Davison (Fifth Doctor) handed over to Colin Baker (Sixth Doctor) – though I did watch the Eighth Doctor/Paul McGann TV movie in 1996. By the time the series was rebooted, I had become a television scholar with a special interest in science fiction and fantasy genres, as well as in representations of gender and sexuality. Even if I were not a science fiction fan, nostalgia alone would probably have encouraged me to watch the all-new *Doctor Who* when it debuted in 2005. I watched *Torchwood* out of similar personal and professional interest, and caught up with *The Sarah Jane Adventures* after being told by my sister, whose daughters loved it, that it was at least as good as the other two *Who*-universe series, if not better.

I am still watching *Doctor Who*, though I have become increasingly disillusioned by its politics of gender and sexuality. As a grown woman I am much less likely to accept uncritically that if I want to identify with heroic, active, capable individuals, then I have to align myself with the male role, especially when this role is an alien who need not conform to the gender binaries still marking twenty-first-century Western society. The refreshing thing about *Torchwood* is its casual dismissal of such conventions by one of its main protagonists, Captain Jack Harkness, a time-travelling alien from the future who blithely ignores our 'quaint little categories' (*Torchwood* 'Day One' 1.2) for gender and sexuality. While *The Sarah Jane Adventures* might seem more likely to offer conventional roles since it is a children's drama expected to 'teach' such roles to young viewers, its avoidance of heterosexual romance and focus on an older female character allows it some latitude in avoiding obvious binary gender distinction. Actor Elisabeth Sladen's death in 2011 brought *The Sarah Jane Adventures* to an end, and *Torchwood* has also been off the air since 2011, though another season is not an impossibility. *Doctor Who* continues, holding its position as a flagship BBC production broadcast on its main channel in the UK, with season 8 sold to 198 territories globally, and ranking as the top seller for BBC Worldwide in the year 2014/15 (BBC 2015a).

In writing this book I have tried to curb, if not entirely suspend, my personal likes and dislikes, and to approach the material with appropriate critical distance. Echoing editor Orthia's introduction to *Doctor Who and Race*, I may write as a viewer and a fan, as well as an academic, but this does not necessarily mean I am defending the series. Rather, I strive, as she puts it, to feel 'confident to criticize to the point where' I 'may seem to actively dislike the programme' (2013, p. 295). I am, inevitably, writing as a female viewer and as a scholar influenced by feminism. To draw on feminist theory, the position I aim for here is a deliberate standpoint and as such may be contested and challenged, even dismissed. I take it, aware of its limitations and potential, because it seems necessary to draw attention, at length, to the standpoint of female viewers and feminist scholars of *Doctor Who* and programmes like it. Taking this standpoint enables an exploration of how many female viewers are marginalised by the series and its approaches, as well as feeling disappointed that it does not offer more given its apparently libertarian views.

This position may seem essentialist at times, yet it is undeniable that women currently experience the world differently to men because of inequalities embedded in societies, at the level of assumption, common practice, or creation. Taking the standpoint of female viewer and feminist scholar does not mean that my views, or the views expressed in this book, are universal: the fact that they are not is part of the point. As feminist standpoint theory argues, no account can be universal or objective:

> The traditional starting point for knowledge is the position of the dominant and, despite assumptions to the contrary, that position is ideologically permeated. This results in partial and distorted accounts of reality, which thereby fail to live up to modernistic standards of impartiality, neutrality and universality associated with a commitment to epistemic objectivity (Bowell 2011).

Consequently, I am not offering this book as an objective analysis of *Doctor Who* and its paratexts. Real objectivity, or what Donna Haraway terms 'the God trick' (1988, p. 582), is unachievable. Certainly as a viewer and a scholar I inhabit some dominant positions (in terms of race and class, for example) and some that are more resistant or marginal (gender). Therefore, while my evaluation of how *Doctor Who* and its associated paratexts and contexts may well be 'biased', it is no more or less biased than other forms of 'situated knowledge' (Haraway 1988).

As is always the case, there is too much television to examine every episode of the three *Doctor Who* series in detail. Given that there are many more television episodes comprising *Doctor Who* than its two spin-off series, at times the analysis may seem to favour it, and this is hard to avoid, especially when it is this series that attracts most public attention.

The book examines two main aspects of gender in the *Doctor Who* universe: the first three chapters deal with how gender is represented in the 'text' of the programmes and their extended narratives, while the last three deal with how gender figures in the various contexts surrounding the series. Chapter 1 examines the role of the 'main' character in each of the three series, analysing and comparing the Doctor, Captain Jack Harkness and Sarah Jane Smith as different – and differently gendered – versions of the hero. Broadening the scope to supporting roles and the ensemble cast, Chapter 2 selects particular 'companions' to examine in detail, exploring how male companions operate in *Doctor Who* and how the ensemble casts operate in *Torchwood* and *The Sarah Jane Adventures*. Naturally, gender does not shape identity in a vacuum, and so in the third chapter various dimensions of identity are examined, focusing on how other factors such as race and ethnicity, age and sexuality inflect all three series' representations of gender. The second section opens with a chapter examining paratexts – spin-offs, extended narratives, and the expanded universe of the television creations – addressing consistencies and differences in the way gender is depicted across the transmedia franchise. The production of the series is the focus of Chapter 5, which examines the series in the context of UK television production, looking at the two male showrunners of *Doctor Who*, as well as female writers, directors and producers across all three series. The final chapter shifts from production to reception, examining how promotional material for the series seeks to manage its reception, as well as analysing press coverage and responses from audiences and fans.

While this structure aims to offer the reader an overview of the franchise from various perspectives, it remains an overview, analysing selected examples and thereby inevitably neglecting others. Given the recent number of scholarly articles and informed internet debate around the *Who* universe and its representations of gender (many clustered around the 50th anniversary of *Doctor Who*), it seems likely that other significant examples will be taken up in analysis that might build on, challenge or complement the arguments posed here.

1

MAIN MAN?

While the irascible Twelfth Doctor may have attracted criticism during his initial season (8), season 9 suggested a slightly different approach. As *Vanity Fair* reported, 'When Capaldi's Doctor entered this season riding a tank and wailing on a guitar, audiences knew the Time Lord had undergone a major overhaul' (Robinson 2015). Yet both the tank and the guitar signify traditional constructions of masculinity, suggesting that the 'major overhaul' is relative only to the previous season, and not to the Doctor's long history.

This chapter examines the leading characters in *Doctor Who*, *Torchwood* and *The Sarah Jane Adventures*, focusing on how the Doctor and Jack Harkness offer variant masculinities and comparing these male protagonists with Sarah Jane Smith's version of mature femininity. The centrality of the Doctor, and the nature of Sarah Jane and Jack as companions and recurring characters who eventually take the central role in their own spin-off series, is also considered. As the Introduction has outlined, *Doctor Who* is in a rather unique position in terms of its main character and 'his' representation. The science fiction conceit of Time Lord regeneration means that the Doctor's personality can be rebooted every time a new actor takes on the part. However, the Doctor will always be at the centre of the series and, at the time of writing, has always been presented as 'male'. The first part of this chapter aims to examine what kind of protagonist the Doctor is and how this is gendered. Inevitably, the series is 'stuck with' the Doctor and, while its science fiction premise suggests this is not strictly necessary, its own structures and mythos dictate that its protagonist will continue to be male.

Of course, it is neither the only TV series nor the only contemporary BBC family drama to maintain a male hero. A mainstream TV product does not necessarily have to conform to conventional gender structures even if it is stuck with a premise that seems to uphold them. BBC One's other recent prime-time family dramas like *Merlin* (2008–13) and *Robin Hood* (2006–9) had to negotiate this too, often attempting to impose twenty-first-century models of gender on stories that are, however loosely, set in earlier historical periods and focus on male heroes. Anyone familiar with the complete run of *Robin Hood* knows that the characterisation of Marian as an independent woman was effective. Over two seasons we saw her challenge Robin's authority and heroism, and act the lady by day and a masked superhero fighting for social justice by night. In fact, this representation was so effective it became problematic for the show's narrative and its positioning of Robin as hero: her story concludes by repositioning her as a love object fought over by two men (Robin and Guy) and eventually as Robin's dead true love. In the case of *Merlin*, fantasy allows some latitude in reinterpreting the traditional story and its conventional gendering of heroic king, uniquely powerful wizard and evil witch queen, and a shift in focus from Arthur to Merlin also potentially displaces conventional models of heroism. *Merlin* included the sword-wielding Morgause, but of course she was sister to Morgana and thus more of a female action villain than a hero. (Notably, both Morgause and Morgana have effectively been ousted by Uther and his establishment of a male dynasty). This is a fairly typical strategy: women who have power are positioned as evil. In addition, the colour-blind casting of Guinevere was not entirely well received and, given her role in most versions of the Arthurian story, the series worked hard to give Gwen a real role in the drama, mostly as the working-class (servant girl) moral conscience to Arthur and even sometimes Merlin. She did have one or two fight scenes, but she was never up to Morgause's standard. And once Arthur was king and they were finally married, Gwen had very little to do. Except turn evil at Morgana's behest, of course. The fate of Britain rests on the shoulders of a young man, after all, not a young woman.

Doctor Who has some of the same problems to contend with, and similar strategies are apparent in the rebooted series, as outlined below. The second and third sections of this chapter explore the main characters of the spin-off series *Torchwood* and *The Sarah Jane Adventures*, as Jack Harkness and Sarah Jane Smith move from being companions of the Doctor to protagonists in their own right. Jack may appear to be a regular hero, cast in a typical – perhaps even stereotypical – mould, yet his representation complicates the notion of masculine heroism and offers a more direct critique of traditional masculinity than the Doctor, something partly possible because the series was intended (at least initially) for a niche rather than mainstream channel, and it addresses adult viewers rather than a family audience. Jack also shares *Torchwood* top billing with Gwen Cooper, indicating that this series is not reliant on standard male heroes. *The Sarah Jane Adventures* offers us the first female lead for a series in the 'official' *Doctor Who* universe, and Sarah Jane's age and gender provide new ways to look at heroism and leadership, especially given the series' positioning as a children's drama.

THE DOCTOR: A DIFFERENT HERO?

'If only he wasn't so different.'
'Evolution of the Daleks' 3.5

The Doctor is not a traditional hero, but seems to be a very British one. He tends to prevail through ingenuity, intelligence and persuasion rather than strength and superior firepower. While he is confident, even arrogant, about his own abilities, he often seems rather unassuming until he has scoped out the situation and starts to take charge. The Eleventh Doctor tells Clara that he generally wins through by being able to 'talk very fast, hope something good happens, take all the credit. Generally how it works' ('The Time of the Doctor' 8.X). While this statement is slightly self-critical, it encapsulates the Doctor's low-key 'heroics'.

He is a time traveller, for example, yet his vehicle is far from impressive. It is made of wood and its camouflage mechanism or 'chameleon circuit' is broken. When seeing another spacecraft Donna Noble, companion to the Tenth Doctor, readily points out, 'That's what I call a spaceship. . . You've got a box, he's got a Ferrari' ('Planet of the Ood' 4.3). Although the TARDIS that transports the Doctor always appears as a blue wooden police box, which makes blending in difficult in some of the places visited, the ability to adapt to surroundings is part of the Doctor's character. He is not a 'big damn hero', he is a 'madman with a box' ('The Eleventh Hour' 5.1). When he carries the Olympic torch at the end of 'Fear Her' (2.11) this signals both his exceptional qualities – torchbearers are often successful athletes – and his ability to appear relatively ordinary: in this instance, the Doctor steps in, literally as a man on the street, to continue the relay when a torchbearer collapses. Likewise, his challenges to the domineering Mr Connolly in 'The Idiot's Lantern' (2.7), which eventually encourage Mrs Connolly to throw her husband out, show that he seeks to effect change on a personal scale, as well as in large-scale political conflicts.

As a product of 1960s science fiction, the Doctor is a reasoning protagonist, an extension of the scientific 'boffin', and his rational and intellectual approach distinguishes him from the typical action hero. His apparent pacifism also works to present him as a different kind of hero. While *Star Trek*'s Captain Kirk is aligned with the American action hero and carries a phaser, the Doctor's signature hardware is a screwdriver, not a weapon. When Vincent van Gogh expresses surprise that the Eleventh Doctor will face a monster alone, objecting, 'You're not armed,' the Doctor responds that he has 'overconfidence' and a 'small screwdriver' ('Vincent and the

Doctor' 5.10). This, and many similar incidents, reinforce the notion that while the Doctor may be 'unarmed' he is definitely not 'powerless', as he points out to his arch-enemies, the Daleks, in 'Doomsday' (2.13).

The rebooted series upholds and routinely draws attention to the fact that the Doctor is particularly averse to guns: 'People with guns are usually the enemy in my book,' he heatedly tells companion Martha Jones in 'The Sontaran Stratagem' (4.4). Yet this attitude is sometimes challenged; here Martha retorts, 'If anyone got me used to fighting, it's you.' Later in the same episode, she points out, 'It's alright for you, you can come and go,' referring to the Doctor's ability to move on while others are left to deal with the aftermath of whatever violent action ensues during his latest intervention. The way those around the Doctor often 'get burned' by being 'too close' is emphasised in this and other episodes, and Martha in particular is reminded that although she is the one who actually travels with the Doctor and therefore chooses to put herself in danger, she is not alone in suffering the consequences. Her family also feel the effects of being associated with 'the oncoming storm' ('The Parting of the Ways' 1.13) and have been imprisoned by the Master ('Last of the Time Lords' 3.13).

At times, his attitudes to those who carry guns and fight for what they believe in make the Doctor arrogant. 'I'm trying to stop the fighting,' he says with exasperation in 'The Doctor's Daughter' (4.6), and is rather nonplussed when his 'daughter' – the genetic anomaly derived from his DNA whom Donna names Jenny – counters, 'Isn't every soldier?' The Doctor's attempts to avoid violence often mean his companions engage in it on his behalf, as pointed out strikingly in season finales such as 'Journey's End' (4.13) and the mid-season finale 'A Good Man Goes to War' (6.7). This becomes a season-long cause of tension between the Twelfth Doctor and ex-soldier Danny Pink in season 8.

While not a typical hero, the Doctor's exploits saving worlds and people across time and space inevitably make him the object of hero worship and myth-making. This is made apparent early in the rebooted series during 'Love and Monsters' (2.10), which follows Elton Pope's attempts to track and record the Doctor's appearances. This is one of the first 'Doctor-lite' episodes, featuring the Doctor and Rose Tyler only briefly, as a means of emphasising the elusiveness of the Doctor's appearances on Earth. In the very first episode of the rebooted series Rose tries to find the Doctor after meeting him briefly, and is shown visiting Clive, who has a website tracking and recording sightings of the Doctor ('Rose' 1.1). This establishes his ability to appear and disappear throughout history right from the start. In 'The Snowmen' (8.X), Madam Vastra tells Clara that the demoralised Eleventh Doctor 'is not your salvation. He is not your protector,' but this *is* the role he repeatedly takes in successive episodes and seasons, especially in relation to his female companions. Those who come into contact with the Doctor are often dazzled by his 'overconfidence' and his take-charge attitude, as well as his 'difference' to the standard male hero. 'You make them want to impress you,' says Rory to the Eleventh Doctor in 'Vampires of Venice' (5.6), his tone implying that this is not always a good thing.

Certainly, despite refusing to carry weapons, the Doctor has a dark side, derived from his alien perspective. The series tends to present him as a male human, and his physical appearance reinforces this: 'You look human,' Lady Christina de Souza observes in 'Planet of the Dead' (4.15), and the Doctor simply replies, 'You look Time Lord'. At times, though, episodes signal a fundamental distinction from human experience. In 'The Lodger' (5.11) the Eleventh Doctor reveals his plan to go undercover and investigate strange happenings in a house in Colchester, telling Amy, 'All I need to do is pass for an ordinary human', eliciting outright amusement on her part. The Doctor's ability to travel through time and space, leading a life very different to most of those he meets, often makes him feel 'naturally' superior. 'I'm a Time Lord,' he reveals to Martha, at their first meeting. 'So, not pompous at all,' she observes ('Smith and Jones' 3.1). When he does have to experience 'ordinary' life, as in 'The Poison Sky' (4.5) or 'The Power of Three' (7.4), he complains about it bitterly: 'I'm stuck on Earth like an ordinary person,' he whines to Martha in 'The Poison Sky'. Donna often challenges the Doctor about this arrogance, and her willingness to do so helps define their relationship, which is characterised by a bickering sibling dynamic. She complains that he has an ulterior motive in choosing companions: 'It's not so you can show them the wonders of the universe, it's so you can take cheap shots' ('Planet of the Ood' 4.3). Likewise, in 'The Time of Angels' (5.4) Amy realises that the Eleventh Doctor is visiting museums and looking at ancient artefacts as a means of demonstrating that his life is vastly different to that of most people. 'Oh, I see – it's how you keep score.' Without the baseline of others' lesser knowledge and experience, the Doctor's abilities would seem much less impressive. He does, as is acknowledged more than once, like to show off. Rarely is this arrogance dented, though every now and again it does happen. In 'The Doctor's Daughter' Jenny confidently instructs him to 'Watch and learn, father,' before showing off her own impressive skill set (4.6) and leaving him momentarily speechless.

His alien nature is most often identified in relation to emotion. In the very first episode, Rose marvels, 'You *are* alien,' ('Rose' 1.1), when the Ninth Doctor apparently 'forgets' that Rose's friend Mickey is dead. (In fact, Mickey is not dead – though he has been turned into an Auton and Rose does not realise the process is reversible. Nevertheless, the impact of the Doctor's attitude to Mickey's apparent death is still felt by Rose, and by the viewer.) Likewise, in Donna's debut episode, 'The Runaway Bride' special (3.X), she is taken aback by the Doctor's reaction to human suffering: 'They were dying and you stood there like a stranger,' she berates him. During the season 6 opener, 'River Song', Amy and Rory, confused by different time streams, witness the Eleventh Doctor being shot only to meet him shortly afterwards, behaving with carefree abandon, in a diner. Outraged, River slaps his face and tells him: 'This is cold. Even by your standards this is cold' ('The Impossible Astronaut' 6.1). Here the Doctor is not being callous and insensitive; he is a different version to the Doctor they just saw killed, yet 'even by your standards' reminds viewers that the Doctor *does* frequently disregard human emotions and views of relationships. In fact, Emma Grayling, the empath who meets the Doctor and Clara when they investigate a supposedly haunted house, tells Clara, 'Don't trust him. He has a sliver of ice in his heart' ('Hide' 7.9). This ice rarely melts.

However, in the two-part story 'Human Nature' and 'Family of Blood' (3.7 and 3.8), the Doctor hides out on Earth by concealing his Time Lord essence and memories in a watch and effectively becoming human. As John Smith, teacher at a boys' school in 1913, he loses some of the Doctor's qualities – 'God, you're rubbish as a human,' complains Martha in 'Family of Blood' as she has to rescue him – but gains others. He gradually develops a romantic relationship with the school's matron, Joan Redfern. 'He gave me a lot of things to look out for,' Martha reflects. 'That wasn't one of them. What sort of man is that?' Once he regains full awareness of his Time Lord nature, this emerging love withers almost immediately: Joan fell in love with John Smith, not the Doctor, and sees a real difference between them. When the Doctor asks her to travel with him, to 'start again,' she asks whether anyone would have died had he not appeared 'on a whim' and then dismisses him when he cannot answer: 'You can go.'

Thus, part of the Doctor's role as male hero, however 'different,' is a reluctance to form lasting emotional attachments. He is a lone traveller, moving through time at a different speed to most, without even the reassurance of family ties. 'I don't do family,' the Ninth Doctor tells Rose in 'Aliens of London' (1.4). When the Tenth Doctor becomes a genetic parent in 'The Doctor's Daughter', it is no surprise that he is highly dismissive of any claim that Jenny is his daughter and that therefore he should behave with parental responsibility and even love. It is Donna, not the Doctor, who names

Jenny, yet when she tells him he has 'dad shock' *she* is shocked that he confesses to having been a father before, presumably because she cannot see any sign of it. Generally speaking, the Doctor is not averse to interacting with children, but this tends to happen more along the lines of the Eleventh Doctor wallowing in the role of eccentric 'uncle' during 'The Doctor, the Widow and the Wardrobe' (7.X). (The latter, being a Christmas special, is admittedly perhaps more than usually indulgent.) Generally, he tends to avoid family situations. When Donna invites him to Christmas dinner following their first adventure together ('The Runaway Bride'), he agrees but then sneaks off in the TARDIS.

This aloofness comes from the Doctor's experience of travelling space and time at will, but much of the drama in the rebooted series arises from his companions helping to ground him and prevent him becoming *too* alien and distant. The danger that comes with the Doctor's adventures is clearly signalled from the start: 'He brings the storm in his wake' (1.1); he is 'the oncoming storm' (1.13); 'he's like fire and ice and rage' (3.8). As mentioned, while he eschews guns, he is not averse to his companions committing violent acts in his name. Davros baits him with this in 'Journey's End' (4.13), inviting him to 'show [Rose] your true self' and explaining, 'You take people and you fashion them into weapons. Behold your children of time. . . murderers.' The Eleventh Doctor even introduces River with the words, 'This is my friend River: nice hair, clever, has her own gun. And unlike me, she really doesn't mind shooting people. I shouldn't like that. Kinda do, a bit' ('Day of the Moon' 6.2). River's training as a psychopathic, weapon-toting assassin should earn her his contempt, but instead he marries her.

Having travelled alone for some time, the Tenth Doctor almost walks away from a doomed Mars mission team, but turns back and saves their leader, Adelaide Brooke ('The Waters of Mars' 4.16). When she discovers that she should have died with her team, she tells him, 'This is wrong. I don't care who you are' and promptly commits suicide to right the course of time. 'I've gone too far,' the

Doctor concludes. Thus, the Doctor is shown to need companions as a way of keeping him 'safe' and healthy. The choice he makes in 'Waters of Mars', it is strongly implied, comes about because he has no one to challenge his foreknowledge and the action arising from it. In this way, his distant coldness is presented as a retrievable flaw and the companion is its solution. 'You alright?' asks Rose after he reads Reinette's final letter in 'The Girl in the Fireplace' (2.4). 'I'm always alright,' he replies, while his demeanour suggests otherwise. Donna in particular acts as a balance. When he tells her, 'I don't need anyone,' at the end of their first adventure, she retorts, 'Yes, you do. Because sometimes I think you need someone to stop you' ('The Runaway Bride'). When they are reunited in season 4, after his short-lived travels with Martha, he admits, 'You were right. Sometimes I need someone' ('The Fires of Pompeii' 4.2). This strand runs throughout the rebooted series, resurfacing as the Eleventh Doctor tries to let Amy and Rory live their own lives by seeing them less frequently. Craig, who first met the Doctor in 'The Lodger', has another encounter with him in 'Closing Time' (6.12), and it is striking that while the episode focuses on Craig's changed circumstances – he is now living with Sophie and they have a baby (Alfie, aka Stormageddon) – there is some emphasis on how Craig can help the Doctor. 'He needs someone. He always needs someone. He just won't admit it' ('Closing Time').

The intimacy of the travelling companions' relationship in the TARDIS lends itself to the new emphasis on heterosexual romance between the Doctor and his companions. This becomes more apparent when the Tenth Doctor travels with Rose and continues across the tenure of David Tennant and Matt Smith as the Tenth and Eleventh Doctors. An assortment of young female companions suffer largely unrequited love for him, or certainly feel a strong attraction to him, despite other, ongoing relationships. This is aligned with the Doctor's presentation in the reboot as a sexually attractive and even sexually active male. 'I will gobble you up, pretty boy,' says the alien entity known as the Wire in 'The

Idiot's Lantern' (2.7). Lynette Porter argues that this helped make the reboot successful in the US, stating that nothing 'cross[es] cultures and attract[s] young female viewers' like 'love interests' (2012, p. 86).

Rose 'gets' the Tenth Doctor eventually, but only in the form of the alternate version that grows from his severed hand in 'Journey's End' (4.13). 'I'm never going to leave you,' she tells him in 'Doomsday' (2.13). Typically, when she says 'I love you,' he does not reply; and much further along he asks, 'Does it need saying?' ('Journey's End'). Only the cloned Tenth Doctor can actually articulate the words, apparently, and even then we do not hear them, because he whispers in her ear. The 'real' Tenth Doctor's aloofness is not compromised by making a declaration of love, just as in 'Family of Blood' during John Smith's relationship with Joan Redfern. Here, Martha confesses, 'He is everything to me. . . and he doesn't even look at me' (3.8), but eventually she chooses to leave him, stating: 'This is me, getting out' ('Last of the Time Lords' 3.13). The Doctor himself later admits to Donna, 'She fancied me,' thus leaving himself open to Donna's teasing, 'Mad Martha. . . charity Martha' ('Partners in Crime' 4.1). The humour here allows the series to sidestep the emotion, and the Tenth Doctor to distance himself from Martha's pain. When Donna later witnesses River's emotional suffering at the Tenth Doctor's unfamiliarity with her – 'He looks right through me' ('Silence in the Library' 4.8) – she cannot feel much sympathy because it is the first time she, and the Doctor, have met River. Later this emotion undercuts River's independent character when she declares, 'I refused to kill the man I love' ('The Wedding of River Song' 6.13, see also Jowett 2014).

CAPTAIN JACK HARKNESS: THE 'WRONG' HERO?

The Doctor may have a dark side but the nature of the programme, and its appeal as family or mainstream television viewing, mean that he is, nevertheless, the hero of the series. In fact, when Captain Jack Harkness appears in *Doctor Who* during 'The Empty Child' (1.9) their versions of masculinity and heroism are deliberately set against each other. Jack appears as the brash American, sporting a flamboyant outfit, tethering his shiny spaceship to Big Ben, using alien technology readily and flirting with almost everyone. The Ninth Doctor's low-key clothing, sonic screwdriver and northern accent offer a sense of understated Britishness in keeping with the spirit of the Blitz. The basis of Jack's character is established here and he reappears in subsequent episodes of *Doctor Who*, yet he is positioned and developed somewhat differently in *Torchwood*. As many commentators and scholars have noted, this is partly owing to the different address and target audience for the new spin-off series, which debuted on BBC Three, a niche channel. Far from being the stereotyped, all-American action man he might appear at first viewing, Jack comes to embody the 'wrong' hero (in 'Utopia' 3.11 the Doctor tells Jack that because he is 'a fixed point in time and space' he is painful for a Time Lord to even look at 'because you're wrong'), and his representation, often playfully, challenges typical aspects of masculinity.

Jack is a time-travelling alien who, through contact with a time vortex ('The Parting of the Ways' 1.13), becomes effectively immortal and survives many lethal attacks, appearing to die but always reviving afterwards. He adopted the identity of an American officer ('Captain Jack Harkness' *Torchwood* 1.12) and thus even his name is not his own. Jack is never quite what he seems. He is also positioned very differently to the Doctor from the start because, though he may be the leading man in *Torchwood*, he fills this role alongside the series' female protagonist, Gwen Cooper, whose involvement with and eventual recruitment by Torchwood affords the viewer a 'way in' to the new spin-off. In some ways this structure might seem to parallel the Doctor and his female companion, and there is arguably an imbalance of power between the two since Jack leads the team, and Gwen is the novice. Yet Gwen is equally, if not more, important to the series than Jack and he is not the sole focus of the drama. In addition, *Torchwood* fields an ensemble cast, situating Jack (and Gwen) in a rather different environment to the Doctor. For instance, despite some uncertainty in using the ensemble in early episodes, the first two seasons take the typical strategy of focusing on different characters in weekly instalments. Thus, some foreground Ianto Jones ('Cyberwoman' 1.4), others Owen Harper ('Out of Time' 1.10, 'Dead Man Walking' 2.7, 'A Day in the Death' 2.8) or Toshiko Sato ('Greeks Bearing Gifts' 1.7, 'To The Last Man' 2.3), alongside arcs involving the whole team, and stories about Jack and Gwen. *Torchwood: Children of Earth*, because it functions more like a miniseries and only has five episodes, and also because the Torchwood team is significantly smaller (following the deaths of Tosh and Owen in season 2), has less latitude in this respect. Still, its narrative structure exploits different groups of characters in different locations doing different things.

Jack seems to fit the mould of the action hero, and his conventional good looks also suggest a typical, even stereotypical, presentation. The physicality of the cinematic action hero, Yvonne Tasker argues, is conventionally focused on bodily control and the preservation of the perfect hard body, as epitomised in the 1980s movies she examines (1993). In this scenario, the body of the male hero, while displayed for the viewer in spectacular ways, demonstrates invulnerability and wholeness during fights and under threat, yet is never really compromised. As Stacey Abbott, among others, has noted (2013), the more recent trend for darker, damaged male heroes emphasises vulnerability, whether physical or psychological, and genres inflected by horror (as *Torchwood* definitely is) might choose to literally open up their male heroes to the viewer, often in scenes of torture designed to exhibit abject male bodies. The very real vulnerability of these characters results in lasting 'damage' that is the primary invitation to identification and engagement. Sympathy is elicited for such characters precisely because they are *not* invulnerable, unfeasibly resilient heroes.

At the same time, however, the level of damage that can be inflicted on such characters is often excessive because, while vulnerable, they are often more than human (as with Angel, the vampire with a soul, from *Buffy the Vampire Slayer* and *Angel*, or Jack) and thus capable of withstanding extreme pain. When they are not superheroic or superhuman (like Batman, or the Winchester brothers from *Supernatural*), they are directly involved in extraordinary situations that require them to behave like superheroes. Thus Jack, while distinctive among the other characters in the *Doctor Who* universe, is not unusual in the contemporary landscape of fantasy television. Because *Torchwood* is a spin-off based on minor allusions to the Torchwood Institute in *Doctor Who*, featuring an almost entirely new cast of characters, the creators of the series are free to tap into this trend and repurpose it to fit the evolving mythos of the series.

Tasker notes that action heroes are rarely sexualised, despite romance often appearing to be their reward (1993), but Jack is highly sexualised and highly sexed from his debut in *Doctor Who* onwards. This sexualisation sets him apart from many other dark, damaged male heroes and anti-heroes. Generally speaking these types carry too much responsibility to embark on lasting romantic relationships, and tend to conceal their true role in saving the world, making such relationships problematic. A dark hero like Angel even suffers from a gypsy curse apparently preventing him from finding happiness through sex. While such characters may be free to conduct more fleeting liaisons for the purposes of sexual satisfaction, as Dean Winchester does, this tends to undermine their moral position and is thus underplayed, seen as a flaw, or used for comic effect. Not so with Jack, who shamelessly flirts with many of those he meets and has a history of sexual conquests and relationships that spans centuries. Even the *Doctor Who Character Encyclopedia* describes him as 'cheeky and flirtatious' (Loborik, Gibson and Laing 2013, p. 32).

This representation is in keeping with *Torchwood*'s position on BBC Three, and its marketing as the 'adult' version of *Doctor Who*, and its timeslot after the UK TV 'watershed' of 9pm (when children might be assumed no longer to be watching). Jack is not the only character in *Torchwood* who has a sex life: rather this is seen as part of the appeal – it is darker and sexier than its predecessor. The season 2 trailers for both the BBC and BBC America emphasise this as a selling point, showing scenes of violence and sex. Even during later appearances on *Doctor Who*, Jack revels in his own attractiveness: when the Doctor asks him. 'What are you taking your clothes off for?' in 'Utopia' (*Doctor Who* 3.11), he responds, 'I look good, though,' and in 'Dead of Night' he is confident that barman Brad cannot resist him (4.3).

The Doctor's ambivalent relationship with violence has already been discussed, and Jack directly contrasts this: he uses action, weaponry and hardware, and is prepared to kill as well as to allow others to die. His wartime costume signals a somewhat old-fashioned construction of the action man, and Jack is often depicted in marketing images posing with guns. This can, perhaps, be read as just another flamboyant performance, and indeed is sometimes played for laughs ('What is it with you, Red Baron? You got Snoopy up your ass?' taunts CIA agent Allen Shapiro in *Torchwood: Miracle Day* 4.8), but Jack's willingness to kill has caused some scholars to see him as 'perhaps one of the darkest, or morally ambiguous/pragmatic characters, on television in the early 2000s' (Porter 2012, p. 102).

Jack's approach to violence and tough decisions are elements of his dark side. In 'Cyberwoman' (1.4) Ianto conceals his girlfriend, Lisa, who has been converted by the Cybermen, in the basement of the Torchwood Hub. Eventually Lisa attempts to convert other members of the team, and seems uncontrollable, despite Ianto's belief that she can still be saved. Jack issues an ultimatum, at gunpoint, that Ianto must kill her, otherwise Jack will kill them both himself. 'You act like a hero but you're the biggest monster of all,' Ianto angrily retorts. Jack's ability to see the bigger picture and act for the greater good is presented as cold and distances him from his human colleagues. Moreover, despite his enjoyment of flirting and his eventual romance and sexual relationship with Ianto, Jack sometimes seems to reject emotional attachments. After the events of the season 1 finale, he simply leaves the team to carry on without him, and the first episode of season 2 ('Kiss Kiss, Bang Bang') sees them floundering without his knowledge and bickering about his absence. Facing a difficult situation, Tosh notes that 'Jack would know' what to do, while Owen wearily states, 'Well, Jack's not here.' Of course, Jack swoops in and saves the day, somewhat puzzled when the team do not welcome him with open arms. 'You left us, Jack!' Gwen shouts, trying to convey their disappointment and sense of abandonment.

In other episodes, though, Jack shows an emotional side. Like the Doctor, his immortality separates him from human companions who age and eventually die. The span of his memories and the scale of his experience means that, again like the Doctor, he tends to live in the moment and continually moves on. Yet he does have memories and regrets. After Gwen's wedding ('Something Borrowed' 2.9) we are offered a brief glimpse of Jack looking through what appears to be a box of keepsakes, and in *Torchwood: Miracle Day* he refers to taking companions, as the Doctor does, to help stave off his loneliness and isolation ('Immortal Sins' 4.7). Thus, while initially presented as a high contrast to the Doctor, Jack actually has much in common with the Time Lord.

Torchwood offers foils to highlight key parts of Jack's character. Captain John Hart appears in season 2 ('Kiss Kiss, Bang Bang', 'Fragments' 2.12, and 'Exit Wounds' 2.13) and acts as an obvious parallel to Jack. In some ways he is an exaggeration of Jack's more excessive tendencies ('God, he's worse than Jack,' marvels Owen in 'Kiss Kiss, Bang Bang'), while in others he functions as contrast or nemesis. A former lover, John highlights Jack's lascivious nature; he flirts indiscriminately, and uses paralysing lipgloss to incapacitate anyone unwary enough to kiss him. Writer Chris Chibnall says that with 'John you see the way Jack could have gone, and probably did, for a little while' (in Wilkes 2008), suggesting that Jack's desire to redeem himself after a life of conning people is one of the factors that makes him a hero.[1]

Jack's other, more consistent, foil is Gwen, the uniformed police officer who stumbles across Torchwood's activities in the very first episode and subsequently pursues the team until Jack recruits her. Although Jack's character does not easily fit into traditional binary constructions of gendered and sexual identity, he and Gwen often seem to be diametrically opposed. If Jack frequently appears cold and calculating in protecting the regular human world from knowledge of aliens and is himself both an alien and alienated from typical human concerns, Gwen almost always serves to represent emotion and human warmth. Jack is flamboyant and excessive, bringing a touch of the exotic into mundane life through his period clothing and American accent; Gwen's down-to-earth attitude reminds us of the domestic and everyday activities that continue despite alien incursion. This is played as a version of 'opposites attract', with an undertone of unresolved sexual tension simmering beneath Gwen and Jack's interactions. However, Gwen is contrasted, not just with Jack, but with every member of the Torchwood team because of her stable ongoing relationship outside the team. When she is welcomed to the Hub, she rapidly evaluates the others and, with some disbelief, asks, 'None of you have partners?' Gwen's investment in her boyfriend and later husband, Rhys Williams, and then her daughter, Anwen, is what she fights for and what keeps her grounded in the 'real' world. She and Jack share a lasting bond, not least as, latterly, the surviving members of Torchwood Cardiff. Yet however suspicious others might be of her bond with Jack, from Rhys' intermittent carping about it, to the bridesmaids' gossip at her wedding ('Something Borrowed'), the series repeatedly makes clear that Gwen's romantic and sexual loyalties lie with Rhys, and she will not give up her family for Jack or for Torchwood.

This is, perhaps, somewhat conventional in terms of gendering and the feminine, yet it certainly produces many critiques of Jack's leadership and personality. When he advises her on how to deal with Rhys in 'Combat' (1.11), Gwen scathingly asks, 'Do you always know best, Jack?' suggesting that while he may know how to approach alien hunting, demonstrable success in lasting relationships is lacking. Gwen also draws attention to Jack's immortality. In *Torchwood: Miracle Day*, when they are reunited, she responds by telling him, 'I started to think it would be like some kind of fairy tale. I'd be an old woman and you'd turn up out of the blue and visit my granddaughter. I'd be ancient and you'd be exactly the same' (4.2). In this series, alone again following the death of his lover Ianto in *Torchwood: Children of Earth*, Jack frequently tries to assert his bond with Gwen, perhaps a means of consoling himself. After going AWOL and picking up a barman, he drunkenly calls her, asserting, 'We don't need anyone, right Gwen?' but fails to elicit much sympathy as his call is interrupted by a Skype exchange with Rhys and baby Anwen (4.3). This characterisation of Jack as increasingly isolated is also complicated by the introduction of Rex Matheson in this fourth season. Rex functions largely as competition, and, as Porter notes (2012, p. 110), he and Jack are often paralleled in terms of action, leadership skills and sexual activity (though Rex is conventionally heterosexual). Rex even becomes immortal at the conclusion of the season narrative. Such were the parallels between the two that it seems that Rex was potentially being set up as a replacement for Jack, but as there has been no continuation of this narrative on television, their relationship has not developed further.

Jack's importance to *Torchwood*, as unfolding narrative and as branded product, is clear. In part, he signifies what is exotic and pleasurable about *Torchwood*; his alien origin and unnaturally extended lifespan both contribute to his position as team leader. *Torchwood* opened with Jack's voice-over in the first two seasons, so he explains the show's premise to the viewer ('The

twenty-first century is when everything changes') and also introduces Torchwood itself ('outside the government, beyond the
police'). Thus, he is an authority from the start, the recognisable
voice of the series, and though Gwen also contributes voice-over
in later episodes, this tends to emphasise emotion and empathy, as
when she leaves a video message thinking the world is ending in
Children of Earth ('Day Five' 3.5), or describes her father's life and
approaching death in *Miracle Day* ('The Blood Line' 4.8). Similarly,
despite the shared importance of the two characters, especially in
seasons 3 and 4 when they provide continuity for long-term viewers, it is Jack whose image brands *Torchwood: Miracle Day* in most
promotional material. This is, presumably, driven by the desire
in US publicity for the new joint venture to use a familiar face in
advertising, and the assumption that British actor Eve Myles would
be much less recognisable than John Barrowman. Nevertheless, it
means that Jack is the face as well as the voice of *Torchwood*.

SARAH JANE SMITH: THE FEMALE HERO

Sarah Jane Smith is described in the *Doctor Who Character
Encyclopedia* as 'one of the Doctor's closest companions' (Loborik,
Gibson and Laing 2013, p. 153), and her tenure as a travelling
companion spans the classic as well as the rebooted series. She
has certainly interacted with more incarnations of the Doctor
than other companions, meeting the First, Second, Third, Fourth,
Fifth, Tenth and Eleventh Doctors (though some of these were
in the classic series reunion episode 'The Five Doctors' of 1983).
Unlike the Doctor or Jack, Sarah Jane is all human and has no
special 'superpowers', yet she becomes a 'defender of the Earth'
in her own spin-off series, *The Sarah Jane Adventures*. In order to
do this, however, she has to overcome a tendency to define herself by her relationship with the Doctor, rather than as her own
person. This is somewhat ironic given that she was originally, as

Elisabeth Sladen points out, 'the show's nod towards the nascent Women's Lib movement' and Sladen's decision that Sarah Jane could 'make herself heard [...] simply by making her a strong character' (Sladen and Hudson 2012, p. 83) contributed much to the character's popularity.[2]

Given the nature of the Doctor's characterisation in the new series, and especially the heart-throb popularity of David Tennant as the Tenth Doctor, Sarah Jane's guest appearance in 'School Reunion' (2.3) is a painful experience for the character. She is struck by how she has aged, waiting in vain for him to come back for her while he, apparently, has simply moved on, selecting a series of new, young companions to share his adventures. (I have written elsewhere about the particular dynamics of the rebooted series' 'girls who waited'. See Jowett 2014, and also Chapter 3, for the way the Twelfth Doctor, played by the much older Capaldi, changes this dynamic.) Another aspect of Sarah Jane's 'reunion' with the Doctor is the initial tension between her and current companion, Rose. Rose's nominal boyfriend, Mickey, notes that the situation is 'every man's nightmare' with the Doctor having 'the missus and the ex' meet. Mickey and the episode thus position Rose and Sarah Jane as both romantically interested in the Doctor, in competition for his attention, or even affection. Indeed, Hannah Hamad describes this scenario as a conventional 'depiction of generational disharmony and toxic sisterhood' (2011).

Eventually, though, Sarah Jane accepts her successor, telling Rose that she is 'more than a match for' the Doctor, while Rose learns about the Doctor's continual need to move on: 'This is really seeing the future,' and she realises, 'You just leave us behind.' The Tenth Doctor extends an invitation for Sarah Jane to come with them in the TARDIS, but she declines: 'Time I stopped waiting for you and found a life of my own.' When she begins her own adventures, she is apparently following through on this statement, although in the first episode she refers obliquely to her time with the Doctor, explaining to Maria that she is single because 'There was only ever one man for me. And after him, nothing compared' ('Invasion of the Bane' 1.X).

Sarah Jane's interactions with the Doctor are not over yet, however: she appears in 'Journey's End' (*Doctor Who* 4.13) as one of several companions from past episodes assembled to help the Doctor defeat the Daleks. Here, she cannot quite cast off her attachment to the Doctor and surrenders so that she can follow the TARDIS. The Tenth and Eleventh Doctors also appear in episodes of *The Sarah Jane Adventures*, potentially reversing the dynamic by positioning him as a guest in *her* series, yet the Tenth Doctor at least retains significant sway over her character (see below).

Initially leading a solitary life that might seem odd or unusual to others, Sarah Jane becomes in her own series a parent to alien 'children' Luke and Sky, a role model for neighbours Maria and Rani, and an important confidant for Clyde, her son's best friend. Yet her previous life and her doubts about it regularly affect how she feels and thinks about her current situation. Even in season 3, she admits that because she 'spent so many years alone, I find it difficult to trust anyone' ('The Madwoman in the Attic' 3.2). However, the youth of her companions, appropriate for a children's series on CBBC (the dedicated BBC channel for children), means that she can form a bond with them that bypasses her distrust of adults. At the conclusion of the season 1 story 'Eye of the Gorgon' (1.3) Maria reads Greek myths with Sarah Jane in a scene of female bonding that exceeds anything shown in *Doctor Who* or *Torchwood*. Naturally, Sarah Jane also opens up to her adopted son, telling Luke about her own parents, who died when she was just a baby, leaving her to be raised by her aunt ('The Day of the Clown' 2.2). This backstory offers further explanation of Sarah Jane's independent life with very few ties to others, and thus when the subsequent season 2 story 'The Temptation of Sarah Jane Smith' (2.5) allows Sarah Jane to go back in time to 1951 and meet her parents, the encounter has all the more emotional impact. The 'temptation' of the title is for Sarah Jane to do something for herself, rather than being a 'defender of Earth' – 'All these years I've been putting others first.' Perhaps most poignantly, viewers discover that Sarah Jane's command, 'Mr Smith, I need you,' used to activate the alien supercomputer in her attic (see also Chapter 2), echoes the notes her mother and father exchanged and adds a layer of feeling to her action adventures.

Young companions Maria, Clyde and Rani all have scenes with their families that contrast their differently inflected interactions with Sarah Jane. Such glimpses are frequently set in the heart of the domestic, family space – in the kitchen. Rani's father, Haresh, is often seen cooking for the family, and he and Rani regularly discuss what they might have for dinner. This also reverses traditional gender roles and although Rani and her mother, Gita, often poke fun at Haresh's cooking, Gita is never seen cooking, and is more often shown going to work. This domestic activity, with Haresh sometimes wearing an apron, seems designed to demonstrate that while he is a strong authority figure because of his position as head teacher of the local school attended by all the young people, Haresh has a warmer personality when at home. Similarly, although we see much less of Clyde's home life, he enjoys a close and relaxed relationship with his mother, a single parent. Clyde forms a strong bond with Sarah Jane (perhaps because he is used to female authority, having been largely raised by his mother), and when his absent father returns in season 2's 'The Mark of the Berserker' (2.4) Clyde's fears that he is similar to his father are shared with Sarah Jane. Notably this scene takes place in a sitting room and we rarely see Sarah Jane cooking, even for Luke or Sky, and the kitchen of her house is not a key location. In contrast to the family homes of Maria, Rani and Clyde, Sarah Jane's home tends to be presented as a communal workspace rather than a typically domestic space.

Indeed, during 'Mona Lisa's Revenge' (3.5), Sarah Jane describes herself as 'a lonely, frosty woman in a big house who knew more about aliens' than people, until she met Luke and Maria. In the pilot episode, she is described by Maria's school friend Kelsey as 'the mad woman', but Maria sees her rather as 'a bit glamorous' ('Invasion of the Bane'), perhaps because she is solitary and independent. Sarah Jane often regrets getting her companions involved in dangerous activities, but although she has more authority because of her age and her experience, she is not always shown to be 'right' because of this. Moreover, the series allows the younger characters much more agency than they might have in *Doctor Who*: in a series aimed at younger viewers who might be expected to identify with them directly, they are the central protagonists. 'We chose you, you didn't choose us,' Clyde tells Sarah Jane, trying to reassure her that she is not responsible for their participation in her investigations ('The Madwoman in the Attic').

When Rani looks back on her life as an older woman from 2059 in 'The Madwoman in the Attic', she tells a young character (who parallels herself and Luke) that Sarah Jane was 'mysterious and moody and, oh, you did not want to get on the wrong side of her' but also that 'She changed my life.' Rather like the Doctor, Sarah Jane can be slightly aloof, but the relationship her companions develop with her is rewarding and even life-changing. If the Doctor, as Rory notes, makes people 'want to impress' him, then Sarah Jane too brings out the extraordinary in people who spend time with her, though less emphasis is placed here on them trying to 'impress' her, and more on them wanting to do the right thing. When Clyde is trapped in a nightmare of a dead-end future in 'The Nightmare Man' (4.1) the main figure in his dream is a mocking, elderly Sarah Jane on a mobility scooter, who derides his failed attempts to make something of himself, in direct contradiction of how their relationship helps instil confidence in him.

Sarah Jane, then, is presented as a lone wolf, a solitary investigator and thoughtful action hero comparable with the Doctor and Jack, though perhaps slightly more approachable. In season 1's 'The Lost Boy' (1.6) she evades and incapacitates a pursuer on a motorcycle and Sladen notes with pride that 'we've had the biggest explosion' of all the *Who* series (Sladen 2012). Even her clothing, updated for the twenty-first century but designed to echo her classic *Doctor Who* costumes, codes her as an action hero. She commonly wears boots, trousers, shirts and a signature waistcoat, mixing styles that might be considered masculine with a more feminine hairstyle and appearance,[3] and overall this outfit is reminiscent of other adventurer heroes like Indiana Jones and Lara Croft. Sarah Jane also has her own distinctive vehicle, like other TV investigators, and one of 'her' Doctors, the Third, who drove a yellow Edwardian-style roadster called Bessie: Sarah Jane's car is a 1991 Nissan Figaro, a model retro-styled to resemble a car from the 1960s. Along with the Victorian house she inhabits, the car adds to her quirkiness and aligns her with the past (a possible shout-out to her tenure in classic *Who*).

Yet Sarah Jane's frequent use of hi-tech gadgets to assist her, including Mr Smith, the alien computer that is cached in the attic and emerges at her command; her sonic lipstick; and K9, the robotic dog from the classic series, mean that she is by no means behind the times. Mr Smith, the male-voiced computer, is perhaps a dig at the sultry female-voiced computers of other SF and action-adventure series, and although his title domesticates him somewhat (as with characters insisting on calling Amy Pond's boyfriend, Rory, Mr Pond) it does not offset his alien nature. Likewise, the sonic lipstick is reminiscent of both River Song and Captain John's dangerous cosmetics, without the sexualisation; perhaps it is a more mundane and disguised version of old Amy's sonic 'probe' ('The Girl Who Waited' *Doctor Who* 6.10). The Doctor (and River's) sonic screwdriver is unlikely to be overlooked as a technical gadget, while the lipstick is more cleverly camouflaged given Sarah Jane operates in a public sphere that is largely unaware of the existence of aliens. Hamad sees the sonic lipstick as an 'over-determined signifier of postfeminist femininity', an icon 'deployed time and again as a visual shorthand for [...] empowered femininity' (2011). Yet the very fact that it is an 'over-determined signifier' might position the sonic lipstick as a performance of femininity, rather than the real thing. Indeed, Sladen refers to it as 'very camp' and reveals 'It was going to be blue, but I said, "No it has to be pink"' (in Richardson 2007a, p. 28). Arguably it could even suggest that Sarah Jane does not need an actual lipstick, just a useful tool.

'Sarah Jane is the man!' exclaims Clyde in 'The Temptation of Sarah Jane Smith' (2.5), yet although she is presented much like male heroes, Sarah Jane is often dismissed by male characters like Karg the Sontaran ('The Last Sontaran' 2.1) because she is female. She is, of course, successful in defeating such male antagonists and her character is most tested by villains who are, or appear to be, older women. Thus, Mrs Wormwood in season 1, Mona Lisa in season 4, Miss Myers in season 5 and particularly Ruby White in season 4 challenge Sarah Jane, as she meets forceful women much like herself. These characters act as foils for Sarah Jane, presenting contrasts and similarities that illuminate and develop her own story.

When Ruby White appears in 'Goodbye, Sarah Jane Smith' (4.6), Clyde says, 'She's exactly like you.' Ruby apparently saves the world from a dangerous meteor strike, emulates Sarah Jane's doorstepping as an investigative technique, and even moves into Bannerman Road. She drives a red sports car and wears a signature red coat. As Ruby first competes with and then befriends the group around Sarah Jane, Sarah Jane herself seems to decline, losing her memory and her confidence. Her doubts about whether she should be involving children in dangerous work are revived, and her recent loneliness following Luke's departure for university is emphasised. She even says she has to 'get Luke's tea' in a rare moment of domesticity that further undermines her usual businesslike self. Her vulnerability under what is eventually revealed to be Ruby's manipulation is powerfully presented and when Sarah Jane hands over her mission to Ruby, it seems that everything she is, the woman who leads what Ruby calls 'the most exciting life on the planet', has been betrayed. As Ruby's prisoner, following this defeat, Sarah Jane is then forced to witness Rani and Clyde's responses to her apparent abandonment of them, emphasising how powerless she is to control both the situation and the perceptions of those who love and respect her. Aptly, Rani's mother, Gita, strongly defends Sarah Jane: 'That's not her style,' she assures her daughter, 'she would never, ever just run off.' This act of female solidarity, despite the vast gulf between Gita and Sarah Jane, restores Rani's faith in her female mentor.

While Sarah Jane exists as a hero in her own right, then, she is not invulnerable. In fact, perhaps more than the Doctor or Jack, she is at risk of losing herself. Several stories track a kind of erasure of her: Sarah Jane is replaced by Ruby, literally erased from history in 'Whatever Happened to Sarah Jane?' (1.5), and becomes almost unrecognisable to her young companions (and possibly also to the audience) when she finds romance in 'The Wedding of Sarah Jane Smith' (3.3). Given that she starts out her own series after vowing to remake her life and stop pining for the Doctor's return, it is striking that so many stories undermine and directly attack this hard-won independent identity. The two male protagonists of the other *Who* series may experience the occasional doubt, and regeneration/immortality certainly inflect and shape their sense of self, yet both are usually confident and even arrogant about their own abilities and their identity as heroes. As an older woman (see Chapter 3), Sarah Jane has a much less secure and less visible place in the world, which often seems to attack her by attempting to literally erase her autonomy. In both 'Goodbye, Sarah Jane' and 'Whatever Happened to Sarah Jane' this is effected by rival female characters who attempt to take her life, acts that could be construed as motivated by jealousy. Hamad describes Sarah Jane's childhood friend in 'Whatever Happened to Sarah Jane' as 'duplicitous and murderous', classing this as 'one of many depicted instances of toxic sisterhood and monstrous femininity' (2011), though I would suggest that such instances stand in contrast to the intergenerational female solidarity depicted between Sarah Jane and Maria or Rani.

'The Wedding of Sarah Jane Smith' likewise undermines Sarah Jane's independence and sense of herself, yet the effect here is even greater because it involves the Tenth Doctor. In this story Sarah Jane's companions become suspicious because she keeps lying about her whereabouts and they are worried about what she is hiding from them. It turns out she is hiding a romantic relationship. While her suitor, Peter, seems unobjectionable, his effect on Sarah Jane is undeniable: she wears a dress for the proposal dinner and is shown confusing her sonic lipstick for a real one. She has to be saved by the Doctor, not the young people she has mentored, when this is revealed as all part of a plan by recurring villain the Trickster. At the end of the story Peter states that Sarah Jane 'gave [him] the strength' to withdraw his agreement to the Trickster's plan, enabling the Trickster to be defeated. Some tension is evident in this story between the excitement of Luke, Rani and Clyde finally getting to meet the Doctor, who is as inspiring as they expected, and the realisation that he treats Sarah Jane rather cavalierly. Rani corrects him when he calls Sarah Jane 'Sarah', and Luke 'can't believe the Doctor ran off like that' following the wedding's cancellation (3.3). The farewell scene is similarly tense: Sarah Jane asks the Doctor if it is the last time she will see him, and he begs her not to forget him (as though she had not preserved his memory for years). Yet Sarah Jane is able to rise above this, and the other threats to her identity as an autonomous, heroic older woman, and regain her sense of self. Arguably, her identity is even reinforced by the story titles, which each include her name, asserting her as the hero of this series, however much her enemies try to erase her.

All three protagonists of the *Who* television series, then, differ from the norm in one way or another. While the Doctor and Jack's distinctiveness might be attributed to the fact that they are alien, Sarah Jane's is almost entirely predicated on the combination of age and gender – she is one of very few older female heroes on television. This situation in itself may have come about because of Elisabeth Sladen's memorable performance of Sarah Jane in the classic series, leading to her immense popularity, as well as her willingness to reprise the role, first in guest appearances and eventually in her own series. This need not undermine the significance of her character and its success, though, being children's drama, it may have less impact than a similar hero in a prime-time popular series like *Doctor Who*.

2

COMPANIONS AND ALLIES

The majority of recent scholarship on gender in the *Doctor Who* reboot has focused on female companions, and the series' emphasis on heterosexual romance between the Doctor and his companions. While this will be touched upon here, this chapter will also examine male companions in *Doctor Who*. The Doctor inevitably dominates his own series, and forms close bonds with his current female companion, yet the other spin-off series have rather different dynamics at work among their ensemble casts, and the mixed-gender team featured in *Torchwood* and the 'family' of companions presented in *The Sarah Jane Adventures* are both examined, developing ideas raised in the previous chapter.

While the actor playing the Doctor may change, the character is, according to the series' narrative logic, continuous, if not consistent in personality. Certainly any given Doctor tends to last longer than the companions, who generally come and go more rapidly. The basic cast of characters within the series comprises the Doctor plus companions. As outlined from the start of this book, *Doctor Who* cannot really avoid a certain power imbalance between the Doctor and his companions. Since the 2005 reboot, it has most frequently featured the Doctor plus one main companion, presenting a rather different, perhaps more intimate, relationship than the classic series, which varied between one and multiple companions. While so-called 'Doctor-lite' episodes such as 'Love and Monsters' (2.10), 'Blink' (3.10), 'Turn Left' (4.11) and 'The Girl Who Waited' (6.10) have allowed minor characters or alternate companions/timelines to take precedence over the Doctor and his current companion, these tend to be few and far between. The scenario presented in 'Turn Left' (4.11) is more indicative of the show's usual operation: the episode shows the repercussions of the Doctor's absence for all his companions and spin-offs, so, for instance, a news broadcast tells us that Sarah Jane, Luke, Maria and Clyde die in a hospital along with Martha. Likewise, the two-part 'The End of Time' (4.17 and 4.18) exploits emotional impact from seeing the Tenth Doctor visit past companions before his impending regeneration into a new personality. This regeneration provides a slight shift (aligned with a change of actor playing the Doctor and a new head writer) in how the Doctor/companion relationship is structured and, for the first time, the Doctor is shown travelling consistently with two companions, Amy Pond and Rory Williams. Rory will be discussed in more detail below.

Torchwood, as outlined above, is premised on a team, does not privilege any named character in the title and operates as an ensemble drama, though at times this is more successfully executed than at others. Nevertheless, Jack's flamboyant character tends to predominate in publicity for the series and, as examined below, the other male characters in the series tend to be overshadowed by him. *The Sarah Jane Adventures*, despite including Sarah Jane's name in the title, and even in many episode titles, also follows – rather more consistently – the ensemble cast model, with the story sometimes following one character or set of characters, and sometimes another. As children's television drama, the audience might be expected to identify most strongly with youthful counterparts who must therefore be given major roles to play. Sarah Jane is thus rescued by her young friends and companions as well as rescuing them herself, and saving the world is always a team effort.

The varying audiences and markets for each series also inflect how relationships and characters interact. Despite its family viewing remit, Piers Britton argues that the new *Doctor Who* ends up 'privileging sexually charged relationships over other kinds of friendship and intimacy' (2011, p. 140), and this chapter touches on what effect this has on representations of gender, in terms of companions. It has already been noted that Jack Harkness is necessarily slightly different in *Doctor Who* than he is in *Torchwood*, and Lynette Porter observes that while Jack's stories in *Doctor Who* are never 'adult' (though his first appearance does include him flirting with both men and women), the more 'adult' tone and content of *Torchwood* does not necessarily provide increased character development. Rather, she argues that 'Relationships sometimes take a back seat to *Torchwood*'s more graphic dialogue or depictions of sexual activity' (2012, p. 106). *The Sarah Jane Adventures* has, again, perhaps more latitude for development: the majority of its main characters are growing up and may therefore be expected to change and, moreover, this development offers potential for drama and conflict within their relationships with Sarah Jane, and with each other. *The Sarah Jane Adventures* also, as might be expected from children's television, includes parents and families as well as friendships, offering a wider range of interactions and types of close relationships more consistently than either *Doctor Who* or *Torchwood*. In addition, it often covers serious everyday topics that affect young people, such as divorce, death and homelessness, alongside alien visitations.

'NOT A KISSY-KISSY KIND OF LOVE'? FEMALE COMPANIONS

As Britton points out, 'any movement to include stronger women in the classic [*Doctor Who*] series was compromised by the lack of real change in their relationships with the Doctor' because any female companion was 'dependent on or ancillary to the male hero' (2011, p. 111). In some respects this has not changed in the rebooted series, though Antoinette Winstead goes so far as to state that in the reboot, 'the heroine's journey took center stage […], reflecting a 21st century sensibility towards the role women play in not only science fiction, but also horror and action-adventure genres' (2013, p. 229). Winstead and others are partly identifying what writer, and eventually showrunner, Steven Moffat sets out as a premise for the reboot: 'The Doctor's the hero but they're the main character' (in Porter 2012, p. 87). This is an extension of the previous operation of the series: the companion is, for the audience, the way into the action and drama of the Doctor's alien existence.

The agency and positioning of the female companions is indicated at times by having them provide voice-over narration for particular episodes, as with Rose in 'Army of Ghosts' (2.12), or Amy in 'The Beast Below' (5.2). The series remains the Doctor's story but the companions occasionally get to tell it in their own words, translating an alien experience for us and mediating it through their (gendered) humanity. Porter also points out that in the BBC America broadcasts of season 5, Amy narrates a prologue before every episode (2012, p. 15), and Porter notes that 'By omitting her name, the narrative invites viewers to put themselves vicariously in Amy's place' (p. 17), alluding to the role that companions have played for decades in both the classic and rebooted series. This makes an interesting comparison with Gwen's more frequent voice-overs in *Torchwood*, as discussed in more detail below.

One other notable development in the rebooted series, as already mentioned in the previous chapter, is the possibility of romance between the Doctor and his young female companions. While Jody Lynn Nye suggests that actually showing such romance would defy logic – 'A true alien would no more be interested in mating with humans than we would with a plant' (2010, p. 110) – strong hints of romance persist, albeit unresolved or unrequited, a standard device in television drama. Britton and Hills even suggest that unresolved sexual tension is a particular recurring theme in the work of Russell T. Davies, head writer/ showrunner for the reboot in its initial stages (Britton 2011, p. 117; Hills 2010, p. 38). This tension, which persists to varying degrees from Rose to Clara with only Donna really escaping it, inevitably positions these women at a disadvantage, with the Doctor appearing even more superior and in control, even of personal relationships.

This is particularly the case for Martha, who is defined by Andy Frankham-Allen in his book *Companions* as 'rebound girl' (2013, p. 263). As outlined in the next chapter, Martha's character is full of potential but her unrequited love for the Doctor defines her, over-riding other traits, and eventually her unreturned affection causes her to stop travelling with the Doctor altogether. Of course, reading this unequal power dynamic in terms of the characters, it is true that 'the Doctor does not overtly deprive Martha of her agency'; rather 'the narrative heavily circumscribes her capacity to act "in character"' (Britton 2011, p. 134). Or, as Shoshana Magnet and Robert Smith? more bluntly put it, Martha's 'character is completely subsumed beneath the puppy-dog eyes arc she's given' (2010, p. 157) – though her character is, perhaps, partially redeemed during her appearance in *Torchwood* season 2. This pattern of romance and unrequited love does not apply to Donna, whose greater maturity and more sibling-like bond with the Tenth Doctor paves the way for Amy – the next conventionally attractive young companion – to engage in a slightly more complex flirtatious relationship with the Eleventh Doctor.

As Porter notes in her analysis of the transatlantic appeal of the *Doctor Who* series and its spin-offs, the emphasis on hetero-sexual romance seems designed to 'cross cultures and attract young female viewers' (2012, p. 86). The relationship between the Eleventh Doctor and 'sexy' companion Amy, Porter argues, 'attracted plenty of fanboys of all ages everywhere' (2012, p. 87), and in her analysis this is less a structure related to character and narrative than a strategy, or at least a significant opportunity, for extending the series' appeal to an American audience. While British television may have a tradition of social realism and nurturing acting talent, 'American audiences expect beautiful young actors in an action series, and the Doctor and Amy fulfil those roles,' she observes (p. 88). However, Amy's appearance (in both senses) was controversial in the UK, jeopardising, for some, the family nature of the series by including a character who was too sexy, appearing in her debut episode in a faux police officer's uniform as a kissogram. Piers Wenger, executive producer for this season, offered a rather dubious 'defence' of Amy's representation:

> The whole kissogram thing played into Steven [Moffat]'s desire for the companion to be feisty and outspoken and a bit of a number. Amy is probably the wildest companion that the Doctor has travelled with, but she isn't promiscuous. She is really a two-man woman and that will become clear over the course of the episodes (in *Telegraph* 2010).

Likewise, the casting of Peter Capaldi as the Twelfth Doctor signalled a shift in this dynamic and even before Capaldi started filming, the official line stated that the Twelfth Doctor would not be romantically associated with Clara, as though to pre-empt any criticism over an age-gap relationship. This decision tends to be attributed to Capaldi himself: 'It's quite a fun relationship, but no, I did call and say, "I want no Papa-Nicole moments."[4] I think there was a bit of tension with that at first, but I was absolutely adamant' (in Rudd 2014). Showrunner Moffat has also suggested that casting Capaldi means the end of a particular type of representation:

> The last two Doctors have been your 'good boyfriend' Doctors. [...] I think it was time for the show to flip around a bit. The new version of the show is quite old now. It's very old [...] We need the kick-up-the-arse Doctor, in a way, to frighten you and make you think, oh, it's a different show again (in DoctorWhoTV 2014a).

While Moffat positions this as a decision about revitalising the series' basic premise and dynamic, it is certainly no coincidence that the 'frightening' and 'kick-up-the-arse' Doctor is performed by the oldest actor to regularly play the character since William

Hartnell in the 1960s. Yet, even when the 'boyfriend' doctors held sway, companions were not always – or at least not only – female.

RORY WILLIAMS: 'THE BOY WHO WAITED'

While female companions tend to be characterised by their relationship with the Doctor and with those they leave behind, Rory Williams, the first major male companion of the reboot, is primarily defined by his relationship with Amy Pond, another companion. Just as Mickey Smith sometimes travels in the TARDIS alongside the Ninth and Tenth Doctors because of his connection with Rose Tyler, Rory follows Amy when she begins to travel with the Eleventh Doctor. Mickey is the necessary precursor to Rory, and sets up several key characteristics for a male companion in the rebooted series.

'[A] bit of a no hoper, Mickey is at first timid and cowardly in the face of alien threats, but shows a great talent for hacking into advanced computer systems,' Jason Loborik, Annabel Gibson and Moray Laing explain (2013, p. 118). As Rose Tyler's boyfriend, Mickey's subordinate role is established and he is generally overshadowed by Rose and her mother Jackie, as well as by the Doctor. Often featuring as comic relief, his pining after Rose is set up as rather pathetic, and while the audience is positioned at times to sympathise with him, it is consistently implied that Rose can do better than Mickey – and her travels with the Doctor seem to prove this. In 'Boom Town' (1.11), teamed in action with the dashing and heroic Captain Jack, Mickey ends up with toilet paper round his ankles. He quickly realises that he is trailing the field as a man in Rose's life – 'It's always going to be the Doctor, it's never me' – but is incapable of changing this situation. In 'School Reunion' (2.3), on witnessing Sarah Jane and Rose meeting as well as seeing K9, he has another epiphany: 'Oh my God, I'm the tin dog.' This prompts him to ask if he can accompany Rose and the Doctor in the TARDIS, but leads to an exchange in the next episode that puts him on the level of pet, rather than boyfriend or lover. When Rose tells the Doctor, 'You're not keeping the horse,' he quips, 'I let you keep Mickey' ('The Girl in the Fireplace' 2.4).

In the episode following this, however, Mickey is given more backstory, as Rose tells the Doctor how Mickey was raised by his gran, with whom he still has a strong family bond ('Rise of the Cybermen' 2.5). As the parallel timelines underline, Mickey's hacking talents finally allow him to become his own man, when he joins the resistance (2.6) and 'a more heroic and grown-up Mickey eventually returns' to merit the subtitle 'talented companion' (Loborik, Gibson and Laing 2013, p. 118). At this point, however, Mickey fades from the televised story of *Doctor Who*, returning only briefly in special appearances of multiple past companions, and eventually marrying Martha Jones.

In many ways, then, Mickey sets a template for male companions as subordinate to females and as, essentially, companions at one remove, since both Mickey and Rory only travel in the TARDIS because they are following a woman. Loborik, Gibson and Laing dub Rory the 'caring companion' (2013, p. 149), and go on to describe him as the 'long-suffering childhood sweetheart' of Amy, and 'at first rather timid and suspicious of the Doctor'. He is, according to this official guide, 'caring and sensitive' and 'remains devoted to Amy and eventually marries her'. This devotion is seen as his driving force, since he 'stops at nothing to get her back' when she is abducted by the Silence during season 6.

Britton suggests that companions (even when male) embody 'dependent, vulnerable femininity' in contrast with their champion and rescuer, the Doctor (2011, p. 114), who controls the TARDIS and thus the fate of those who travel with/in 'her'. Rory's presentation certainly does little to contradict this characterisation. He is even objectified by the embodied TARDIS in 'The Doctor's Wife' (6.4) when 'she' refers to him as 'the pretty one'. While Amy is 'the girl who waited' she is rarely described as passive by viewers or commentators. Rory, however, seems 'dependent' on Amy for direction: he follows her through their childhood and adolescence, waiting for her to notice him as more than a friend (as seen in 'Let's Kill Hitler' 6.8). His devotion to Amy is such that, when he becomes an Auton, he waits for centuries to pass so that she can be freed from the Pandorica and her life saved – leading the Doctor to call him 'the boy who waited' ('The Big Bang' 5.13). He dismisses the sacrifice involved in this patient waiting, later saying, 'I don't remember it all the time' ('The Day of the Moon' 6.2).

Rory's devotion is thus a defining feature and reinforces his 'caring' profession: he is a nurse, and throughout his adventures with Amy and the Doctor he is often seen tending to the wounded or reassuring the anxious. Unlike Martha Jones, who trains to be a doctor, Rory's medical skill is presented less as knowledge and expertise and more as nurturing, in line with his caring personality. As a nurse, he stays in the background, offering support, while the Doctor takes centre stage. Even when Rory teaches an emergency medical programme in life-saving techniques, the context of this scene ascribes his motivation to his love for Amy, who has been taken into the sickbay of an alien ship, and helps position his training as affect rather than action ('The Curse of the Black Spot' 6.3). In contrast with Sontaran Strax, who remains a warrior first and a nurse second, providing comedic effect when the two impulses clash, Rory's nursing is credible because his whole character is predicated on caring for others.

Most of the female companions who travel with the Doctor in the rebooted series have some kind of family to situate them in 'real life' and offer them something to return to. Given that Amy's parents are absent from her childhood, Rory provides the stability of family for her: he is a reliable, caring element she can come back to.[5] Yet from the start, their story casts doubt on whether she really desires this stability: 'Flesh and Stone' (5.6) reveals that she left with the Doctor on the night before her wedding to Rory (the camera pans round the empty room, fixing on a wedding dress hanging waiting). Her allegiance to both, and the question of whether she can maintain two such significant ties, provides much of the drama as the three travel together, since it highlights Rory's 'vulnerability' (as Britton puts it), that is, his love for Amy and his fear of losing her.[6] Amy kissing the Doctor in 'Flesh and Stone' can be interpreted as an attempt at seduction, and competition between Rory and the Doctor for her loyalty and affection is frequently hinted at. While Amy might choose to travel with the Doctor to see wonders and experience alien worlds, as well as – potentially – because she is attracted to him, Rory does it to be with her. When he meets the Doctor again after waiting for centuries for Amy as an ageless Auton, and asks only about her, the Doctor points out, 'Your girlfriend isn't more important than the whole universe.' Rory immediately responds, 'She is to me!' 'Welcome back, Rory Williams!' says the Doctor, identifying this as the core of Rory's character ('The Big Bang').

Amy may be uncertain about whether she wants to settle down and have a family, but Rory is not. The couple are shown across several seasons at various stages in their lives and he is consistently presented as desiring and enjoying a stable family life of domesticity. When they experience different realities during 'Amy's Choice' (5.7), Amy and Rory are shown as a married couple back in Leadworth, expecting a baby, with most of their scenes together taking place in the kitchen, the traditional domestic heart of the home. Amy is offered a choice between this idyllic life and a life of adventure with the Doctor, bringing previous tensions to a head. The confusion between 'realities' is resolved when both are discovered to be illusions, and Amy does not have to make the choice alluded to in the episode title, yet Rory articulates *his* choice: 'I want the other life… happy, settled' with a baby. Likewise, in 'Asylum of the Daleks' (7.1), the couple have separated, with Rory claiming that a 'basic fact of our relationship is that I love you more than you love me' and explaining that he gave her up to allow her to enjoy a happy life without him. At this point Amy confesses that she gave him up because she knows he wants children and she cannot have children following her capture while pregnant in 'A Good Man Goes to War'. While other companions may feel that they have put their lives on hold to travel with the Doctor continuously, Rory and Amy show another possibility: having a 'normal' life while travelling with the Doctor periodically. (Subsequently, Clara does the same.) Their domestic life is often shown through doorways, as they leave for an adventure, or as the Doctor temporarily enters their world, and 'The Power of Three' (7.4) plays this for laughs, emphasising how mundane interactions with opticians, washing powder and yogurt cause the Doctor much frustration and boredom when he comes for a more lengthy stay. (Another side is shown in 'A Christmas Carol' (6.X) when Amy and Rory dress up in the honeymoon suite while on a cruise, reliving Amy's kissogram outfit from her debut episode.)

Despite the many jokes about Rory as one of Amy's 'boys' (Britton 2011, p. 138) and eventually as 'the brand new Mr Pond' ('That's not how it works,' he complains in 'The Big Bang'), this remains how he is defined. In 'The Girl Who Waited' (6.10), Rory's reaction to a version of Amy grown old waiting for rescue from another time stream is extremely powerful, especially when she demonstrates that her memories of him are precious, even after thirty-six years without him. (When instructed by the Doctor to 'think the most important thought you ever had', Rory is taken aback to hear her sing 'Macarena'. 'Our first kiss', he realises). He is anxious to save her, but is told that only one Amy can remain in the TARDIS and he will have to choose between the old and young versions. 'This isn't fair. You're turning me into you,' he complains to the Doctor. In this episode, Rory tells Amy, 'You and me. Always', and this desire for eternal togetherness defines him, and her, till the end. In season 7 the weeping angels trap Rory in 1930s New York City ('The Angels Take Manhattan' 7.5), and Amy chooses to return to live out her years with him, rather than continue to travel with the Doctor.

TORCHWOOD: OWEN, GWEN AND RHYS

Given the team dynamic of *Torchwood* outlined in the previous chapter, and the dyadic nature of the relationship between Jack and Gwen, it is hardly surprising that the other males in the Cardiff Torchwood team tend to be overshadowed by Jack's anti/heroic and flamboyant performance of masculinity. In the opening episode of season 2, which sees the team trying to carry on in Jack's absence, the alien they are pursuing describes them by function: 'doctor, carer, technician, office boy' ('Kiss Kiss, Bang Bang' 2.1). Owen, in this description and in contrast to both Rory and Martha in *Doctor Who*, is a doctor but not a carer (that is Gwen), and this coldness is part of what defines his character, as well as, perhaps, aligning him with Jack. 'Office boy' assigns Ian to the most subservient position among the various team members, a categorisation reinforced by him frequently being referred to as the tea or 'coffee boy'. The season 2 finale, 'Fragments' (2.12), provides flashbacks of the team being assembled by Jack, and in some ways this backstory demonstrates selection for particular qualities, regardless of gender or character. Jack is clearly the leader and the alpha male, leaving both Owen and Ianto to accept their designated roles and, occasional outbursts aside, Jack generally remains unchallenged except by Gwen. (Even said outbursts are after her arrival and thus, perhaps, encouraged by her own challenges to or questioning of Jack's leadership.) The first episodes of season 1 certainly suggest that the team has been working together for some time without asking many questions about each other at all.

Owen is a 'scientist' and a proponent of rationality rather than emotion, though his physical appearance and presentation do not always denote the typical medical doctor. Of all the Torchwood team, he vaunts his lack of human connections, implying that he enjoys his relatively solitary life, especially given he can easily find sex whenever he wants. His callousness is highlighted by his response to Toshiko's unrequited love, or infatuation, with him. Owen is clearly aware of it, but chooses to ignore it, and the fact that he starts a sexual relationship with Gwen suggests both that he does not care about Toshiko's feelings and that he is not against workplace 'romance'. His connections are hardly depicted as 'romantic', however, and are largely sexualised. Indeed his introduction to the viewer shows him effectively conducting date rape, when he uses some kind of spray to attract a woman in a bar. Her boyfriend objects, and Owen simply includes him too. This suggests that Owen is not overly concerned with strict definitions of sexual orientation (like every member of the team, as emphasised in the opening episodes of season 1), although he usually prefers women. Presumably Owen could, and has, conducted similar short-term sexual liaisons before, but the way he attracts his partners in this instance presents him as an aggressive sexual predator who does not care about consent between adults so long as he gets what he wants. This is certainly a somewhat risky strategy for the series, and has been interpreted as unacceptable criminal behaviour by some (see, for instance, Dunn 2010; Barron 2010, p. 223). As a result, Owen's cold and uncaring nature is established beyond doubt and is reinforced by subsequent words and actions.

It might be expected that Owen will somehow be redeemed as the series unfolds, and this does happen, though he is dead before another, more emotional, side to his character is fully revealed. His softer side is hinted at in 'Out of Time' (1.10) when he starts a relationship with an older woman, Diane Holmes, a pilot from 1953 who is transported, along with two passengers, to the present day when her aircraft flies through the Cardiff Rift. In this storyline Owen begins by helping Diane adjust, though her independence and progressive thinking make this less difficult than it is for the other time refugees. It is also clear that, like Owen, Diane is accustomed to, and enjoys, short-lived sexual relationships rather than more stable, romantic attachments. The two begin an affair. Owen seems to open himself to more than a sexual relationship as he realises that Diane misses flying, the activity that provided her with valued independence, as well as a sense of her own skill and daring. She is desperate to fly again, but though he tries to make this happen, modern regulations and her lack of contemporary qualifications mean that she will have to wait weeks for flying lessons. Eventually Diane attempts to replicate her manoeuvres in the hope of flying back through the Rift to her own time. Owen realises this and rushes to the airfield to try to prevent her from leaving, but he cannot persuade her to stay. Thus – with some conscious dramatic irony perhaps – the first woman he seems to care about beyond sexual satisfaction chooses to leave him.

In 'Adam' (2.5) an alien affects all members of the Torchwood team, erasing some of their memories while adding false memories of his place in their lives (as Adam), and thus rearranging their personalities. With Owen, this turns him into the office geek, complete with spectacles, and also reverses the unrequited love between him and Toshiko so that it is Owen who suffers while she ignores him. Adam tells Jack that 'all [Owen's] cynicism [is] gone' and Owen is 'selfless, happier'. While this reversal is temporary and 'resolved' by the whole team taking the memory-wiping drug Retcon (used by Torchwood to erase memories of alien encounters from civilians) and forgetting Adam's existence, for the audience it serves to further undermine Owen's outward appearance of cynicism and callous carelessness.

His final redemption, in narrative terms, comes with his death. In other series this might mean that Owen sacrifices himself to save the team and is thus redeemed: because *Torchwood* celebrates difference, it means that Owen dies, is redeemed, and only then sacrifices himself as part of the team's work. At the end of 'Reset' (2.6), Owen is shot and is brought back from the dead by the Resurrection Glove (an alien device seen in previous episodes). The following episode ('A Day in the Death' 2.7) deals intimately with Owen's feelings about this, and he comes close to expressing a wish to die when he encounters a woman, Maggie, about to commit suicide herself. One of the things Owen most misses from his mortal life is sex, though the episode also highlights other sensual experiences like eating or touching that he can no longer enjoy. These emotions are expressed through a direct voice-over from Owen as well as through his conversation with Maggie, an atypical approach. While voice-over is used to frame some other episodes and to 'brand' the series in its opening sequence, it is not adopted consistently throughout an episode before this one. The episode begins with the words, 'Three days ago I died and they think I'm fine. But they're wrong.' Allowing the audience access to Owen's subjective viewpoint is an easy way to build sympathy for a character who, until now, has seemed remote and unattractive. With many of Jack's traits but lacking his larger-than-life vibrancy, Owen simply seems cold, and he certainly never plays the hero. 'A Day in the Death' opens up some of his interior thought processes and suggests that perhaps he just keeps his feelings to himself. In this episode Owen is seen genuinely interacting with people outside of Torchwood, and even trying to help them come to terms with their own problems, but it is not until the season finale that a reason for his previous detachment is presented.

In 'Fragments' Jack remembers the process of assembling the team following a major attack, and it is revealed that Owen had a fiancée, Katie, when Jack met him. She appeared to be suffering from early-onset Alzheimer's but it turned out to have been an alien parasite in her brain, which was diagnosed as a tumour. Jack was too late to prevent the parasite from releasing a gas that killed Katie as well as the surgeons trying to operate on her: this tragedy has left Owen grieving and ready to shut himself off from human contact and intimacy. Jack offers him a way to take a kind of revenge, by helping to track down and resolve other alien incursions. Owen's coldness is thus reframed as a form of protection against feeling this kind of grief and hurt again. While not excusing some of his worst behaviour, this reframing allows the audience to engage emotionally when Owen is killed a second time by choosing to stay in a nuclear plant and make it safe before it causes a catastrophic explosion ('Exit Wounds' 2.13). Particularly because his death is coupled with Toshiko's, and she helps Owen by talking him through the process of venting the system, Owen's second death allows this example of damaged masculinity to be laid to rest, if not entirely redeemed.

The development of Owen's character tends to shadow Jack's, while Gwen's complements him. Rory follows Amy into adventure, becoming a companion and traveller in the TARDIS himself, but Rhys, Gwen's boyfriend and eventual husband, tends to remain an outsider, despite taking part in some Torchwood activities. Notably both Rory and Rhys are defined by a relationship with a woman who overshadows 'their man' because of an interaction with the extraordinary. This does not mean *they* are extraordinary, and indeed both Rory and Rhys function as ties to the everyday and especially to the domestic.

Gwen is far more domestic and 'ordinary' than Amy, however, partly because of the nature of the *Torchwood* series and its Welsh setting, and partly because she is, perhaps deliberately, less 'sexy'. The initial presentation of the two characters – Amy in a 'sexy' kissogram police officer outfit and Gwen in a 'real' police uniform complete with high-visibility vest – suggests as much. While the camera tends to dwell on Amy's long legs, short skirts and tumbling hair in *Doctor Who*, Gwen's freckled face and the gap between her front teeth are emphasised in *Torchwood*. US viewers of *Torchwood* were, according to Porter (2012, p. 65), inclined to be critical of these physical features as they are unlikely to be highlighted on US television, though other commentators imply that Gwen has much more depth than Amy achieves.

Gwen is more sympathetically written and certainly has more interiority and subjectivity than Amy and many of the other *Who* companions display. Yet, like them, this rounding of her character into three dimensions is largely achieved through the domestic and her ties to it. Gwen's family tend to be wheeled out when she needs depth, or when the series needs some emotional punch. In the first two seasons, the vehicle for this is her relationship with Rhys, and in *Miracle Day* it is her sick father and her baby daughter, Anwen. One of Gwen's first observations, on being introduced to the team after gaining official entrance to the Torchwood Hub, is, 'none of you have partners?' ('Day One' 1.2) and later she worries that her job with Torchwood, however much she loves it, is 'changing me' ('Countrycide' 1.6). Inevitably it does change her, given that it introduces Gwen to new worlds and new ways of seeing. Her awareness affects her relationship with those she knew before joining Torchwood, like PC Andy Davidson, who still proves useful to her and whose apparently unrequited feelings towards her remind us that Gwen is far from perfect in her handling of relationships. Like Owen, Gwen is not above exploiting the affection of others for her own ends. Furthermore, as already mentioned, despite her long-term relationship with Rhys, Gwen finds herself attracted to Owen and has a passionate sexual fling with him.

Rhys is a constant in Gwen's life, and this means that he is sometimes regarded as mundane – even boring – compared with her alien encounters. When Jack asks her about Rhys in 'Combat' (1.11) she rather dismissively replies, 'He'll get over it, he always does,' and in this episode she indulges herself by confessing her affair with Owen to Rhys, but then gives him Retcon knowing he will forget what she told him. This not only constructs Gwen as tested morally or ethically by her job but also highlights how her attachment to Rhys runs the risk of becoming hollow if she cannot honestly share her experience with him. In 'Meat' (2.4), the first episode where Rhys is really involved in the action of the team, the drama of finding an exploited alien creature being used for 'meat' is continually cross-cut with domestic arguments between Gwen and Rhys. Finally he asks angrily, 'Am I a habit you just can't be arsed to break?' By the end of this episode Gwen affirms that her boyfriend is a hero, and refuses to lie to him any longer, yet the tension between her job and her domestic life continues.

This comes to a typically over-the-top climax in 'Something Borrowed' (2.9), when Gwen is infected by a shape-shifting alien and ends up heavily pregnant for her wedding day. This strange occurrence is never really explained to her friends and family, who thus make assumptions about Gwen and her relationship with Rhys and with her work. The marriage takes place, however, and she and Rhys commit to each other publicly. The wedding guests are given Retcon so they forget the alien, but Gwen refuses it as she wishes to have an honest relationship with Rhys. By the beginning of the third season, the miniseries *Children of Earth*, Gwen is pregnant with a daughter, though typically Rhys learns this only after she tells Jack (when Jack finds her scanning her body using equipment in the Hub during 'Day One' 3.1). Gwen and Rhys have a heated exchange in this series about whether she should have children because of her job ('Day Five' 3.5). By the fourth season they are together with the baby, at least to begin with, though domestic harmony is again disrupted by the demands of Torchwood.

ALIENS IN THE FAMILY: LUKE, SKY AND MR SMITH

Jack and the Doctor are both aliens who attract human companions, but *The Sarah Jane Adventures* features a human protagonist who takes at least two aliens as not only companions but adopted children. This reversal allows the series to explore the often unsettling experience of growing up via alien characters trying to fit into a human world, though some have argued that, in doing so, it undermines its female title character. Hannah Hamad describes Sarah Jane's return to *Doctor Who* in 'School Reunion' as 'a post-feminist cautionary tale of the abject singlehood that awaits the Doctor's discarded companions' (2011). Certainly this episode does tend to present Sarah Jane as 'abject' in constructing her identity around an absent, male figure, and in doing so it draws attention to how the spin-off series has to recontextualise the character as hero rather than 'victim'. *The Sarah Jane Adventures* appears to rectify this by positioning Sarah Jane at the centre of her own story. However, as Hamad notes, 'the extraordinary scenario whereby the heroine of a children's sci-fi action-adventure series was a childless single woman approaching her sixties proved to be predictably short lived', and by the end of the first instalment Sarah Jane 'fortuitously acquires a fourteen-year-old son' (2011). Sarah Jane, Hamad argues, thus becomes a character much closer to convention in terms of gender representation by becoming a 'mother', though Hamad does not address the fact that Sarah Jane is much older than the average mother of a fourteen-year-old, nor that this 'family' arrangement, while diegetically unremarked upon, is in many ways less than conventional.

Porter describes one of the main attractions of *The Sarah Jane Adventures* for young people as 'attractive young actors doing the things typically middle-class teenagers do, as well as having atypically adventurous lives' (2012, p. 121). This view is perhaps a little superficial and does not take into account that Luke and Sky are 'doing the things typically middle-class teenagers do', without actually *being* typical teenagers. This emphasises the message of the series: that anyone, however apparently isolated, can find friends and 'family' who will accept, love and support them. Sarah Jane's own isolation and solitary existence in the years between leaving the TARDIS and bonding with her group of young companions in Bannerman Road means that this desire and need for security and companionship is not one-way, and shows that adults can feel it too. Sarah Jane's 'family' is a chosen family, not a biological one, and since she does not have a partner, she is not placed within a conventional binary dynamic, potentially allowing her to be a 'parent' rather than simply a 'mother'.

Thus, the show engages with the typical science fiction strategies of estranging the everyday at the same time as making the fantastic seem ordinary, at least for some. In the first story proper of season 1 ('Revenge of the Slitheen' 1.1), Clyde comments that Luke and

Maria are 'beyond weird', but he is soon so caught up in having alien encounters alongside them that 'weird' becomes normal. The same process applies to Luke and Sky, life forms who are adopted by Sarah Jane and have to learn to live, or at least pass, as human children. This learning process is most detailed with Luke, who is a regular character for three full seasons before leaving for university at the start of the fourth. The development of Sky's character is cut short by the premature end to the series brought about by Elisabeth Sladen's death.

The very first *Sarah Jane* story, 'Invasion of the Bane', introduces Luke, an 'Archetype' made by the alien Bane from human DNA to further their experiments on people. The Archetype helps Sarah Jane and Maria to defeat the Bane and escapes with them after the Bane's operation is destroyed, whereupon Sarah Jane decides to adopt the Archetype, and calls him Luke. Thus, Luke is technically human, yet his early life means that he does not think or behave like a typical fourteen-year-old human male. He has been designed to be more intelligent, but lacks experience of social situations, having been the Bane's prisoner all his life. Luke finds an ally in Maria, who has just moved to Bannerman Road with her father after her parents' divorce, and the two start a new school together, both feeling out of place. That he first meets Maria when both hide from the Bane in the ladies' toilets seems to highlight that he has missed the social conditioning of growing up in a society still largely structured by a gender binary. In 'Revenge of the Slitheen', Luke and Maria meet and eventually team up with Clyde, another pupil at their school, providing Luke with his first male friend and someone who can tell him how a teenage boy is 'supposed' to behave.

This interaction is often played for laughs, contrasting Clyde's clowning and 'cool' with Luke's logic and geekiness, yet both exchange ideas about what it means to be a young man in a contemporary environment. Producer Matt Bouch notes that the 'gender balance' of the series' regular cast changed from the first special episode: 'It felt like a rather feminine programme because you had Lis [Sarah Jane], Yasmin [Maria] and Porsha [Kelsey] – three female characters – and then you had Luke who wasn't a classic butch male lead, he was a lost boy' (2007, p. 30). The introduction of Clyde, then, is a conscious decision by the creative team that, in Bouch's words, 'paid real dividends because we've been able to explore masculine friendship and boys growing up' (2007, p. 30). Clyde and Luke start bonding seriously in 'Warriors of Kudlak' (1.4) when they investigate strange occurrences at a laser-tag gaming centre.

Clyde is one source of information for Luke about fitting in, and Luke also shares his worries and anxieties with Sarah Jane, his adoptive mother. In 'Secrets of the Stars' (2.3) the group investigate an astrologer and Luke discovers that not having a birthday is something else that makes him unusual. He tells Sarah Jane that he is always finding 'new things […] to make me feel different' and the two later have a discussion about competing meanings of being, or feeling, special that concludes with them choosing a date for his birthday. As might be expected from a teenager, however, there are also sometimes tensions between them as Luke 'grows up'. In season 3, Luke and Sarah Jane are at odds over his untidy room, a typical bone of contention between parent and teenager ('Mona Lisa's Revenge' 3.5), and the story concludes with them joking about him being a normal 'messy' teen. These conversations bracketing an alien adventure function to restore normality and, particularly in the conclusion, provide reassurance about the strength of human relationships. They are not confined to Luke: Maria, Clyde and Rani also have such moments with Sarah Jane at the end of episodes, suggesting that strong bonds can be found outside as well as inside family structures.

When season 4's 'The Nightmare Man' (4.1) features a villain who preys on victims by apparently making their worst nightmares come true, the narrative centres on Luke's insecurities about leaving home to go to university a year earlier than his peers. His nightmares feature Clyde and Rani mocking him, as well as Sarah Jane rejecting him, and play on his fears about being replaced in their affections by someone else. While it is clear that Luke soon recognises that these are not just nightmares but a concerted attack, the insecurities they play on are both understandable and realistic. In the conclusion of the story, Luke rallies Clyde and Rani to help him after they also come under attack, getting through to them by telling them, 'I need you,' and talking about how all three work so well as a team that the threat cannot defeat them if they stand together. Poetic justice is served on the Nightmare Man when it is trapped in a dream of Sarah Jane talking endlessly about her 'brilliant son', a neat way of again reinforcing the genuine love between the two characters, despite Luke's anxieties and their impending separation as Luke departs for university.

If Luke's character serves to debate models of masculinity and what it means to be a friend and a son, the introduction of Sky provides an opportunity for Sarah Jane to have an adopted daughter, a new dynamic different from her mentoring of Maria and Rani, both of whom have supportive and loving parents of their own. 'Sky' (5.1) sees a baby left on Sarah Jane's doorstep at the same time as a meteor crashes into a local junkyard. Sarah Jane takes care of the baby, assisted by Clyde. Eventually the team discover that the baby is a 'weapon' in a war between 'fleshkind' and 'metalkind' and has been grown by the fleshkind to help defeat their enemies. Ultimately, as one of these enemies approaches, she transforms from a baby to a girl of around twelve. Sky's origins thus mirror Luke's: both are 'created' or grown artificially by aliens as part of a hostile project, and neither get to 'grow up' normally until they start to live with Sarah Jane – and even this is not exactly 'normal'. Having a female child second time around avoids simply repeating the same elements of Luke's adoption by Sarah Jane, and there is more drama and urgency in Sky's debut, since Sarah Jane has to convince her not to be used as a weapon as well as having to deal with two alien species. Sky's destructive potential as a 'bomb' also has to be defused. It is revealed that Sky was left on Sarah Jane's doorstep by the mysterious Shopkeeper from 'Lost in Time' (4.5), who explains that he and his parrot, the Captain, are 'servants of the universe'. Given the option of leaving with them, Sky chooses to remain with Sarah Jane, who adopts her as she did Luke.

Sky's alienness is more pronounced than Luke's – when told she is a girl, she asks, 'What's a girl?' ('Sky') – though the small number of episodes she appears in offer little time for her character to develop, and perhaps start to change. As a result, her alien nature is emphasised without being slowly eroded, as with Luke. For instance, Sky calls Sarah Jane by her name, rather than using 'mum' or another familial term. She and Mr Smith – the alien supercomputer – are the only characters not affected by 'The Curse of Clyde Langer' (5.2), and Sky never turns away from Clyde as his friends and family do under the influence of the curse, and even tries repeatedly to defend him to them. This enhances a sense of her as different, as well as offering hope in an undeniably grim storyline about homelessness and rejection.

It is worth noting, of course, that because the majority of characters in the series are so young, and Sarah Jane is presented largely as a 'defender of the Earth' rather than a professional journalist, *The Sarah Jane Adventures* manages to sidestep many potential 'problems' with gender roles. Few of its main characters are seen engaging in paid work, and most do not worry about a career structure, while the younger characters have a limited amount of family responsibility and no dependents. On the whole, problems with families and familial relationships are raised but not gendered, largely because they are positioned as individual and/or emotional rather than strictly social. Rani, the only younger character to live with two heterosexual parents, receives no discouragement from either Gita or Haresh in pursuing her own goals and interests, and while Haresh might have a better-paid job than Gita, both work outside the home. Haresh's overprotectiveness is focused on his wanting the best for his daughter rather than trying to limit her opportunities. While Gita and Sarah Jane are unlikely ever to get along comfortably, this is presented as a clash of personalities rather than any form of competitiveness, and they are united in opinion at various points (see also Chapter 3).

Moreover, despite Hamad's comment about 'toxic sisterhood', the series at times challenges the 'hegemonic discourse that reinforces women's rivalry' in order to 'undermine the possibility of women's bonding, sisterhood, and friendship that allow the collective building of social and political power' (Lemish and Muhlbauer 2012, p. 171) by showing Sarah Jane mentoring both Maria and Rani. In particular, this works against what Dafna Lemish and Varda Muhlbauer identify as the way such 'discourse pits older women, as a tremendously valuable resource of experience, wisdom, and skills, against young women rather than as supportive of them' by, for instance, 'transferring social capital that might strengthen younger generations of women' (2012, p. 171). Luke's intellectual abilities meant that he would be valued within certain social circles, but he still had to learn from Clyde how to acquire 'social capital' and from both Clyde and Sarah Jane how to cope with being a teenager. Sky, on the other hand, does not have heightened abilities – unless we count her self-confidence – and, like both Maria and Rani, she benefits from her relationship with Sarah Jane, whose 'experience, wisdom, and skills' cover both the real and the alien, and who consciously mentors all of the young people she forms bonds with. The replacement of Kelsey with Clyde discussed above, as well as offering more emphasis on masculine friendship also, as Bouch notes, served to '[throw] the Maria/Sarah Jane relationship into sharp relief as they are much more of a unit' (2007, p. 30). This sets a strong precedent for Sarah Jane's mentoring of the young women, and in 'The Last Sontaran' she tells Maria that it's been like having the 'daughter I'd always wanted' (2.1). The mentoring part of her role – as opposed to surrogate parenting – is seen more overtly with the arrival of Rani, given Rani's ambitions to become a journalist and thus to learn from Sarah Jane professionally as well as personally.

There is, of course, a further 'alien' member of Sarah Jane's 'family' who resides at Bannerman Road: the 'supercomputer in the attic' usually referred to as Mr Smith. This supercomputer is powered by a Xylok, a crystalline alien being that Sarah Jane discovered could communicate with more mundane computers. Mr Smith appears to be a typical masculine authority – rational, scientific and capable of complex intellectual feats. Hamad sees this 'supercomputer, a masculinised voice of intellectual superiority and authority' (2011) as problematic. His 'superiority' is undoubtedly true, though it can be argued that this presentation is not without irony. Mr Smith is voiced by Alexander Armstrong, best known for his work in comedy, and the person chosen to voice Danger Mouse, hero of an animated parody about a Bond-style secret agent, when it was rebooted for CBBC in 2015. As Mr Smith, his voice talent is equally parodic: whether the supercomputer is a reliable ally, a bickering sibling (arguing with K9) or an evil alien force (season 2), its superiority is emphasised, or even exaggerated. Like other alien artefacts or life forms, 'he' functions to remind viewers that the extraordinary is continually present in the everyday lives of Sarah Jane and her companions, rather than serving as something that normalises her, as a husband called Mr Smith would do.

Moreover, despite having a voice full of authority, Mr Smith has no real agency. He is fixed in location, though he can hack into remote systems, and remains in the attic, usually hidden, while the other characters move around and engage in adventures. Hamad finds the verbal cue that brings the supercomputer out of hiding ('Mr Smith, I need you') to be full of 'patently troubling connotations' (2011), presumably interpreting it as reliance on 'his' intellectual capacity and superiority. Yet, recalling Sladen's attitude to the sonic lipstick as a parodic or 'camp' signifier, Mr Smith can be read in the same way: given that this action-oriented series features a female hero, it reverses the *Star Trek* model of a female-voiced computer serving men, providing instead a male-voiced computer serving a woman and her teenage companions. Even Mr Smith's voice might reverse the often sultry tones of feminised technological voices, providing an apparently authoritative tone that is actually willing to act on behalf of whichever ally calls it out of hiding. And calling it 'Mr Smith' seems like another little joke: Sarah Jane does not have, and does not need, a husband. This is stitched into the story during the events of 'The Temptation of Sarah Jane Smith' when we discover that the verbal cue consists of the same words as a note between Sarah Jane's parents, and was a shared joke between them. The family joke now embraces the alien supercomputer, making Mr Smith part of the chosen family of *The Sarah Jane Adventures*.

Overall, the representation of non-familial bonds takes precedence in the series because of its premise, yet familial bonds are not denigrated because of this. Even though both Maria's and Rani's mothers often provide comic relief, it is never suggested that they do not love their daughters. Thus, Gita may behave erratically when confronted by the extraordinary figures and events that the young people and Sarah Jane now take for granted (as when she imagines being on *Newsnight* after an encounter with an alien in 'The Vault of Secrets 4.2), but she always takes a strong position on family, assuring Rani that Sarah Jane would never leave Luke ('Goodbye, Sarah Jane Smith') as well as telling Sarah Jane how good a mother she was to Luke following his departure ('Sky'). In fact, the best interests of the young people they care for are the one thing guaranteed to unite Gita and Sarah Jane. Nor does Rani's relationship with Sarah Jane undermine her family bonds: in the second part of 'The Temptation of Sarah Jane Smith' Rani is really tested when, in an alternative timeline, she sees her mother traumatised and beaten down, and this provides all the incentive she needs to set things right and save her mother.

It is clear that the presentation of the main character in each *Who* universe series is partly developed through their interactions with others, whether companions, colleagues or even adopted children. Their gendering, and that of all characters, is also affected by intersections with other facets of identity, as examined in more detail in the next chapter.

3

MULTIDIMENSIONAL IDENTITY

When characters can travel in time there are many possibilities for situations challenging and complicating their identities. Clyde Langer, from *The Sarah Jane Adventures*, gives a spirited defence of Britishness to a group of Nazis ('Lost in Time' 4.5), while the memorable recurring character Madame Vastra in *Doctor Who* introduces herself and her companion with the words, 'Good evening. I'm a lizard woman from the dawn of time and this is my wife' ('The Snowmen' 7.X). It is almost impossible to debate gender representation in isolation. Therefore, this chapter addresses intersections of gender with race, age and sexuality, taking a closer look at characters such as Martha Jones, Mickey Smith, Clyde, Rani Chandra, Toshiko Sato, Wilf Mott, Ianto Jones, Vastra (the 'lizard woman') and Jenny (Vastra's wife), as well as the Doctor, Jack and Sarah Jane. Given the extensive use of Earthbound stories in the reboot, as well as production of all the series by BBC Wales, notions of contemporary Britishness, nationality and class form a particular background to these representations. The twenty-first-century reboot of *Doctor Who* seems to make a conscious effort to represent diversity: Lindy Orthia observes 'the new series' assertive engagement with a cosmopolitan Britain – a Britain not only diverse with respect to race, but also sexuality, gender, regionality, class and sub-culture' (2013, p. 3). This is partly a sign of the times but it is also in line with the BBC's public service remit, and some have ascribed it specifically to Russell T. Davies in his role as head writer or showrunner. Emily Asher-Perrin, for instance, notes that Davies 'had a penchant for diversifying his casts in everything from colour to sexual orientation' (2013, p. 65), and Rosanne Welch recounts his comments on the experience of watching TV with 'a minority family, frankly it's embarrassing to see how they're presented or how little they're represented at all' (2013, p. 69). (Davies' role as 'author' of the reboot is discussed further in Chapter 5.) The spin-off series follow suit even more clearly given their larger casts. *Torchwood* foregrounds Welshness alongside alien Jack and Toshiko's Japanese heritage, as well as including a range of sexualities, while *The Sarah Jane Adventures* depicts several single-parent families, and Clyde and Rani are key characters representing a multicultural Britain.

Antoinette Winstead notes of the early female companions of the rebooted *Doctor Who*: 'All three women, despite class and ethnicity, are limited and constrained by their assigned familial roles – roles they wish to escape' (2013, p. 232), suggesting that gender overrides other factors in terms of social identity. Yet Iona Yeager contends: 'When Donna and Rose travel to the past, they meet persons of all social classes who resemble them [...] there is no need to stress that they are meeting the persons who helped shape their cultural and political history.' (2013, p. 24). This is not the case for companions who might be ethnically or regionally marked, such as Martha or Amy, and Yeager notes how Amy 'both a child and young adult, speaks often of her Scottish heritage and her dislike of English culture' (2013, p. 24). As Orthia points out, 'while the Doctor may aspire to a world in which race does not matter, the programme is not culturally neutral' (2013, p. 4).

'The Doctor has always been, to this day, a white elite male' who, moreover, as Vanessa de Kauwe points out, 'enjoys the practical benefits of the elite in that he has absolute social, political and financial freedom thanks to TARDIS technology' (2013, p. 144). As a result of 'this privileged position he never experiences the ongoing complexities and sustained difficulties of racial relations' (p. 144), or indeed of inequalities based on class, gender or sexuality. This is why it is important to take different standpoints in examining it.

The perhaps unconsciously hegemonic nature of the series is also reflected in the times and places the Doctor and his companions visit: as Stephanie Guerdan comments, 'We glorify western history so much, but Asia and the Middle East have millennia of exciting historical events that have remained untapped on the show' (2013, p. 76). Certainly, Britishness is celebrated through adventures that include well-known writers such as Shakespeare ('The Shakespeare Code' 3.2) or Charles Dickens ('The Unquiet Dead' 1.3), while although Nefertiti appears in one episode ('Dinosaurs on a Spaceship' 7.2) she functions more as a historical 'name' than a rounded character with a distinct personality.

In this sense, *Doctor Who* 'always *presents itself* as opposing racist oppression' and oppression of all kinds, but it does so 'with varying degrees of success' (Orthia 2013, p. 293; original emphasis). Quality as well as quantity are relevant when examining diversity of representation. Having greater numbers of characters from 'minority' groups does not necessarily mean that a programme or cultural product tackles issues of inequality or under-representation, and it is often tempting to label different representations simply as 'positive/negative' or 'progressive/conservative'. Representation in popular culture is generally more complex, however: the impulse to address inequalities and under-representation can exist in tension with commercial and industrial factors, as well as attracting criticism about tokenism or role models. *Doctor Who* and both spin-off series have a broad spectrum of supporting characters suggesting diversity, as might be expected of programming from a public service broadcaster. The ways they tackle issues of race/ethnicity, age and sexuality intersect with their representation of gender producing particular approaches to identity and to characterisation.

While this chapter focuses largely on other areas, *Doctor Who* and its spin-offs engage regularly with notions of social class and how this inflects identity. The first season of the reboot presents a Doctor with a distinct regional accent (and class implications) and a companion variously described as a 'shop girl' or a 'chav' (as Lady Cassandra calls Rose in 'The New Earth' 2.1, though clearly this is meant to emphasise Cassandra's snobbishness). 'Father's Day' (1.8) serves as a kind of celebration of Rose's ordinary family life; the alternate version of Jackie Tyler, Rose's mother, seen in 'Rise of the Cybermen' and 'The Age of Steel' (2.5 and 2.6), is positioned as nouveau riche; and in the same two-part story Mickey reminds Rose of how far they have both come 'from the old estate' (2.6). These allusions to class positioning and how it persists in British society are revisited through Donna, the 'temp from Chiswick' and details of her lower-middle-class life. In many ways, *Doctor Who* implies that by taking the opportunity to travel in the TARDIS with the Doctor, companions from any background can become 'extraordinary' – a kind of neo-liberalism in action.[7]

Gwen – or rather actor Eve Myles – from *Torchwood* first appears in a *Doctor Who* episode as servant Gwyneth. 'She saved the world. A servant girl. And no one will ever know,' says Rose, highlighting the invisibility of the servant class, even as she is aligned with it through her friendly conversations with Gwyneth ('The Unquiet Dead'). Such servants are often female, and both Rose and Martha end up in service jobs while undercover with the Doctor, Rose as a dinner lady in 'School Reunion' (2.3) and Martha as a maid in 'Human Nature' and 'Family of Blood' (3.8 and 3.9; see below for more on this two-part story). While Gwen's social class is slightly undetermined in *Torchwood* itself, Ianto's background is revealed in *Torchwood: Children of Earth* as parallel to Rose's and Mickey's when he visits his sister Rhiannon on 'the old estate' he clearly left behind some time ago, aspiring to a much more middle-class lifestyle and career ('Day One' 3.1). Rhiannon later tells Gwen that Ianto's romanticised tales of his father the master tailor are 'shit' (their dad 'worked at Debenhams'; 'Day Five' 3.5) and thus Ianto is (re)positioned as buying into false consciousness and self-improvement by dressing, speaking and behaving in approved middle-class ways. *The Sarah Jane Adventures* is perhaps most firmly rooted in British middle-class life, though as demonstrated below, it does offer other diversions from conventional norms.

RACE AND ETHNICITY

The 2005 *Doctor Who* clearly does signal 'assertive engagement with a cosmopolitan Britain' (Orthia 2013, p. 3) and as David Butler notes, early episodes include what might be deemed '"positive" examples of cultural and "racial" mixing' such as Mickey and Rose, Brannigan and cat Valerie, Vastra and Jenny (2013, p. 23). However, the series has come under fire for a 'failure' to present consistent and significant roles for non-white actors/characters, a situation managed slightly differently in the two spin-off series. Both the Doctor and Jack, as discussed in previous chapters, can be seen as fairly typical contemporary heroes in terms of their damaged white masculinity, though Jack's omnisexuality adds an extra twist. The Doctor may be alien, Firefly points out, but 'the character is informed by whiteness and the racial anxieties of the show's white British creators, such that the Doctor embodies a number of characteristics of whiteness' (2013, p. 17; Firefly does not elaborate in this short piece on what these characteristics are, though provides a selection of key texts on whiteness for readers). Likewise, despite Jack's immortality and sexuality offering a different spin on this, he still embodies the same white middle-class privilege the Doctor enjoys. Detailed examination from a range of perspectives on both classic and new *Who* appears in *Doctor Who and Race*, and necessarily I can only sketch some of the key points here in relation to my own focus on gender. The discussion therefore picks up characters already mentioned in the previous chapter, such as Mickey and Martha, as well as showing how Clyde and Rani are presented differently.

For some viewers and commentators, the mere presence of non-white characters is not enough when the nature of their roles is produced by what Linnea Dodson identifies as 'conscious colour-blindness, unconscious racism' (2013), which in turn impacts on their reception and interpretation by those with differing levels of privilege and/or awareness. 'What the BBC was really blind to,' she argues, 'was how characters of colour were consistently cast as unloved and/or servants' (2013, p. 31). The characters of Mickey and Martha have both attracted some attention in terms of how, or whether, race/ethnicity is a factor in their representation. While it might seem a positive move to present without comment 'cultural and racial mixing' in Rose and Mickey's relationship, Mickey's representation, as already discussed in Chapter 2, is more comic or pathetic than heroic. Although he travels in the TARDIS with the Doctor and Rose, he is often overlooked, and his role in the series downgraded from companion to recurring character. As Orthia points out, this stemmed at least in part from the BBC itself:

> Although Mickey (played by Noel Clarke) was a regular char-acter from the first episode of the new series in 2005, the BBC did not include him among its lists of companions until well after Freema Agyeman was cast as Martha in late 2006, causing numerous fans to question why (2013, p. 7).

In addition, Dodson notes that the British press also ignored Mickey's role: 'the *Daily Mail* called Martha Jones the first black companion' (2013, p. 32).

Dodson argues that while '[v]iewed objectively, Mickey was the type of character usually called the salt of the Earth' (2013, p. 31), that is, he was a potentially positive representation in line with the BBC's principles of diversity, in practice the narrative undermines this and presents him instead, as the Doctor calls him, as 'an idiot'. This is because Mickey is rarely offered his own point of view, and episodes only infrequently allow viewers access to his thoughts and emotions (as in 'Rise of the Cybermen' 2.5 when he complains about being 'a spare part'). Rose and the Doctor tend to be the focus, and thus Mickey is presented through their eyes. Rose seems to see Mickey as a hindrance to a life of adventure with the Doctor, while the Doctor, as Dodson observes, 'can't even be bothered to remember his name' (2013, p. 31).[8] This is at least partly aligned with Mickey's role as both domestic and dependable – he is associated with the mundane and everyday rather than with adventure and excitement. Even when he eventually shows that he can be a hero, leaving to pursue rebellion in a parallel universe (taking over from Ricky, an alternate of himself), this does not change his character because it effectively removes him from the (television) narrative, and subsequent appearances are fleeting. Dodson even argues that his exit can be read as a direct result of his treatment: 'He's so desperate for respect that he's willing to leave not just them [Rose and the Doctor] but his home universe behind, taking nothing but the clothes he's wearing' (2013, p. 31).

Much the same could be said of season 8's Danny Pink, whose character fits the same model of disposable boyfriend. For Clara he comes second to adventures in the TARDIS, and he is regularly insulted by the Doctor. While the emphasis here might be slightly different, given the Twelfth Doctor's characterisation as impatient and generally irascible (suggesting that his attitude is unjustified), Danny follows more or less the same trajectory as Mickey. Likewise, his treatment by Clara is a little less cavalier than Rose's devaluing of Mickey, but Clara still lies to Danny about her adventures with the Doctor, even to the point of telling him she has called a halt to them ('Mummy on the Orient Express' 8.8). Clara only realises her true feelings for Danny after his death (which is very mundane – he is run over by a car while talking to Clara on his mobile phone in 'Dark Water' 8.11). Though he returns after his consciousness is revived, he is still dead, but finally ends up in a cyber body, allowing him to help save the world ('Death in Heaven' 8.12). Like Mickey, Danny is only able to become a hero at the point where he is written out of the narrative.[9]

This tendency to undervalue non-white characters can also be traced across Martha's character arc. 'Rebound girl' Martha is undermined from the outset, and it is unfortunate that this role coincides with a major character of colour. While Mickey is generally treated with 'colour blindness', Martha's race is occasionally commented upon, and this could be an opportunity to tackle issues of representation, or the history of racial inequality. Yet various commentators argue that this opportunity is missed, and that Martha is undervalued in a similar fashion to Mickey, despite displaying heroic qualities.

In 'The Shakespeare Code' Martha is conscious that her appearance in the late 1500s might be cause for alarm: 'Am I alright? I'm not going to get carted off as a slave?' she asks the Doctor. This might indeed be a valid and pressing concern for Martha, but the Doctor at first does not seem to understand the comment and then dismisses it: 'I'm not even human. Just walk about like you own the place. Works for me.' Thus, as Firefly observes, 'the role of whiteness is normalized – nobody else *could* "own the place"' but a white male (2013, p. 18; original emphasis). This certainly seems to be an example of what Orthia describes as 'the relationship between life experience and seeing race' (2013, p. 292) – Martha's lived experience gives her a different perspective to the Doctor, who is to all intents and purposes a middle-class white male. Moreover, while some praised the episode for actually acknowledging Martha's blackness ('Though the Doctor blows off the question, I believe my first reaction to that line was *thank you*,' K. Tempest Bradford 2010, p. 169), others believe it could have gone further in terms of its exploration of history. 'The script silences Martha's opportunity to voice her opinion regarding the institution of slavery, and denies her character agency to view her black British ancestors' experience in context' (Yeager 2013, p. 23).

Later in the episode Martha is offended by the way Shakespeare refers to her (as 'Ethiop' and 'delicious blackamoor lady'), saying, 'I can't believe I'm hearing this.' Her comment can be seen as a calling out of racist language from the past, but it is once more brushed off with little concern. Yeager states: 'The Doctor describes Martha's reaction as "political correctness gone mad" and suggests the only offence is Martha's hypersensitive reaction' (2013, p. 23), trivialising Martha's concerns and, by implication, her lived experience. It might be true, as Yeager suggests, that the episode does not tackle the history of slavery in Britain because 'portraying these elements of British history would either be too disturbing for family viewing, or serve as instigators of ethnically divisive dialogue' (2013, p. 24), but neglecting to comment tends to further undercut the series' investment in liberty and autonomy.

Likewise, in 'Human Nature', Martha's presence in 1913 initially appears to trouble early-twentieth-century attitudes about race and class, but the emphasis of the story undermines and undervalues her. Yeager even argues that the episode positions the era's race and class prejudice as part of an innocent era before the crisis of World War I (2013, p. 25). In this two-part story (continued in 'Family of Blood'), the Doctor is undercover as a human teacher, John Smith, at a boys' school. He cannot even remember that he is a Time Lord, reinforcing his appearance as simply a white, middle-class, heterosexual male. Although Martha does retain her memories, she works at the school as a maid. Courtney Stoker observes that Martha – a middle-class doctor in training – is the only new companion 'with much power in her own world' (2012, p. 122), and thus her role as a servant here might appear to be a reversal intended to be absurd, or to be an obvious injustice that social change rectifies in the future. Yet instead, Stoker argues, Martha's maid's uniform functions as a 'visual amplification of her relationship to the Doctor, not a deviation from it' (p. 124), given the tendency of the series to position Martha as caring for the Doctor but having her 'service' continually taken for granted by him. Likewise, Bradford also notes that Martha functions, more than other female companions, as caregiver, working in a shop during 'Blink' (3.10) to support the Doctor while he tries to get them home: 'Why the Doctor can't also get a job is never explained. Nor why a highly educated person such as Martha would end up in a shop, a career path often held up in the Whoniverse as highly undesirable and something to escape from' (2010, pp. 171–2). These observations highlight mixed handling of Martha's character and the intersections of her gendered identity with race and class.

The 'Human Nature'/'Family of Blood' story foregrounds the 'tragic' relationship between 'Smith'/the Doctor and school nurse Joan Redfern, apparently possible when the Doctor is human but impossible when he regains his identity as a Time Lord. This serves, of course, to shift attention away from Martha and her sacrifice and onto the Doctor. When Martha tells Joan that she is a doctor, and comes from a world where women can *be* doctors, rather than just nurses, this seems to be an opportunity to illuminate history. Joan responds that even if this were possible there would 'hardly [be] one of your colour', a reminder of Martha's 'place', as determined for Joan by her skin colour. Yeager points out that there are documented examples of black female doctors during this period and therefore while they may not be commonplace, they are not unheard of (she gives details of three; 2013, p. 25). In fact, Yeager implies that the series could play a role in educating its viewers about this neglected history but instead prefers to focus on the romance plot featuring white middle-class characters.

As noted above, Martha is one of very few companions to leave the TARDIS of her own accord, 'a moment many have pointed out as Martha's strongest' (Stoker 2012, p. 122), yet the severing of her ties with the Doctor is protracted, with more than one goodbye. Dodson observes that in each scene where the two part, supposedly for the last time, 'the Doctor never gives her a word of praise' (2013, p. 32), in direct contrast to other companions like Rose and Donna. In particular, Martha's story in the season 3 finale ('The Sound of Drums' 3.12 and 'The Last of the Time Lords' 3.13) can be read as reinforcing her role as a devalued companion who services the Doctor while receiving neither praise nor acknowledgement of her sacrifice and heroism. In this story, Martha spends a year 'walking the Earth' to spread the word about the Doctor and find help to defeat the Master. This ostensibly frames her as a hero, yet the fact that it, inevitably, happens off-screen minimises Martha's contribution and emphasises that it is done to serve the Doctor. Certainly it can be interpreted as conveying that 'people of colour are expected to laud the power of white male heroes to liberate – to be maids, not masters, of liberation' (Firefly 2013, p. 19). Moreover, this positioning extends to Martha's whole family. Dodson notes that 'To underline the racial imagery [in 'Last of the Time Lords'], Martha's entire family of successful professionals are reduced to literal slaves of an abusive master' (2013, p. 32), presenting another unfortunate image of potentially positive black characters.

Torchwood has a more diverse ensemble cast from the start, seemingly by design. Toshiko Sato is a member of the team in seasons 1 and 2, Ianto's girlfriend is black, and Martha joins the Torchwood team briefly when they need a medical doctor after Owen's death in season 2. On the face of it, the series consciously presents a diverse range of characters. In addition, while some of Martha's *Doctor Who* episodes seemed to miss opportunities to engage with the histories of people of colour in the UK, Toshiko's ethnic identity is highlighted when she and Jack are transported to a Cardiff dance hall in 1941 ('Captain Jack Harkness' 1.12). Martha's skin colour leads to reminders of her 'place' in the era just prior to World War I, and during World War II Toshiko is called a 'Jap' and tells Jack how her grandfather was persecuted when he came to live in London.

Dunn argues that Toshiko fits stereotyped representations of Oriental characters – 'she is a cipher of exotic appearance, constructed by Western culture' (2010, p. 118) – and notes that 'her Japanese heritage is referred to as her distinguishing feature on several occasions' (p. 118). However, in this episode the danger to Toshiko because of her ethnicity is acknowledged to be very real, and the fact that Tosh needs to be 'rescued' and her presence explained or even vouched for by Jack also acknowledges the powerlessness of people of colour in earlier eras. Similarly, the easy acceptance of those attending the dance hall that Tosh is a patriot helping decode Japanese radio transmissions might seem to be a positive move. Writer Catherine Tregenna observes, 'The beauty of having Toshiko there is that she knows Pearl Harbor is coming' (2007, p. 43), as do the audience. At the same time, though, the episode is primarily focused on Jack and his adoption of the identity 'Captain Jack Harkness' from an officer who is killed in action shortly after this meeting (as mentioned in Chapter 1). As well as drawing attention to Toshiko's ethnic otherness, the epi- sode highlights Jack's sexual otherness when he dances with and kisses the 'real' Captain Harkness in public. Given the flamboyant nature of Jack's character, and the characterisation of Toshiko as someone who likes to stay in the background, Toshiko's story here is definitely overshadowed by Jack's, valorising the otherness of a white male over a woman of colour.

Certainly, Toshiko's representation seems to oscillate between her ethnicity being marked and unmarked: unremarked upon by a soldier from 1918, yet noted by some characters in the twenty-first century. Like Martha in *Doctor Who*, Tosh's family is affected by her work – during the flashbacks in 'Fragments' (2.12) we see her committing espionage because her mother is being held hostage by those forcing her to steal plans for a 'sonic modulator'. She and those holding her mother are captured by UNIT, yet Jack saves her from being condemned as a 'traitor' by offering her a job at Torchwood, noting that the plans she stole would not have worked, but she 'fixed' them so they would. Thus Tosh's brilliance is estab- lished but she needs a white male to find her 'place' and make an effective contribution to society. Moreover, her role as technology expert also fits stereotypes of East Asian characters as intelligent and nerdy (particularly in the US, East Asian Americans have been labelled the 'model minority' because of high achievement in education).

In *The Sarah Jane Adventures*, the ethnic identities of Rani Chandra and Clyde Langer generally go without comment. Indeed, Rani's character might be said to challenge stereotypes of female passivity because of her ambition and drive to succeed, as well as her willingness to face danger. Her father, Haresh, the school headmaster, is generally presented as a model middle-class citizen and a caring parent. Gita, Rani's mother, on the other hand, is routinely used as comic relief and presented as somewhat silly and often unaware of what is going on with those around her, as already noted in the previous chapter. This may not be directly connected with ethnicity, of course, and Garner points out that Rani's predecessor Maria had a (white) mother who was similarly characterised: both, he says, are 'self-absorbed and oblivious' (2010, p. 167). This makes sense in terms of offering a contrast to Sarah Jane, the 'good' adult and role model, even as it seems to devalue mothers in particular. (Maria's father, Alan, is as caring and warm as Haresh, and becomes involved in at least one adventure.) Rani and her family seem to be entirely British in terms of their cultural identity and ethnicity is never their 'distinguishing feature', as Dunn argued about Toshiko.

On a couple of occasions Rani's ethnic identity is marked, first in 'The Temptation of Sarah Jane Smith' when she tries to find a time-travelling Sarah Jane and repair a damaged timestream. The need to take action overcomes any inhibitions Rani might have about being an 'ethnic person in the Fifties' (following Sarah Jane, she travels back to 1951), but the fact that she is conscious of her 'difference' in this earlier, rural and much less diverse Britain makes viewers aware of it too. Similarly, and perhaps most notably, her ethnicity is marked during the season 4 story 'Lost in Time' when each young character is transported to a different time. Rani finds herself in the Tower of London in 1553, and befriends Lady Jane Grey – her presence explained as a lady in waiting 'arrived from the East'. This might seem to parallel the way Martha was positioned as a servant in 1913, yet here Rani becomes the confidante of Jane

Grey and manages to offer her genuine comfort as well as helping to save the world (a contribution that is fully acknowledged). In this way, Rani still has agency and her subjectivity is foregrounded (her part of the story is told from her point of view, without contesting interpretations). Moreover, when Rani realises that she cannot save Jane from inevitable death, this experience of history is positioned as a valuable learning experience that helps Rani mature: in other words, the story is focused on her.

Clyde's situation is perhaps a little different, given the mixture of class, gender and ethnicity in his characterisation. While never directly acknowledged, Clyde's flippant attitude seems to be a result of other people's perceptions of him. Luke, the alien-grown Archetype, becomes a model school student and leaves Bannerman Road on a fast track to Oxford University, apparently overcoming the limitations of his situation – perhaps unsurprisingly given he has access to the privilege of a white middle-class male. Clyde also struggles with aspects of his identity, and this is complicated, at least implicitly, by being black. While Mr Smith tells Clyde in season 1, 'You're not as stupid as you pretend to be' ('The Lost Boy' 1.6) and Sarah Jane comes to value him as a member of the team, we see Clyde continually denigrated by Haresh as an unsuitable friend for his daughter because of his lack of interest in traditional academic achievement. Clyde's artistic ability is high-lighted in more than one story: during 'Mona Lisa's Revenge' (3.5) he wins an art competition, but only because Luke has submitted some of his work without telling him. This uncertainty about his own talent and ability to achieve is generally papered over by Clyde's clowning and façade of 'cool' in a much more sympa-thetic manner than with Mickey in *Doctor Who*. Mickey was the object of ridicule; Clyde uses comedy as a means of constructing his identity and making himself likeable. He is also, perhaps as a result of being largely raised by his mother, less concerned about defining gender boundaries, though he is clearly aware of them. He cooks dinner for himself and his mum, Carla, once a week

('Mark of the Beserker' 2.4), and befriends Sky when she joins Sarah Jane's 'family', even being designated best babysitter when she first appears.

In 'Lost in Time' (4.5) Clyde finds himself near a Norfolk village during 1941. Here, he meets an evacuee from London, George, and the two succeed in foiling a Nazi invasion. Clyde's insistence on talking back to authoritarian adults is valorised in this episode: he is dismissed as 'a negro' by the German officer Koenig but displays a strong sense of patriotism in his stirring response about the Nazis' 'blind, stupid prejudice' causing them to lose the war. The fact that he works with (white British) George to defeat the Nazis, who have infiltrated with the help of the apparently all-British white school mistress, signals diversity as part of this conception of patriotic Britishness. The story may be overly optimistic about Clyde's easy acceptance by George and the other inhabitants of Norfolk, yet his identity as black British is underlined when he uses his mobile phone to distract the Germans and it plays the opening of Tinie Tempah's rap hit 'Pass Out'.

AGE

Age and ageism is perhaps even more insidious in terms of representation. Most of the Doctor's companions in the rebooted series have been young and attractive, as has the Doctor himself – until the departure of Matt Smith and the debut of Peter Capaldi. The Doctor has only really had one companion who is unambiguously old: Wilfred Mott, Donna's grandfather, played by veteran British actor Bernard Cribbins. Cribbins had played a companion in the 1966 film *Daleks: Invasion Earth 2150 A.D.*, so his casting as Wilf around forty years later recalls the long history of the series and its characters, while Cribbins' role on children's series like *Jackanory* (1965–96) and more recently *Old Jack's Boat* (2013–) situates him as a father and grandfather of British culture.

If Rory and Mickey are companions at one remove, drawn in by their connection to Amy and Rose, Wilf is likewise connected to the Tenth Doctor because of his granddaughter, Donna. Wilf's character certainly might be termed a positive portrayal of an older character. In keeping with Cribbins' established persona, Wilf is depicted across all his appearances as a 'wise and gentle old man' (Loborik, Gibson and Laing 2013, p. 197). A family member at one generational remove, he acts as necessary support for Donna, who is often at odds with her mother, Sylvia. Thus he is positioned as someone who might readily engage viewer sympathy and his frequent displays of affection for the outwardly abrasive but inwardly insecure Donna justify her love for him, as well as adding depth to her character's history. Wilf becomes a companion in his own right during the 2009–10 New Year special, helping the Tenth Doctor defeat the Master and then, tragically, becoming the cause of the Doctor's regeneration ('Journey's End' 4.17, 'The End of Time' 4.18). In this adventure, Wilf is still a figure of comedy and affection, but the sacrifice the Doctor makes on his behalf allows him to be taken seriously. In the *Doctor Who Character Encyclopedia*, this shift in emphasis is highlighted: 'A soldier in his younger days, Wilf's heroic qualities never left him' (Loborik, Gibson and Laing 2013, p. 197). However, it may only be Wilf's age – and the distance from his military past – that allows him to seem simultaneously heroic yet affectionate, emotional and gentle.

Older female characters have historically been few and far between on television, and science fiction is no exception. The rebooted *Doctor Who* has been criticised for apparently insisting that female companions must be young and attractive (see Johnson 2014) – the exception being Donna, who is one of the most convincing (and popular) of them. Lynette Porter notes that Amy has not acquired much life experience and 'her attitude thus seems abrasive and annoying rather than mature and ballsy' (2013, p. 257), while Helen Kang observes that to her, Rose and Martha 'felt juvenile as characters' (2010, p. 41). Donna's age and maturity, coupled with her lack of romantic interest in the Doctor, make her more inclined to speak her mind, repeatedly challenging his authority. 'Listen, I don't know what kind of kids you've been flying around with in outer space,' she tells him in 'The Fires of Pompeii', 'but you are not telling me to shut up' (4.2), insisting that he hear her voice and her opinions. In this episode she sways the Doctor, who returns to save the family they have met when the volcano erupts. Donna's tenure was much shorter than other companions' (presumably because of Catherine Tate's other commitments), and she was succeeded first by Amy, and then by Clara, in a return to the more conventional attractions of youth.

Older female characters tend to appear in the series on a regular basis, but are generally featured in the same way as characters of colour – as guest stars (like Madge Arwell or Mercy Hartigan) or recurring roles (particularly River Song, but also Harriet Jones, Kate Lethbridge-Stewart and Madame Vastra). As I have argued elsewhere (Jowett 2014), River is a particularly controversial character and her relationship with the Eleventh Doctor was criticised partly because of the apparent age difference between them (that is, the visible age difference between the actors), causing her to be characterised as a 'cougar': 'there's a bit of the cougar in Kingston's on-screen relationship with 28-year-old Matt Smith' (Duncan 2011) – cougar being slang for an older woman who seeks out younger men for sexual relationships. Potentially, River fits Kathleen Rowe's model of the 'unruly woman' (1995) and often displays characteristics or behaviour – especially sexual behaviour – that might be considered inappropriate for her age. She is ultimately constrained by her function in the narrative, and by her problematic character development, despite Alex Kingston's best efforts. (See the next chapter for more on River outside of the television series.)

With the tenure of Tennant and then Smith, the Doctor has also become 'young' and attractive, embodied by more youthful actors who became heart-throbs (see Williams 2011). The

50th-anniversary special episode 'The Day of the Doctor' (7.14) contrasted this with the War Doctor played by John Hurt, in his early seventies. In conversation with his later incarnations, the War Doctor observes their fetishisation of youth/youthful appearance and asks, 'What is it that makes you ashamed of being a grown-up?' He also questions the prevalence of heterosexual romance: 'Is there a lot of this in the future?' he asks the Eleventh Doctor as the Tenth Doctor kisses Queen Elizabeth I.

Hurt, with a 50-year acting career spanning six decades, tends to overshadow Tennant and Smith because of his experience. Smith admits, 'Me and David would be climbing the walls but Johnny just needs to do one tiny thing, and that is the scene' (2013). The War Doctor was never set to be a permanent incarnation, though he has become popular with fans, and also features in one spin-off novel to date (see Chapter 4) and some comics. His character hinted at how an 'older' Doctor might function in the post-2005 series. The announcement that Smith's replacement would be 55-year-old Peter Capaldi then offered further possibility for change, both in how the Doctor was being presented and in his relationship with companions. As Catherine Johnson observes, 'his age marked a significant departure in new *Who* from casting younger male actors in the title role' and she argues that these concerns 'emerged within the series itself, particularly in the opening episode. [...] Here Clara stood in for the disgruntled viewer upset at the transformation of the youthful, handsome Matt Smith into the old, dour and Scottish Capaldi' (2014).

Torchwood also tends to eschew older main characters in favour of the young and beautiful: despite Jack being literally unkillable and therefore living for centuries (while his 'age' is difficult to determine), he is still played by an actor who at his last appearance in the role was yet to reach 45. *The Sarah Jane Adventures*, on the other hand, features a youthful cast alongside a heroic older woman, something of a novelty for action and science fiction. While Alan Jackson (Maria's father) skateboarding in 'Whatever

Happened to Sarah Jane?' (1.5) is played for laughs as doing something inappropriate for someone of his age, Sarah Jane regularly and competently takes on aliens and, with the help of her young companions, saves the world. Producer Matt Bouch picks this out as distinctive, saying that he 'liked the idea of having an older character and a team of youngsters because that's an interesting emotional dynamic *and you don't often see that*' (2007, p. 29; emphasis added). At the same time, however, he says: 'The dynamic between an older woman and a younger group of people led you down a more traditional storytelling route. She became this kind of surrogate parent.' Bouch uses the word 'parent' here and not mother, but calling this 'a more traditional storytelling route' suggests he is aware that it taps into gendered stereotypes and characterisations (as discussed in Chapter 1). That he then describes Sarah Jane as 'this kind of Yoda/Merlin character, who has specialized knowledge and a magical world who can guide our characters' indicates how the series – and its producers – is perhaps unaware of how to develop a female hero without resorting to masculine archetypes (Bouch 2007, p. 29). It is rather unfair to single out Bouch here, yet the apparent contradictions in his comments speak to the complexities and contradictions in Sarah Jane when she becomes the title character in her own series.

After conducting a 'thematic analysis of the stereotypes of older women prevalent in the media', Dafna Lemish and Varda Muhlbauer found 'three recurring types: the controlling mother; the plain, uneducated, but good housewife; and the bitch-witch older woman' (2012, p. 170). Arguably, all three of these stereotypes are present in *The Sarah Jane Adventures*, but none adequately describe Sarah Jane herself. Likewise, Maricel Oró-Piqueras, in an examination of the TV series *Brothers and Sisters*, argues that 'the media has been ungenerous by neither constructing nor spreading a positive image of the aging process in women,' again suggesting a very narrow range. Bouch's description of Sarah Jane as Yoda or Merlin actively overturns a stereotype identified, perhaps rather sweepingly, by Oró-Piqueras: 'The aging and old woman has been represented as either a motherly and grandmotherly figure or the evil woman who uses her experiential wisdom to manipulate others' (2014, p. 20). Sarah Jane, in contrast, uses her experiential wisdom, her knowledge of the universe from her travels in the TARDIS and her subsequent adventures, to help, nurture and protect others in ways that go beyond stereotypical 'mothering' or 'grandmothering' and align themselves, as Bouch's parallels suggest, with powerful mentor figures. Moreover, her approach to alien adventures also challenges the way older women 'continue to be located within the world of emotions in which rational thought is lacking and behavior is uncultured' (Lemish and Muhlbauer 2012, p. 170). In her own series, Sarah Jane is most vulnerable when she is uncharacteristically distracted by emotion, much like a male hero.

Yet, like many other older women characters, including River Song, Sarah Jane's position as an autonomous single female is often contradictory. Lemish and Muhlbauer point to the 'growing presence of women in many media-related professions, as well as the devotion of several mature celebrity-actresses to issues of gender equality (including acting such roles, as well as directing and producing movies themselves)' as factors that 'have resulted in innovative images of older women, mainly in the film and television industries' (2012, pp. 172–3; see Chapter 5 for more on women working in television production). The most obvious place these images might occur is in domestic drama, and the US examples Lemish and Muhlbauer offer of 'strong, multi-dimensional older women' tend to be 'matriarchs and occasionally overbearing mothers who incorporate elements of counter-hegemonic portrayals of mature womanhood' situated within a family and domestic context.[10] Powerful female characters also appear in the public or professional sphere (Lemish and Muhlbauer cite Candice Bergen in *Boston Legal* and Christine Baranski in *Private Practice*; 2012, pp. 172–3), and this is where Sarah Jane seems to fit best. Her role, though, falls between the public and the domestic, the professional and the familial, as already noted in Chapters 1 and 2. She is neither a demonstrably successful, powerful professional (her articles are rarely seen and her journalism is used primarily in the TV series as a cover for her 'real' investigative work), nor a biological matriarch, and her strength as a hero is kept secret from all but her closest allies. Thus, her heroism is as invisible as older women generally become in a youth-fixated society.

This is not to say that Sarah Jane is without privilege or real-world power, however. Sherry Ginn notes that while *The Sarah Jane Adventures* 'provides the viewer with many exemplars of a woman living her life on her own terms' the conditions of its title character's life enable both her autonomy and her heroism:

> Those terms include having a large amount of money and teenage children, the first to allow her the luxury of not having to worry about how to pay the bills, and the second of not having to worry about diapers and childcare (2013, p. 250).

Sarah Jane's large detached house, well-kept and distinctive car and apparently endless time to devote to investigating alien happenings are signifiers of class as well as familiar trappings of the male hero. This aligns her with her young allies, who have no adult responsibilities as yet and are all from comfortable middle-class backgrounds, even those from single-parent families. Arguably this is necessary for the narrative premise to work effectively, and perhaps Sarah Jane earns her living while the teens are at school.

Thus, like most other 'positive' representations of older women on television, Sarah Jane's character 'ignores the majority of older women who are not rich, not White, not "hot", and not leading associates in famous law firms or medical practices' (Lemish and Muhlbauer 2012, p. 174). In this case though, for some, Sarah Jane *had* been young and 'hot' and was now, visibly, older. Her character, as Porter notes, is partly about 'continuity' (from the classic series to the audio adventures to the rebooted series to her own spin-off), and Porter concludes that this makes Sarah Jane 'a far less controversial or mercuric [*sic*] character than' Jack or the Doctor (2012, p. 126). Yet Ross Garner observes that while the Doctor is regenerated into different, generally youthful, actors, and Jack continues to be unkillable and ages indiscernibly, 'the *embodied presence* of Elisabeth Sladen reprising the role she had left 30 years earlier' (2013a, p. 194; original emphasis) makes Sarah Jane different to both these *Who*-universe heroes. Garner is primarily concerned with nostalgia and responses to Sarah Jane's return in the reboot and her own series, but nevertheless he highlights the way that an actor 'reprising his or her role also emphasises the passing of (extra-) diegetic time, as the ageing body of the performer – in this instance Elisabeth Sladen as Sarah Jane – affects nostalgic responses by recognizably, but differentially, embodying the character' (2013a, p. 201). This ageing body situates Sarah Jane's character firmly within a 'real' universe, one that might see aliens visiting from other planets or dimensions, but one that she and her allies cannot leave, any more than they can bend the physical laws of time in the way the Doctor and Jack do.

As several scholars have noted, Sarah Jane's ageing body is also presented in particular ways, 'managed' Hannah Hamad suggests, by being positioned 'as what Sadie Wearing calls a "subject of rejuvenation" […] facilitating a culturally apposite re-entry into postfeminist culture' (2011). Sarah Jane's 'postfeminist' appearance might be indicative of social pressure to disguise the 'signs of ageing': Oró-Piqueras argues that this is necessary for a woman to 'still be considered an active part of society; otherwise, she is made invisible and put aside' (2014, p. 21). The many storylines about erasing Sarah Jane's identity (see Chapter 1) may, consciously or otherwise, have been influenced by this logic, and though she always emerges victorious from these trials, they nevertheless suggest the continuous threat of social invisibility for older women.

The ageing female body, Oró-Piqueras adds, 'is also perceived as "the other" by those younger women who fear ageing as the tombstone that will distance them from social visibility' (2014, p. 21). Arguably this fear underlies the story 'The Madwoman in the Attic' (3.2), which flashes forward to 2059 and shows an older version of Rani who lives in Sarah Jane's attic and remembers her previous adventures. However, in Clyde and Sarah Jane's interactions during the same episode we see, perhaps, a slightly more positive attitude to ageing, one that is able to acknowledge and even poke fun at the different physical embodiment of the characters, and at society's fascination with youth.

During one scene Clyde, typically, questions authority, asking Sarah Jane, 'Are you sure you know where we're going?' leading her to comment that Luke would have complained less. Never one to hold back a snippy rejoinder, Clyde responds, 'I run faster though,' which in turn provokes Sarah Jane to assert, 'I was holding back so you could keep up.' This sparring for the last word continues, even as Clyde reassures Sarah Jane that Rani will 'be okay' and that Sarah Jane is not responsible for the choices the young people make in joining her defence of the Earth. When she tries to refute this he resists, saying, 'You're getting old, you know. Your memory's going.' After a pause, Sarah Jane chooses to accept Clyde's point, and his deflection of tension into humour, laughing and joking, 'You're not going to take an old lady's hand? I might fall if you don't.' Sarah Jane's hesitation here before she joins in the joke indicates her reluctance to concede her age and its effects on her body, something not generally approved in contemporary society. It may even be that she is able to make a joke about her own ageing in this situation because Clyde is not a male who might be romantically interested in her – though ironically it is presumably her age (and the fact that *The Sarah Jane Adventures* is a children's programme) that precludes this. (MILF may be a current term, but GILF is definitely not.)

While the presentation of other older women in the series might fit Lemish and Muhlbauer's model of competition and destructiveness, as noted by Hamad and in Chapter 1, Sarah Jane's centrality challenges it. She might, admittedly, function much like a superhero with special powers – defined by her exceptionalism, rather than her normality. However, given the way the series normalises the exceptional, fitting fantasy into mundane settings and situations, it can be argued that Sarah Jane becomes *the* model of older womanhood, with other destructive versions revealed to be aliens. Overall, as Hamad admits, despite some flaws and contradictions, *The Sarah Jane Adventures* 'was extraordinary for its discursive centralization of a sixty-something single woman with agency and amiability' (2012, p. 175).

SEXUALITY

The most obvious example of a *Who*-universe series that challenges sexuality is *Torchwood*: designed for a niche audience, and originally broadcast in the UK after the 9pm watershed, it set out to include 'adult content' and its first episodes showed every member of the Torchwood team having some kind of sexual contact that defied heteronormativity. Thus, although Jack kisses the Doctor before leaving the TARDIS in *Doctor Who*'s 'Parting of the Ways' (1.13), Richard Berger notes: 'Sexuality is implicit in *Who*, but explicit in *Torchwood*' (2010, p. 74). Likewise, in her essay about 'transgressive touch', Ria Cheyne observes that 'sexual contact is perhaps the most obvious form of touch in *Torchwood*, and the emphasis on the sexuality of the characters is one of the notable differences between *Torchwood* and *Doctor Who*' (2010, p. 44). *Torchwood* explores sexual behaviour, most often without the confines of romance and relationships, so much so that when Amal El-Mohtar argues that audiences might want to be 'shown as well as told about queer relationships on television' he identifies Moffat-era *Doctor Who* as only delivering the telling, while *Torchwood* offers 'a lot of queer sex without meaningful queer relationships' (2013, p. 69). Sexuality is one of *Torchwood*'s most talked-about features and this book will not cover the same ground, but it is worth noting that El-Mohtar's criticism arises from debates about whether representation of 'minorities' is obliged to be 'positive' and representative, or is free to explore whatever avenues it wishes.

There is also some debate about whether 'normalising' sexualities other than hetero is progressive or regressive.[11] Thus, although Alec Charles notes that *Torchwood* 'took for granted that general homophobia was history (quite literally so: TMD [*Torchwood: Miracle Day*] sees homophobia as a phenomenon of the 1920s)' (2013, p. 166), the explicit sex scenes (gay and straight) in *Torchwood: Miracle Day*, enabled by its positioning on the Starz network, also came under fire. *Miracle Day* attracted criticism not for graphically depicting gay sex, but for repositioning Jack as 'gay' rather than 'omnisexual' (see also Porter 2012, p. 99) partly by pairing him exclusively with men, but also via the tension between Rex and Jack. 'Rex doesn't like his jokes too gay,' Jack quips in 'Dead of Night' (4.3), and when Rex asks Jack if he is trying to 'make everyone who's around you gay?' Jack blithely responds, 'That's the plan' ('Escape to L.A.' 4.4). This may make strong, positive statements about male homosexuality (with another layer because of actor John Barrowman's identity as openly gay), yet it arguably reinstates a binary of 'straight' and 'gay' identities, rather than the spectrum of sexualities seen in previous seasons.

In this sense, then, *Doctor Who* might be criticised for implying other sexualities rather than depicting them in detail, and *Torchwood*, in making one of its main characters sexually nonconforming, has to negotiate how a non-heteronormative character might be presented. Can Jack be visibly and overtly non-heterosexual, without having sexuality define his character or simply becoming an 'issue'? In terms of how audiences receive drama series, subtext, slash fiction (a subgenre of fan fiction that focuses on sexual relationships between characters of the 'same' sex, most commonly male–male) and shipping (derived from 'relationship') have all played their part in interpreting characters and their relationships and/or resisting dominant or surface readings. In an era when marriage is not restricted to heterosexual couples across many Western countries, subtext or 'reading into' a favourite series is no longer sufficient, and negotiating character relationships is both more important and more complex.

Relying on subtext and implication now carries the risk of accusations of queer-baiting, and Moffat's tenure as showrunner has elicited such complaints, especially during the Eleventh Doctor's run.[12] Britton seems to see episodes like 'Closing Time' (6.12) as genuine queering of the Doctor (2011), but others perceive such representations as a superficial challenge to heteronormativity, produced by and aimed at heterosexuals. Since this subtextual hinting has never actually become text, it seems that, as Claire Jenkins notes, *Doctor Who* 'demonstrates the commodification of masculinity and male sexuality as a way of reinforcing normative masculinity' (2013, p. 380) and, consequently, of heteronormativity. As Jenkins points out, episodes potentially queering the Doctor sit alongside Amy's 'desire for him', something that effectively 'heterosexualises the Doctor' (2013, p. 385).

Eventually *Doctor Who* introduces a recurring female–female couple: Madame Vastra, a Silurian, and human Jenny Flint. Vastra and Jenny debut in 'A Good Man Goes to War' (6.7), making a cameo appearance alongside Strax, a Sontaran commander, and other characters from previous episodes[13] when the Doctor calls in reinforcements – allies made during his travels – in an attempt to rescue the pregnant Amy. The two reappear, along with Strax, in 2012's Christmas special 'The Snowmen' (7.X), having formed a household in nineteenth-century London. While Vastra introduces herself and Jenny at one point in memorable, unambiguous terms (as quoted at the beginning of this chapter: 'Good evening. I'm a lizard woman from the dawn of time and this is my wife'), the relationship is still somewhat problematic. Vastra is styled as 'the great detective' and is clearly the householder, while Jenny and Strax take on the roles of housemaid and butler respectively. This is, as the dialogue states repeatedly, a 'cover', though why such cover should be maintained when Vastra announces her identity in the terms detailed above is not quite clear. Jenny thus appears to be on a par with Martha in 1913, and with Gwyneth (Gwen's ancestor) in 'The Unquiet Dead' (1.3), part of a dispensable, often invisible servant class. Moreover, given the scheduling of *Doctor Who* as an early-evening, family-friendly series, Vastra and Jenny might exchange innuendo and talk about their relationship but it is rarely acknowledged visually as physical and sexual.

In August 2014, during the season 8 premiere ('Deep Breath' 8.1), the two exchanged an on-screen 'kiss' which attracted some press coverage and received a handful of complaints from British audience members. The six complaints were not upheld by the regulatory body Ofcom, on the basis that 'same-sex' kisses are not treated differently to heterosexual kisses under Ofcom's rules (McCormick 2014). The very small number of complaints suggests that public attitudes are changing and that it is now considered acceptable to depict 'same-sex' kissing in pre-watershed drama. In any case, the 'kiss' was not presented in a sexualised context, given that Vastra does it to share oxygen with Jenny as the characters hold their breath to evade detection by clockwork cyborgs. Therefore, this is as much a 'kiss of life' as a physical demonstration of affection or sexual attraction (or perhaps a 'kiss of life' motivated by such affection and attraction). As has been common within science fiction, this representation allows the series to show a 'lesbian kiss' on screen during family viewing time because it is narratively 'justified' as something other than a lesbian kiss.

In fact, since Vastra and Jenny are an interspecies couple, the relationship offers some distance from what might be considered a 'real' human lesbian relationship: not only is it not a 'kiss', it is arguably not between 'lesbians', depending on how this is defined. Lesbian or gay kisses in other UK early-evening drama have not provided such justification (see *Brookside* in 1994 and Syed and

Christian, who married in a civil ceremony during *EastEnders* in 2011).

Following the introduction of Vastra and Jenny, and the removal of heterosexual attraction, acknowledged or otherwise, between the Doctor and his companions since Capaldi became the Twelfth Doctor, heterosexual romance has largely been confined to Clara's relationship with Danny Pink, which – as noted above – is in itself problematic and ends in Danny's death. However, the transformation of the Master into Missy (also in season 8) raises issues around the series' depiction of sexuality as well as of gender. 'The relationship between the Doctor and the Master has long held a homoerotic edge for many *Doctor Who* fans,' Catherine Johnson points out (2014). Given that the Doctor and the Master have a connection far outlasting the tenure of any companion in the TARDIS, this is perhaps unsurprising. Asher-Perrin talks about their 'heartbreaking codependency' (2013, p. 27; see also El-Mohtar 2013, p. 62). It was therefore a disappointment to many that only when the Master became a woman was this relationship depicted in physically intimate or sexual terms. In this sense, what can be seen as advancement in relation to depictions of gender within the series results in a regression in representations of sexuality. Moreover, gender and sexuality are entwined here with age. Johnson notes, 'At the same time as erasing some of the queerness of the Doctor/Master relationship, the implication of a sexual relationship between Capaldi and Gomez equally contributes to the series' continuing inability to imagine male/female relationships outside of a sexual framework' (2014), and, I would add, outside traditional age parameters.

Perhaps unsurprisingly, given its status as a children's drama, *The Sarah Jane Adventures* shows no overtly sexual relationships, and none of its younger main characters engage even in heterosexual romance relationships.[14] However, CBBC had suggested that the series should have a gay character, and this was planned to be Luke. Davies revealed this in an audio commentary for a special

DVD release (2013). This did not come to pass because Elisabeth Sladen's death put an end to the series and, had Luke come out as gay, it might have attracted criticism since, as the previous chapter outlined, he is far from being a typical young man. Just as arguable, though, is that Luke's sense of not being 'normal' lends itself to this representation.

The refusal or at least sidelining of sexuality in the series is part of the presentation of Sarah Jane as an older woman, as discussed above. As Lemish and Muhlbauer argue: 'Glorification of women's external appearance as the most central characteristic of a woman's essence is directly related to the media's overemphasis on the portrayal of women as sexual beings whose central function is relegated to being objects of male sexual desire and pursuit' (2012, p. 169). In *The Sarah Jane Adventures*, and in children's drama generally, women are not necessarily depicted in this way. In line with *Doctor Who* and *Torchwood*'s emphasis on action, adventure and heroism, the third spin-off series also takes these as key factors and Sarah Jane's centrality to the narrative means that the depiction of her character diverges from the usual emphasis on female sexuality.

This is not to say that the series is 'progressive' or challenging norms: Sarah Jane's appearance is, if not conventional, at least acceptable in terms of normative femininity, as are Maria's, Rani's and Sky's. It is also worth pointing out that Sarah Jane is depicted as exceptional because of her adventures on the TARDIS and her role as protector of Earth, and therefore her appearance might equally suggest that she is not an ordinary woman in her sixties. In addition, as alluded to earlier, older women are often invisible in social terms, and therefore not seen as sexual. If the most common portrayal of older women that might be considered positive is as a motherly or grandmotherly figure, then, as Oró-Piqueras summarises (2014), it offers an asexual image, leaving images of young women to connote sexuality. Since Sarah Jane is a mother by proxy, she fits this model, and when her younger allies discover that she is in a romantic relationship with a man ('The Wedding of Sarah

Jane Smith'), it is only ever depicted in terms of companionship and affection, never sexually. At the conclusion of this story, Sarah Jane's relationship is revealed to have been manipulated by the Trickster as a means of creating chaos, suggesting that Sarah Jane is not, after all, feminine or conventional enough to attract a man's attention romantically or sexually.

This fits with Sarah Jane's at times awkward positioning as a professional older woman. However, since she rarely works with adults, accepting the help of children instead, Sarah Jane does not conform to the typical representation identified by Lemish and Muhlbauer: 'representations of older, sexy women frame them as powerful and successful in the prestigious workplace, threatening, and even dominating, male colleagues and competitors' (2012, p. 174). Sarah Jane is removed from the arena of adult relationships, substituting the alien technology known as Mr Smith for her 'husband', and where she is put in a position that requires her to 'threaten or dominate' she more frequently faces (at least nominally) female villains, as noted in Chapter 1. Like other depictions of successful professional women, Sarah Jane is 'childless, hav[ing] only fleeting intimate relationships (if at all), and [...] entirely devoted to [her] career and professional accomplishments' (Lemish and Muhlbauer 2012, p. 174), at least until her adoption of Luke and then Sky. Even after this, her depiction is still focused on her 'professional' role as protector of the Earth, rather than as 'mother' in a purely domestic context. Thus, she is potentially aligned more with older female detectives like Miss Marple or Jessica Fletcher (*Murder, She Wrote* 1984–96), where 'as spinsters [...] their portrayal is focused on their detective skills rather than their family, emotional, or sexual experiences' (Oró-Piqueras 2014, p. 21).

The series, for several reasons then, offers a departure from the prescription of romance. Friendship and mentorship are shown to be more important than myths of romance, which rarely, if ever, feature in conversation. It is even possible to argue that heterosexual relationships are generally shown as negative or failing since single-parent families are the 'norm', with Rani the only character whose parents remain happily married. Sarah Jane's brushes with heterosexual romance or desire turn out badly. She never knew her parents, since they died when she was a baby, and therefore was never provided with a model of heterosexual marriage to follow. In 'The Temptation of Sarah Jane Smith' (2.5), when she is able to travel back through a time portal and meet them for the first time, her parents are depicted as having a loving relationship. However, this is situated far in the past and also does not last, albeit because they sacrifice themselves to save the world.

It is not possible to address and explore all the dimensions of identity offered by the three television series, though this chapter has attempted to highlight some of the ways in which race, ethnicity, class and sexuality inevitably affect representations of gender. Whether this happens in a rather didactic and idealised fashion, as in *The Sarah Jane Adventures*, or in a provocative and highly self-conscious way, as in *Torchwood*, even a brief examination demonstrates how complex these intersections are, meaning that they are often interpreted variously.

4

PARATEXTS

The Unfolding Franchise

A s well as the television series themselves, the *Doctor Who* franchise also encompasses a range of what Jonathan Gray refers to as 'paratexts' (2010), from webisodes, games, audio adventures and books, to companion programmes such as *Doctor Who Confidential* (2005–11), *Totally Doctor Who* (2006–7), *Torchwood Declassified* (2006–11), and *Sarah Jane's Alien Files* (2010). Gender representation across this spectrum, therefore, has potential for diverging from the representational strategy of the series. The character of Bernice Summerfield, featured in novels and audio spin-offs from 'classic' *Doctor Who*, for instance, arguably provides a clear link to the new female companions, particularly River Song. Of course, the spin-off series themselves can be considered paratexts of *Doctor Who*, in that they expand the *Who* universe and develop particular characters from it. *Torchwood* and *The Sarah Jane Adventures* 'each construct their own mini-verse within the larger universe hinted at in the original series' (Evans 2011, p. 27). Various scholars have addressed issues of overlap between the different series, with Ross P. Garner suggesting that an 'intertextual barricade' existed initially between *Doctor Who* and *Torchwood* because of the latter's more adult address (2013b), while Lynette Porter argues that references in *The Sarah Jane Adventures* to *Doctor Who*, and especially the classic series, are kept to a minimum as they are unlikely to engage its target audience of children (2012, p. 121).

Of course, paratexts of any kind are not necessarily there to support or to subvert gender representation in the 'parent' text. There are obvious reasons why they have proliferated. Even for a public service broadcaster like the BBC, paratexts help build both programme brands, and audiences for those brands. Catherine Johnson notes that in recent years,

> When the BBC was under pressure to encourage the uptake of digital technologies and to increase its commercial revenue, developing programmes as branded products that could be exploited through trademark and copyright law across a wide range of extensions across multiple media emerged as an important commercial strategy (2013, p. 97).

The BBC now practises 360-degree commissioning, making or commissioning not programmes but bundled projects, and is moving, as Elizabeth Evans observes, to being a 'content provider' rather than a television service (2011, p. 35). The BBC has not been slow to exploit the rebooted *Doctor Who* as a worldwide programme brand, and has used it, as Johnson outlines, to deliver one of its six 'public purposes': 'delivering to the public the benefit of emerging communications technologies and services' (BBC n.d. a). The *Doctor Who Adventure Games*, Johnson notes, aim to fulfil this purpose, and BBC's head of TV content for iPlayer, Victoria Jaye, states, 'They really are aimed at taking a big broad audience, three generations of Who fans, into the internet platform' (in Johnson 2013, p. 105). Likewise, Porter, in her book on the franchise as a transatlantic success, discusses the BBC's launch of its *Doctor Who* Facebook page, and iTunes sales (2012, p. 133), while Evans examines the Tenth Doctor on BBC Red Button (a digital interactive service providing extra content) and the interactive episode 'Attack of the Graske' (2011, p. 25). However, Matt Hills argues that while *Doctor Who*'s paratexts *have* been partly driven by this mission statement about technology, the spin-off

Torchwood has 'typically [been] extended via lower-budget media (novels/radio/comic strips/information-based websites)' (2013b, p. 67), suggesting that as a public service broadcaster the BBC must operate with certain limitations.

Indeed the brand – and the BBC – has not altogether avoided the problems that come with new technologies. Evans notes the lack of mobile content (2011, p. 26), while Porter outlines how a technical problem with the *Torchwood* 'Web of Lies' ten-part motion comic/animation series, released online and as an iTunes app alongside *Miracle Day*, caused fan dissatisfaction (2012, p. 109). Content on *The Sarah Jane Adventures* website cannot be accessed using a tablet and runs the risk of becoming obsolete. Evans argues that 'the emergence of transmedia television texts is precisely about utilising the temporal windows inherent in the television schedule' (2011, p. 37), and therefore problems for viewers in other countries in accessing an internationally successful series are likely to militate against effectively doing so.

The rebooted *Doctor Who* and its ongoing unfolding of paratexts operates slightly differently than the classic series, given these industrial and technological shifts. As Evans notes, the audio adventures and novels that are 'tied in' to the classic series and, in part, filled the gap when the series was off the air 'may offer an expansion of the fictional world that was first presented in the television series', but 'they remain not only separate but also ancillary and secondary to it.' She argues that in this earlier era 'there is no integration between the television programme and the other elements of the transmedia text' (2011, pp. 23–4). This resulted in the book series becoming an independent line, completely separate from the *Doctor Who* brand.[15] Given this gap between the 'brand' and the tie-ins, as well as cultural changes in attitudes to gender while the series was off the air, it might be expected that gender representation would shift. By the time of the reboot in 2005, the television landscape had changed: 'In addition to new novels and toys, the BBC also produced games, mobile content and narrative-rich websites, expanding the universe of *Doctor Who* away from the television set more coherently than in its earlier incarnation' (Evans 2011, p. 24). This certainly seems to be the case, yet even the toy lines demonstrate certain attitudes towards gender: the packaging for River's sonic screwdriver is emblazoned with the words 'Tenth Doctor' and even includes a picture of Tennant's Doctor, indicating River's subordinate status even while offering an alternative to the Doctor's signature device.

The *Doctor Who* franchise would not be a successful contemporary television product if it did not have the expected range of multiplatform paratexts. Evans argues: 'New media elements are no longer added on to support or promote a more recognisable form; the balance between the different elements of a transmedia text has become more equal' (2011, p. 33). In this sense, then, the content, and perhaps even the canon, of *Doctor Who* and its universe is widespread, and both viewers and scholars might be expected to see a *Sarah Jane Adventures* webcomic, for instance, as just one part of a larger transmedia story. If, as Johnson observes, this strategy makes 'any inconsistencies across different texts and products more apparent and evident', it also makes 'the corporation's own expansion and exploitation of the series more visible to the public' (2013, p. 108). This was highly evident in the advertising of the 50th-anniversary special *Doctor Who* episodes. Hills observes that this was the first time 'the series has embraced a Twitter hashtag #savetheday' (2014b, p. 166; see also Williams 2013a) and the screening of the main anniversary episode, 'Day of the Doctor', was reported to be the biggest TV event on Tumblr and provoked 1.83 million tweets (p. 168).

In terms of their creative rather than their commercial function, paratexts can fulfil specific purposes in relation to narrative and character. Filling a gap, as *Doctor Who* novels and audio stories did between the classic and rebooted series, is one. The Eighth Doctor demonstrates this since with 'only one televised text and one web-released minisode' devoted to him, this incarnation could be easily ignored, yet, as Paul Booth observes, 'hundreds of hours of non-televised material deepen his story' (2014, p. 199). The reintroduction of Sarah Jane Smith as first a guest in *Doctor Who* and then as a character in her own spin-off series also indicates how paratexts are used: 'Audio adventures,' notes Porter, offer insight into what happened to Sarah Jane 'between leaving TARDIS and "School Reunion"' (2012, p. 125). Likewise, 'several web, radio or print texts helped serve as a transition between the television episodes' of *Torchwood: Children of Earth* and *Torchwood: Miracle Day* (Porter 2012, p. 83), because of the two-year hiatus between them. Paratexts are often positioned on a timeline, and may be advertised as 'before x' or 'between y and z', sometimes even functioning as 'prequels' or 'sequels' to other paratexts (such as *Torchwood: Long Time Dead*, which informs the reader on its front cover that it is 'a prequel to *Torchwood: Miracle Day*').

According to Richard Berger, in *Who* fanfic the 'trick was to maintain a level of fidelity while at the same time exploring new plots and developments' (2010, p. 67). 'Official' paratexts also explore new aspects: 'each proliferation, after all,' states Gray, 'holds the potential to change the meaning of the text' (2010, p. 2). Returning to Evans' evaluation that the BBC's current *Doctor Who* programme brand is being more coherently exploited, and that consumers and producers are taking paratexts more seriously as part of the 'main' narrative, it is hardly surprising that the 'meaning of the text' might be changed by shifts in emphasis. Given that both *Who* spin-off series feature protagonists first featured in another show, 'a level of fidelity' would be expected, even as the separate series raises expectations of 'new developments'. Thus, Porter examines the way both Jack and Sarah Jane were 'transformed as they took on new roles. Sarah Jane became a mother and a mentor. Captain Jack became a citizen of Earth and an integral part of Torchwood' (2012, p. 82). With games and paratexts that do not follow the same structures as television narrative, introductions from characters such as the Doctor or Mickey 'provide a recognizable figure that the audience can relate to and act as a form of narrative branding' (Evans 2011, p. 30), strengthening a sense of consistency across platforms. The fact that Mickey acts as a guide to *Doctor Who* flash games from 2006 demonstrates how paratexts can assign a more prominent role to a character who attracted audience interest but was somewhat neglected by the TV narrative. Paratexts can also address inconsistencies in continuity. Hills notes that *Torchwood* tie-ins can be seen as 'repairing or retconning errors in the TV text' (2013b, p. 67), and therefore as actually re-establishing continuity and consistency. Several scholars note how radio plays like 'The Dead Line' (2009) add depth to Jack and Ianto's relationship, cut off by Ianto's death in *Torchwood: Miracle Day*.

This chapter explores various approaches to paratexts and their representations of gender, looking first at examples that appear consistent with the TV series, then at those that parody their 'parent' texts and might therefore challenge or subvert its gendering.

LICENSED CONSISTENCY

Consistency is perhaps best exemplified by minisodes that fill in chronological gaps between television episodes. For instance, the 'Pond Life' five-part series of minisodes (released on consecutive days leading up to the 2012 season 7 premiere via the BBC's official *Doctor Who* website and then available through Red Button on the day the first TV episode was broadcast) form a serialised prequel, whetting viewers' appetites for what is to come. *Torchwood* episodes continually contrast Gwen Cooper's home life with her Torchwood activities, and this seems to be one way in which it distinguishes itself from its 'parent' text since we rarely see either the Doctor or his companions between adventures. These *Doctor Who* minisodes offer an 'inside' look at the home life of 'the Ponds' (immediately reinforcing Rory's positioning as 'Mr Pond', adjunct to Amy) when they are not travelling with the Doctor and, conversely, of his while they are not with him. The first, dated 'April', shows Amy and Rory in their kitchen drinking wine while listening to a voice message from the Doctor about meeting Mata Hari in a hotel room in Paris, for example. Point of view switches between the Doctor and the 'Ponds', with Rory in particular being rooted in 'normal' life, and the characterisation of Amy, Rory and the Eleventh Doctor established in TV episodes is continued. 'May' sees the Doctor bursting into the Ponds' bedroom while Rory and Amy sleep, and the fact that Rory wearily tells him, 'We have a rule about the bedroom' and concludes, 'I really hate it when he does that' suggests that such disruptions are becoming regular, if not quite mundane.

The tone of this paratext may appear more comedic than the usual TV episodes – writing for Den of Geek, Louisa Mellor describes 'Pond Life' as a 'comic spin-off' and notes that the first four episodes are 'characterised by silliness, frivolous gags, and an Ood on the loo' (2012). Parts 3 and 4, 'June' and 'July', see Rory find the 'Ood on the loo' (accidently transported into the Ponds' home by the Doctor) and then show the Ood carrying out domestic tasks. Rory explains, 'He seems to think he's our butler,' yet the visuals in the montage that follows complicate this masculine gendering: the Ood wears a frilly apron while making beds, hanging out laundry and cleaning windows. Juxtaposing the apron with the typical Ood boiler suit offers a confusion of codes that is clearly meant to be humorous, as is Amy and Rory's discomfort at being served.

The final episode, however, 'had a drastically different tone' as Mellor notes (2012): it depicts the breakdown of Amy and Rory's relationship, forming a direct segue to 'Asylum of the Daleks' (7.1), where they are separated. 'August' opens in typical style with the Doctor fixing the light on the TARDIS roof and babbling about 'inventing pasta', but his usual effervescence is dampened (literally) when he is left on the doorstep in the rain wondering why the Ponds are not at home. He leaves a message on their answering machine in a sequence juxtaposing his usual verbosity with a worried facial expression, and he erases the message once he has finished. This is intercut with Rory leaving the house, in an emotional scene played in silence and slow motion, with Rory showing frustration or exasperation, and Amy putting her hand over her mouth as if to stop herself crying. Later, she re-enters the house alone, and checks the phone for messages before wondering aloud where the Doctor is when she – they – need him. Thus, Amy's intimate connection with the Eleventh Doctor is emphasised, particularly when 'real life' seems overwhelming.

Likewise, the minisode 'The Night of the Doctor' released on the BBC iPlayer and online via YouTube, as well as later through Red Button in the run-up to the 50th-anniversary special in 2013, also seems explicitly intended to fill gaps and, perhaps, to retcon the history of the Doctor's regenerations to 'fix' the plot twist that formed the cliffhanger ending of 'The Name of the Doctor' (7.13). The title is a conscious nod to both the anniversary special and the celebrations themselves ('The Day of the Doctor'), positioning the minisode as a direct prequel. It also functioned as a retroactive continuity link from the 'classic' series to the reboot, since it featured the Eighth Doctor, played by Paul McGann. The Eighth Doctor, as noted above, had only appeared on screen in the ill-fated 1996 TV movie thus far, and Hills discusses how 'The Night of the Doctor' functions to unify classic and new Who (2015, p. 41). Here, the Eighth Doctor regenerates into the War Doctor (John Hurt; Hurt had been introduced as a previously unseen incarnation at the end of 'The Name of the Doctor'). While this reference to the Eighth Doctor might have been obscure to viewers who had only watched the series since 2005, it was welcomed by fans who knew the classic series – one viewer calling it 'Pure unadulterated fanboy heaven' (Richie C 2013) – as well as lauded by the BBC as 'a new creative canvas for storytelling' that 'enabled' producers to show 'something fans had never seen before' (Jaye 2014; see also Chapter 6).

Given the apparent intention of providing continuity, it is hardly surprising that the minisode sticks to presenting the Eighth and the War Doctors as heroic, if damaged, versions of masculinity

not unlike those seen in the post-2005 series. 'Night of the Doctor'
opens with the Doctor interrupting Cass, a female pilot, whose
ship is badly damaged during the Time War. She is repulsed on
discovering he is a Time Lord, pointing out that both Time Lords
and Daleks are obsessed with the 'battlefield' to the point of erasing
any difference between them. Cass' (inevitable) death as the ship
crashes is presented as the final straw for the Eighth Doctor in the
scene that follows, when the Doctor is revived by the Sisterhood of
Karn. This group of female mystics reinforce binary gender roles as
they talk about their instinctive knowledge ('we have always known
in our bones that he would return') but still need a (male) warrior
to stop the war. In order to persuade the Doctor to be that saviour –
he insists, 'I will not fight' – they manipulate him into choosing to
reincarnate as a 'warrior' by reminding him of his failure to save
Cass. He welcomes the pain of this artificial reincarnation, salutes
his former companions (mostly female), and apologises to Cass.
When regenerated as the War Doctor, he takes up Cass' gun belt
as the music reaches a dramatic peak. Thus, the Doctor remains a
reluctant and damaged hero, and female characters serve simply
as motivation, or as plot functions in a manner consistent with
the ongoing series.

Other paratexts take the opportunity to follow up particular
periods or settings. The book *Doctor Who: Summer Falls and Other
Stories* outwardly appears to be an artefact from the TV series. A
novel called *Summer Falls* is featured in the TV episode 'The Bells
of St. John' 7.6, so even the collection's title is a form of continuity.
The book includes two stories which link explicitly to the televised
narrative and feature its characters. 'The Angel's Kiss', by Justin
Richards, refers directly to season 7 of the televised narrative
when Rory is transported from New York City in 2012 back to
1938, only to unexpectedly meet River. Amy and the Doctor find
clues in a pulp detective story about Melody Malone aka Melody
Pond, or River Song ('The Angels Take Manhattan' 7.5). In the
episode, this book is revealed to be written by Amelia Williams

(Amy 'disguised' by adopting her husband's surname), and it contains an afterword to the Doctor. Hills has examined tie-ins that maximise their medium – and this is certainly the case here, with the packaging and Introduction signalling the book's author as 'Amelia Williams', and an afterword providing 'an extract from an interview in Brooklyn Fare, 1969' with her (written by James Goss; 2013, p. 283).

In 'The Angel's Kiss', Melody adopts the typical first-person narrative voice of hard-boiled detective fiction and film noir, translated for gender and filtered by Richards through some aspects of River's characterisation in the TV episodes. In this story, River/Melody, despite her hard-boiled tone, is hyperfeminised through continual emphasis on her looks and suggestions of vanity and predatory sexuality (hints of the 'cougar', as mentioned in Chapter 3). 'She' tells the reader in chapter one, 'I caught a reflection of myself in the glass of the door as it opened. […] Just a quick glimpse to assure myself that everything was buttoned and unbuttoned in the best places and pointing in the right direction' (Richards 2013a, p. 118). Thus, although River retains some of her abilities and poise ('it was the sort of day when deciding what to wear is like planning a military operation. Believe me – I have considerable experience of both'; p. 125), Melody's narration constantly mentions her attractions, implying a self-centredness atypical of the hard-boiled 'dick'. Likewise, although the female movie star Giddy Semestre also featured in the story is not as giddy as she might appear (confessing to Melody, 'I can't act to save my life. Oh, I have no illusions about that'; p. 136), the female characters come across as stereotypes in a pastiche that reproduces and even extends the gender norms of its referent.

The plot centres on a production line using the power of a Weeping Angel to transform hapless victims into endless reproductions of Giddy and her co-star Rock Railton: this process promises a brief moment of youth and beauty but soon decays into accelerated ageing. Drawn into investigating this, River is apparently given her own voice and her own story, but even though the Doctor never appears and River/Melody is acting alone, the story still seems to undermine her. In fact, Rebecca Moore, who provides a 'study' of 'sexism' in *Doctor Who*, suggests that 'when it comes to River Song, it seems that audiences were fooled into thinking she was a strong female character because of her propensity toward violence and some admittedly excellent monologues' (Moore 2014; see also Jowett 2014). These traits are certainly to the fore in this paratextual story, which foregrounds River's least attractive features. River comes very close here to one of the 'recurring types' of older women in TV drama identified by Dafna Lemish and Varda Muhlbauer and mentioned in Chapter 3, 'the bitch-witch older woman' (2012, p. 170) or, as Maricel Oró-Piqueras would have it, 'the evil woman who uses her experiential wisdom to manipulate others' (2014, p. 20). Notably, fan fiction (fanfic) sometimes takes a rather different approach to characters such as River, who seem full of promise yet whose narrative arcs and function reduce them to the same set of stereotypes (see also Chapter 6 on fix-it fanfic).

'Devil in the Smoke', also by Richards, features the Paternoster gang (Vastra, Jenny and Strax) in Victorian London. Like 'The Angel's Kiss', 'Devil in the Smoke' seems to offer development of these popular characters. Yet it still positions them as 'supporting' characters by focusing on Harry, a boy from the workhouse who meets Strax, Jenny and Vastra following a mysterious murder. The story makes no mention that Vastra and Jenny are anything but employer and maid, perhaps using the excuse that Harry is young and his first-person narration to avoid depicting a lesbian or interspecies relationship. So although these stories and this volume pick up on events from and 'gaps' in the TV episodes, they actually provide little 'extra' character information or development. 'Devil in the Smoke', especially, uses Strax for comic relief in a manner consistent with TV episodes, repeating his inability to tell male from female (while it should have become obvious after living on Earth in an era when dress was highly gender-specific), for example.

It also continues to keep Vastra and Jenny at a distance – Harry is in awe of them – so that none of the familiar characters are explored in more depth and no new information is forthcoming about their backgrounds or relationships.

These stories, therefore, do not agree with Gray's statement that cult texts 'seemingly welcome in all manner of other texts and paratexts to delineate small portions of the universe, plotline, thematics, and characterization' (2010, p. 43). In contrast, the first novel to 'star' the War Doctor (*Doctor Who: Engines of War* by George Mann) does exactly this, while remaining remarkably consistent with the television series in terms of gender representation. The story has, more or less, a clean slate to work with since the War Doctor only appeared in one special episode and one minisode, yet the depiction of him in the novel takes pains to develop the character from what is already established, along the lines of a typical *Doctor Who* story. Matt Hills describes how the book was promoted as a War Doctor novel (2015, p. 12), as well as commenting on how it unites the 20th- and 50th-anniversary specials by combining the settings of both (p. 66). The fact that it is, like 'Devil in the Smoke', narrated from the point of view of a new character, here Cinder, allows for some distance from and mediation of the War Doctor's character while situating Cinder as a protagonist in the mould of other female companions.

Certainly, the book's blurb and its description in the BBC online shop sells it as a story about the Doctor, with Cinder not even mentioned until the final sentence. The shop's description specifically states that Cinder is 'a young, female Dalek hunter', though the actual book jacket omits mention of her gender. (Since Cinder does not appear in the cover illustration this might have been considered an enticement for female readers.) Pre-release publicity from the book's author, Mann, as reported by DoctorWhoTV, 'teases what fans can expect', mentioning first 'A new companion!' before reassuring readers that it also offers familiar 'old' attractions such as Time Lords and Daleks (in 'The War Doctor Returns...'

2014). Mann emphasises that the novel is 'a war story' and that 'it's also about the Doctor's personal journey' (in 'The War Doctor Returns...' 2014). In another interview he is asked whether he considered giving the War Doctor a known companion such as Romana or Susan, and replies that 'those characters [...] deserve breathing space, proper stories of their own. This book was always going to be the Doctor's story' (in Kavanagh-Sproull 2014).

Thus, although Cinder initially challenges the Doctor and his attitude – 'Oh, *really*?' She shook her head at the sheer arrogance of the man. '*I* need *your* help?' (Mann 2014, p. 36) – she soon takes up a more conventional companion role. As Mann explains, she is a necessary 'counterpoint' positioning her, consciously or otherwise, as a function rather than a character with any agency. Despite Mann divulging that 'she really became a person to me while I was writing the book,' Cinder is relegated to 'allow[ing] him [the Doctor] to see himself properly for the first time in years' and 'remind[ing] him who he is' (in Kavanagh-Sproull 2014) – presumably by being young, female and planet-bound, or in other words, by her *difference* to the Doctor, as well as through them sharing certain characteristics or experiences ('being alone, drifting, fighting, unfocused'). She is there, like other female companions, to reflect the Doctor back to himself, to transmit his story and to present him as a hero to the reader or viewer. Cinder is established as a survivor and as someone who doesn't suffer fools gladly from the start, yet her brief time in the Doctor's company provides dramatic revelations about herself. 'Then the Doctor had come along [...] and in a few short hours had forced her to face up to this, to recognise that perhaps there were things that could be done, that nothing was as impossible as it might seem' (Mann 2014, p. 75). The Doctor tells her, 'You know, you're quite remarkable, Cinder' (p. 185), but his attitude towards her remains protective and paternalist: 'You're worried about what I might do,' she tells him, 'that I'm going to go and get us both killed' (p. 273). In fact, it is Cinder who dies, and the story ends with the Doctor apologising to yet another dead female companion who put herself at risk because of him.

Peripheral characters, who are present in the television narrative but not developed to any degree, might also have potential for escaping gendered roles and stereotypes. One such opportunity is the audio adventure 'UNIT – Extinction', released in November 2015. Big Finish, the producer of the audio adventures, promises familiarity: 'In this four-story box set, Kate Stewart, Osgood and the UNIT team confront an alien invasion by the Nestene Consciousness and its army of plastic Autons' (Big Finish n.d.). This has made news less because it seems to foreground female characters and more because, as James Whitbrook notes, 'Up until now, the revived-era of Doctor Who has been strictly off-limits to Big Finish for their stories' (2015). Therefore a story about

> Kate actually marks the first time that Big Finish will be allowed to explicitly use a character and plot elements from the 2005-and-onwards era of the show, and obviously, that opens up even more possibilities for other characters to make the transition from TV to audio plays (Whitbrook 2015).

Time will tell how female characters Lethbridge-Stewart and Osgood are depicted in the audio adventure, but despite Big Finish being careful to avoid it, other headlines continue to refer to 'Kate' as 'the Brigadier's daughter' first (see Caron 2015), as do some of those involved in bringing the story to audiences: '"it is wonderful to see the return of UNIT under the Brig's daughter," says executive producer Jason Haigh-Ellery' (Big Finish 2015).

Other official paratexts offer more information about Martha's adventures with the Tenth Doctor, including *Doctor Who: Infinite Quest* (2007), an animated story produced for *Totally Doctor Who*, the CBBC *Doctor Who* bolt-on programme. *Infinite Quest* aired in a sequence of minisodes of around three and a half minutes, and the final story, subsequently released on DVD, is around the same length as a standard live-action TV episode. Here Martha and the Doctor (voiced by Agyeman and Tennant) undertake a 'quest' to retrieve parts of a data chip, travelling to several planets and having various adventures featuring pirates, lizard-aliens and an ice planet. As might be expected, the story, the Doctor and Martha are consistent with established conventions from the main series, but without dwelling on Martha's unrequited romantic feelings, perhaps because these are not seen as appropriate or interesting for a child audience. Yet when *Infinite Quest* is referred to in another paratext, Martha's blog (on a MySpace page set up under the name Martha Jones), it functions almost exclusively to provide an opportunity for her to explain her unrequited love and more firmly establish her in a subordinate, painful position. She recounts some of the Doctor's exploits ('I [...] saw him destroy Baltazar's ship with a spoon'), concluding, 'No wonder I felt the way I did. [...] I love him and that's what makes this all so hard' (Jones 2007).

Like 'Devil in the Smoke', Martha's blog may give a female character her own voice, but it uses that voice to continue, and even exacerbate her gendered position, in this case as an emotional, needy, overlooked companion who serves the Doctor without any hope of her love being reciprocated (see also Chapter 3). The blog does take the opportunity to address the Tenth Doctor's lack of thanks for any of Martha's sacrifices. Recounting events from 'Blink', she notes: 'And then he thanked me, which is also a first!' and emphasises how during this adventure she 'had to get a job' while the Doctor 'stayed on the sofa'. Martha's sense of her own worth is validated by her mention of working in a shop being 'a step down from being a nearly-Doctor' yet simultaneously undercut by her admission that 'it was a bit of a laugh really'. The enjoyable part of this experience may even have been because she 'got on great with the other girls', certainly a different environment than the TARDIS.

And the blog ends with Martha again disclaiming any credit for her heroism:

If Martha Jones became a legend then that's wrong, cos my name's not important. There's someone else. The man who sent me out there. The man who told me to walk the Earth.

And his name, is the Doctor (Jones 2007).

This valorisation of the Doctor is accompanied by confessions that delineate Martha's abject emotional state: 'I have to let him go. And it's going to break my heart but I'll keep on smiling. I'm smiling because I know. I remember it all' (Jones 2007). In the end, Martha's experience of travelling in the TARDIS is the same as every other female companion; she sees it as the pinnacle of her existence and these memories will console her while she tends her broken heart after the object of her affection has left. Despite concluding with a statement about how she 'spent a lot of the time while travelling with him, thinking I was second best. But you know what? I'm not,' the overwhelming impression of Martha here is still, unfortunately, a character 'completely subsumed beneath the puppy-dog eyes arc she's given' (Magnet and Smith? 2010, p. 157).

So do paratexts for the spin-off series adopt similar strategies to Doctor Who and its paratexts? The trailer for season 2 of *The Sarah Jane Adventures* that showed in cinemas exemplifies what Gray sees as a frequent function of paratexts, 'tell[ing] us how producers or distributors would prefer for us to interpret a text, which audience demographics they feel they are addressing, and how they want us to make sense of their characters and plots' (2010, p. 72). The trailer finishes with branding from both *The Sarah Jane Adventures* and *Doctor Who* (an on-screen title 'From the makers of *Doctor Who*' and the current logo), as well as concluding with the CBBC website address, thus positioning the series specifically as a children's drama related to a familiar family entertainment series. Clyde is the main focus of the trailer, and introduces both the main location of the series, Sarah Jane's house, '13 Bannerman Road', and the various characters ('a boy genius', 'a supercomputer in the attic', and a 'girl reporter across the road'), as well as the science fiction elements of the series and its focus on action ('it's dangerous and it's deadly'). While parts of the trailer are taken from the prologue to each episode, extra framing and more action is included, with a handheld camera 'finding' Clyde on Bannerman Road, upward angles presenting Sarah Jane's house as somewhat ominous, fast editing providing a dynamic viewing experience at various key points and the whole thing giving glimpses of episodes to come in season 2.

Clyde's role as our introduction to the series in both the trailer and the repeated episode prologue, which functions as a kind of credit sequence, establishes him as a consistent figure who anchors the series for the viewer. This role foregrounds his relationship with Sarah Jane, as well as with her adopted son, Luke the 'boy genius'. As a 'normal' teenage boy speaking directly to the camera, using informal language and even joking with the listener (he cites the danger of associating with Sarah Jane and then laughs at the thought it might put him off), Clyde also anchors the series in the everyday melodrama of teen friendships and family life, despite the excitement and 'danger' offered by science fiction aliens. He is a young male protagonist to balance the older, female title character, Sarah Jane. Viewers who have already watched the first season will recognise his trademark humour and his desire to seem 'cool', but also know that Clyde suffers the doubts and uncertainties of developing masculinity. His loyalty and willingness to help Sarah Jane defend the Earth are never in doubt – highlighted in the closing dialogue when Sarah Jane asks, 'Ready?' and Clyde replies, 'Always.'

The Sarah Jane Adventures original audio stories tend, in common with many of the *Doctor Who* paratexts and the web comics available through the *Sarah Jane Adventures* website, to extend the television episodes by offering new adventures featuring familiar characters from the various seasons. Thus, for instance, Maria features in earlier stories, to be replaced by Rani later, and Sky is included in the final two. However, the different medium shifts the address slightly, with eight of the ten audio adventures being narrated in the first person by Sarah Jane, voiced by Elisabeth Sladen, and the final two narrated in the third person by Daniel Anthony (Clyde) and Anjli Mohindra (Rani) respectively. This shift means that while the stories generally follow similar patterns and offer consistent representations of the series' characters, they also include 'internal' comments from Sarah Jane (or the first-person narrator) that would not appear in the television episodes. They serve to extend what Garner identifies as the two key genres of the series, science fiction and melodrama (2013), with each adventure opening on a 'normal' day only to be disrupted by unusual events caused by an alien presence.

Thus, the audio story 'The Time Capsule' (2008), by Peter Anghelides, begins with Sarah Jane unexpectedly meeting Clyde at the local supermarket, where he is employed as part of his school work experience. Here, Clyde is described by Sarah Jane as Luke's 'best friend, really', a designation more often applied to girls than boys, signalling Clyde's support of Luke and his social awkwardness. Sarah Jane spends some time describing how Luke enjoys supermarket shopping, an activity most teenage boys would find anathema, and how he helps out an elderly neighbour by shopping for him. Luke's character is rounded out by these details, and similarly the interaction between Sarah Jane and Clyde extends and develops the warm and easy relationship glimpsed in the television episodes. Clyde admits to misleading people about his work experience being 'in sales' and seems slightly embarrassed at being caught out, but Sarah Jane takes his side in the face of the bullying and 'pomposity' of his supervisor, Mr Charlson, who harangues Clyde and the other workers continually.

Likewise, 'The Ghost House' (2008), by Stephen Cole, opens as Sarah Jane chats to her milkman about how a neighbour's house has been suddenly transformed from a more modern dwelling to a Victorian villa. Given that this story moves between the present day and 1884, throwing the usual cast of characters together with a Victorian family as houses from two different time zones blend together, it has scope for some direct address to gender roles and representations, yet this is downplayed. Charles Burden, the owner of the 1884 house, is described as a 'Victorian patriarch' but primarily depicted as a 'very frightened man', especially when his daughter and eventually his wife slip away into the present day. Eventually Burden leads a mob of men, carrying a poker and threatening violent revenge on the aliens who 'abducted' his family, in what can be construed as typical masculine aggression (the contemporary characters are 'sickened' by it). Burden's actions are contrasted with Clyde's attempt to kick down the door of the Victorian villa and 'rescue' Luke and Sarah Jane, which is presented somewhat comically and ridiculed by Sarah Jane – but the contrast is subtle and not directly commented upon. Burden clearly loves his daughter and shows her physical affection, and neither his wife, Beatrice, the maid Clara, nor the daughter, May, seem particularly submissive in the face of his bluster. On hearing a scream, Clyde comments that he thought women in this era 'fainted a lot', only to have Luke suggest that this is 'most probably a stereotype'. The downplaying of a different set of expectations for men and women in the two time periods is narratively justified by the emphasis on the contemporary characters and their roles in a plot involving an alien bounty hunter tracking down two intergalactic criminals, and arguably the story is more focused on action and entertainment than history of any kind.

Rani's mother, Gita, is featured in 'Judgement Day' (2011), by Scott Gray, and this audio adventure extends her characterisation as somewhat self-absorbed and dizzy, and Rani's father, Haresh, as well-meaning but lacking in certain 'masculine' skills (he cannot start the car engine). However, it also notes the affection between mother and daughter, sometimes sidelined in the television episodes in favour of Rani's respect for Sarah Jane and their mentor-protégé relationship. In this adventure, we see Rani refusing to let her mother be teleported away by an energy bubble, grabbing on and going with her in what Sarah Jane calls an act of bravery.

This sits within a plot line that, through alien-induced flashbacks, allows Rani to see Sarah Jane develop as a journalist (Rani's own ambition), and as a defender of Earth via her role at UNIT. At the end of the story, Sarah Jane apologises to Rani about Gita's memory of the events having to be wiped, reinforcing the importance of family ties, though both agree that it is necessary. Sarah Jane also emphasises how she needed to 'justify' herself to Rani as well as to the aliens who put her on trial. The final lines of the story, narrated by Anjli Mohindra, have Rani vowing to tell 'the true story of Sarah Jane Smith' in the future and get her the credit she deserves.

Another relationship developed in this story is that between Clyde and Sky, with Clyde adopting Sky and teaching her how to behave as a 'normal' teen, just as he previously did with Luke. They first appear in the story distracting Rani by dancing to loud drum and bass music requested from Mr Smith in the attic. Given the (technical) gender difference between them, their friendship is not read the same way as that between Clyde and Luke: a security guard in the shopping centre harasses them, focusing on Clyde and telling him not to try and impress his 'little girlfriend' by hanging over the balcony. One implication here might be that Clyde is picked on because he is a young black male, racially profiled as a troublemaker, though this is not spelled out. In addition, any hint of 'inappropriate' romance between Sky and Clyde is dispelled by Sky's immediate rejection of the 'girlfriend' tag. As he did with Luke, Clyde accepts Sky's alien abilities and is generous in his praise: 'Sky Smith, you are the coolest magician in town,' offering a positive view that helps offset other, more negative, perceptions of Sky as a 'weirdo kid'. (Like Luke, Sky's alien origins mean she often speaks or behaves in ways that are not considered 'normal' by others.) These audio adventures, then, fulfil the function of adding depth to established characters, extrapolating as opposed to simply reiterating roles and behaviours seen in the TV episodes.

While *The Sarah Jane Adventures* has relatively few paratexts, Matt Hills notes that 'there is far more official *Torchwood* story content *not* on television than otherwise,' going on to argue that because of this 'analysing *Torchwood* purely as a TV series seems curiously unhelpful' (2013b, p. 65). He does admit, however, that most *Torchwood* tie-ins are 'largely medium-neutral in tone. That is, they use audio or the printed word to approximate and replicate televised *Torchwood* as closely as possible' (2013b, p. 72). Paratexts may choose to do this by providing more detail, by returning to characters or situations or settings that have been left behind as the TV text unfolds. One such example is the radio drama/audio adventure 'The Dead Line', discussed by Porter and Hills (2013b), among others, as a means of commemorating, or even reviving, the relationship between Jack and Ianto. In Cardiff, Ianto's shrine – a tribute to the character by fans who have left messages, pictures and other objects – still exists, long after Ianto was written out of the TV narrative.

Another example is the tie-in novel *Torchwood: Long Time Dead*, by Sarah Pinborough. Not only is the novel written by one of the few female authors featured in the official franchise novel series, it also focuses on a female character killed off in the TV series' very first episode: Suzie Costello. 'I loved her in the show, and totally loved bringing her back from the dead,' Pinborough reveals in a note at the end of the novel, 'Bad girls rock' (2011, p. 251). Certainly, the novel takes Suzie's point of view much of the time, offering an alternative perspective on *Torchwood*'s familiar cast of characters. Yet given that Suzie reappeared in 'They Keep Killing Suzie' (1.8) as a villain bent on taking Gwen's life force for herself, Pinborough is working within certain limitations. The novel does offer insights that perhaps can be seen as particularly gendered (a female character muses on emptying the bin: 'It was a two-minute job and it really didn't matter, but somehow it did, because it was *his* job and by not doing it, he made her feel like *she* didn't matter'; 2011, p. 58), but Suzie must remain a bad girl just as Martha is constrained in *Doctor Who* by her 'puppy dog' arc. This characterisation is achieved through fairly typical means in

Long Time Dead. Suzie's first acquisition is a weapon – 'There was something about a knife that she found reassuring' (p. 31) – and she consistently uses her physical attractions and sexuality to influence other (male) characters. Suzie is herself being manipulated by an outside force ('It was hungry and she was angry'; 2011, p. 32) yet its goals seem to align with hers, and the power she gains allows her to take revenge for past anxieties and uncertainties: 'She felt powerful. Gone were the insecurities she'd felt before – the suspicion that she had never been *good enough*. That she'd so easily been replaced by someone *better*' (2011, p. 111). Jealousy of Gwen is highlighted, in line with events from 'They Keep Killing Suzie', and unfortunately this perpetuates the pattern of women competing with, rather than supporting, each other (see Chapter 3). Pinborough might relish the fact that Suzie is a 'bad girl', but this judgment means that she has to be punished, dying yet again at the end of the story. In BBC Books' *Torchwood Archives*, Jack's case notes conclude that Suzie's return in 'They Keep Killing Suzie' simply 'showed her true nature [...] she must have been damaged for a long time' (Russell 2008, p. 82).

In his brief discussion of *Torchwood: Risk Assessment* by James Goss, Hills suggests that it is an example of tie-ins that 'relativise and refract *Torchwood*'s TV mission statement by re-gendering it' (Hills 2013b, p. 77). This novel charts the visit of an assessor from the Torchwood Institute, an Agnes Havisham, who has known Jack for many years. In the course of her visit, she challenges his suitability to lead the Cardiff Torchwood team, suggesting instead that Gwen should take over. In this way, Hills argues, the story aims to 'offer up condensed, elliptical yet critical commentaries on the limits of TV *Torchwood*: momentarily replacing Jack's masculine authority with the idea of Gwen as leader' (2013b, p. 78). In addition, I would suggest, Jack's 'masculine authority' or leadership style is contrasted here with Miss Havisham's Victorian propriety. Despite softening towards him and even hints of flirtation between the two, Havisham's very different manner and style throw Jack's coldness and often cavalier attitude into sharp relief if, as Hills notes, only briefly.

UNRULY DIVERGENCE: PARODY AND COMEDY

Continuity and consistency, then, seem to be a significant part of *Doctor Who*'s paratexts, consolidating the BBC's 'programme brand' and offering little variation in representations of gender. *Doctor Who* parodies, on the other hand, suggest a slightly different strategy. 'Parody,' argues Gray, 'works as a form of "critical intertextuality" that aims precisely to bump a text of genre's meaning-making process off its self-declared trajectory' (2010, p. 34). This certainly applies to *Doctor Who and The Curse of Fatal Death*, a special episode broadcast as part of the BBC's Red Nose Day telethon for Comic Relief in 1999, while the series was on hiatus. In this 'episode' the Doctor regenerates several times into versions seemingly designed to mock the usual casting decisions, including incarnations played by Richard E. Grant ('cute, sexy and lick-the-mirror handsome'), Jim Broadbent (socially inept fanboy?) and Hugh Grant (more 'cute and sexy') before ending up as a woman, played by Joanna Lumley. It also features the Master ('the camp one'), and emphasises the homosocial as well as homoerotic relationship between them which, now the Doctor is female, can become more than just subtext (see Chapter 6 on Missy). The two Time Lords walk off together at the end of the story, leaving the latest female companion, Emma, disappointed. The Doctor had agreed to 'settle down and get married' to her but 'he' is now female and clearly more interested in the Master than in Emma. The sketch subverts some traditional elements of *Doctor Who* relating to gender and sexuality, but only within a context of heteronormativity can it 'allow' the Doctor and the Master to become openly romantically or sexually interested in each other, and arguably the only reason the Doctor becomes female is to facilitate this.

Tardis Data Core notes that Lumley is the first woman to play the Doctor in an official 'though non-canonical' production (n.d.). Given the tone of the comedy ('Stop showing off', complains companion Emma, and the Doctor taunts the Master for getting 'bosoms' before his own regeneration), which may be a reference to the stereotypical fanboy who is socially awkward and unattractive, it is hardly surprising that one of the main features of the female Doctor is cleavage (boob jokes are always hilarious, apparently).

The *Doctor Who* sketch that featured on John Barrowman's *Tonight's the Night* in 2009 is rather more circumspect, though it shares some features with 'The Curse of Fatal Death', most notably its construction of *Doctor Who* fans as fan*boys*. Russell T. Davies discusses this sketch in *The Writer's Tale* (p. 663), recounting how he was persuaded into it so that Barrowman could offer a part in an 'original' *Doctor Who* scene penned by the current head writer as a competition prize. The BBC press release plays up the authenticity of the experience:

> Offering viewers dream-come-true-wish-fulfilment, BBC One's *Tonight's The Night* is running a competition for one viewer to take part in a specially-written Doctor Who scene, working with the Doctor Who production team, and shot on the set of the TARDIS (BBC 2009).

Davies' scenario, however, sidesteps any confusion about whether this will or won't be canonical by presenting it as, in fan fiction terms, a Mary Sue. ('Mary Sue' is the term used to describe a fan wish-fulfilment story where the author writes a version of themselves into the narrative of their favourite story and gets to save the day). Thus, Barrowman and competition winner Tim Ingham play Captain Jack and alien Sao Til in the TARDIS control room. However, it is made clear that they are 'playing' when they revert to themselves having a bit of fannish fun on being interrupted by David Tennant, who castigates Barrowman for playing with 'his'

TARDIS. (Davies' script as published in *The Writer's Tale* designates 'David Tennant' rather than the Tenth Doctor, and stipulates, 'In normal clothes', but uses 'Captain Jack' and 'Sao-Til'.)

Barrowman himself is presented as the Mary Sue (telling Ingham/Sao Til, 'He's so cool,' as Tennant leaves), thus deflecting any potentially negative characteristics of fandom from Ingham. This parody characterises *Doctor Who* fans as men who are childishly enthusiastic about the object of their affection and swap playground insults with each other – in much the same way as the Doctor and the Master in 'The Curse of Fatal Death'. Moreover, this is not really seen as insulting, and Benjamin Cook responds to the sketch by telling Davies, 'It shouldn't piss off too many fanboys' (*The Writer's Tale*, p. 668). The 2009 sketch draws attention to the fact that both Barrowman and Tennant are self-declared fans of the series, as were many of those involved in bringing the rebooted series to air, including Davies (see Chapters 5 and 6). It is an interesting contradiction, however, that the Mary Sue is a female designation (most definitions give Marty Stu as the 'male' version, but this is a derivation) and is generally ascribed to female fanfic writers, yet here it is applied to fanboys and operates in terms of action rather than romance. Whether this is allowable because both Davies and Barrowman are gay and thus might take the Doctor as their object of desire or affection – as well as of their fandom – is open to interpretation. Barrowman has been discussed by scholars as a key site of intertexuality, given his simultaneous appearance on *Tonight's the Night* and *Torchwood* (see, for example, Williams 2013b).

Comic sketches and parodies related to *The Sarah Jane Adventures* are fairly consistent with the television episodes. The Comic Relief special 'From Raxacoricofallapatorius with Love' (2009) features British comedian Ronnie Corbett as an alien visitor to Sarah Jane's attic. Corbett is perhaps most famous in the UK for being one half of 'The Two Ronnies' alongside Ronnie Barker and so the sketch names his alien character Rahnius, or 'Rani', prompting him, when introduced to the regular characters, to say, 'The two Ranis'. One reviewer derides the sketch as 'embarrassing' but rather grudgingly acknowledges that 'the nation's children will have lapped this skit up, fart jokes and all' (Wolverson 2009). Given that 'The Curse of Fatal Death' contains numerous 'bosom' jokes yet is cited by the reviewer as a success, this is somewhat mystifying. The reviewer recounts cringing all the way through the short sketch and also mentions having 'to endure the cruel jibes of my wife throughout', offering a negative flip side to the childish fanboy enthusiasm given a positive spin in Davies' sketch for *Tonight's the Night*. Rahnius is even more overt than the usual male series villains in deriding Sarah Jane and her companions as 'just a woman and a bunch of kids', and he also mocks the sonic lipstick ('what's next, bionic blusher?'), but given his obvious function as 'comic relief' he is easily defeated, and such comments are designed to show his ignorance of Sarah Jane's heroism and that of her companions.

Porter argues that 'Children in Need specials and proms provided additional ways for fans to see characters in real-life related skits' (2012, p. 80). Yet *The Sarah Jane Adventures* is perhaps unique in the franchise for regularly inviting viewers of its 'overflow' paratexts to move between 'fact' and fiction, between the world of the drama and the real life of those involved in it in a more blended fashion than the usual 'making of' and 'behind the scenes' bolt-on episodes accompanying *Doctor Who* or *Torchwood*.

CBBC Extra – described on the CBBC website as 'a look behind the scenes of CBBC' (BBC n.d. c) – features several *Sarah Jane* specials including 'Chris meets...'. Introduced by Anjli, the sketch adopts a parodically melodramatic voice-over – male, of course, since this is conventional ('Somewhere in Ealing, England, the world...') – accompanying familiar exterior shots of '13 Bannerman Road' until the camera finds a tent in the driveway. Chris, the tent's occupant, explains that he is making 'a documentary' but belatedly realises that if 'Sarah Jane' arrives her car will run over his tent. At this point, he is interrupted by Clyde and Rani (not Danny and

Anjli), who naturally find his presence in Sarah Jane's driveway suspicious. When Chris tells Rani and Clyde he is working for CBBC and identifies his 'boss' as female, this aligns with typical *Sarah Jane Adventures* episodes (see Chapter 1). In a clash of meta-textuality, Chris continues to act like a fanboy, or even a stalker, gushing over Sarah Jane in particular, as well as flattering Clyde by praising his comic-book-style drawings, potentially a kind of fanboy bonding. Rani, on the other hand, is not impressed by his behaviour and remains suspicious even when he compliments her on her fashion sense.

Chris may act like a stereotypical fanboy in some ways, yet in others he subverts gender norms, as when he applies his Plum Crush lipstick ('It's my sonic lipstick') – though notably at this point he is immediately handed some tissues by Rani in a not very subtle hint to remove it. His bumbling antics come to a dramatic end: when confronted with supercomputer Mr Smith, called out by Clyde to address the problem, Chris cannot resist playing with the controls and eventually presses a red button. Given the clash of worlds in this sketch, viewers realise that Chris expects the red button to produce extra content, as this is its function on the BBC, but Rani and Clyde both express horror and try to stop Chris pressing it. The well-known convention of the red button being some kind of destruct mechanism holds true, the screen abruptly fading to interference in a self-conscious departure from the happy endings of the TV stories.

Another 'extra', dubbed 'The Gameathon', has the three young stars of the series take part in 'another barrage of ridiculous chal-lenges' and revels in parodying the excesses of game shows, com-plete with another male voice-over. Here the narrator uses a boom-ing, dramatic voice at odds with the sarcastic comments he makes on proceedings ('What special effects are these?' and 'I'm sorry, I just refuse to say this title'). The challenges have little to do with the series themes or the characters played by the actors, though the level of parody suggests that viewers are expected to be familiar with the conventions of television (and is not a million miles away from the enthusiastic fanboy behaviour seen in the *Tonight's the Night* sketch discussed above, as well as – perhaps – the enthusiastic approach of some children's television).

There is little distinction made in terms of gender in how Anjli, Danny and Tommy are presented, and all three enter into the 'competition' with equal amounts of energy, whether the challenges are physical or intellectual. As with the narrator, however, most of the structuring devices are gendered male. The facilitator of the challenges is the Man in the White Coat, who 'fires' a starting pistol (which is simply his fingers with a special sound effect added) in the first three challenges, and the voice giving the scores ('Graham') is reminiscent of K9. It is not quite clear whether these structuring elements are all masculine because this is part of the parodic nature of the Gameathon, or whether it is unconscious reproduction of male-dominated media.

The way these various paratexts tend to follow the representations established in the television series suggests that there is a desire for a degree of consistency, though whether this comes from the producers of such official paratexts or is assumed on the part of the audience consuming them is not always clear. The next chapter focuses on production of the series, examining how industry 'norms' and gender imbalances affect them.

5

PRODUCTION

Unsung Heroes

Given that *Doctor Who* was itself started under the guidance of producer Verity Lambert, at the time the only female producer at the BBC, it seems that the current franchise has moved on very little. This chapter examines gender in terms of *Doctor Who* and its spin-offs' production history and creative personnel, looking specifically at how certain individuals have become aligned with authorship in relation to the television series.

'Authorship' is always a complex term in relation to popular media, given the collaborative nature of producing it. Bridget Conor, in her study of screenwriting, notes the 'inherent collectivity that downplays and denies claims to individual creative authorship' (2014, p. 1). Yet the changing landscape of digital television has led to a rise of possible 'authors'. 'At the very moment television studies abandoned the author as a viable avenue of inquiry,' Derek Kompare notes, 'television itself began to increasingly foreground its ostensible authors. [...] The "source" of television authorship was re-attributed to the showrunner' (2010, p. 98). While initially US terminology, the showrunner model and the (industrial) need to assign authorship has become so prevalent that 'a US-style "showrunner" model [is] being adopted on a number of high-profile UK series, *Torchwood* among them' (Hills 2013c, p. 201). There are various reasons for this: social media, networked, transmedia viewing habits, and increasing emphasis on 'interaction' with series and the provision of (official and unofficial) ancillary content around them. In the past, cast and crew might have been expected to engage in a few publicity and promotional activities; now, screenwriters or directors might have a certain number of blogs or appearances written into contracts. As a result, 'For television in particular, the explosion of websites, the increase in entertainment news magazines and programs, and the advent of DVD bonus materials and podcasting have made executive producers/showrunners considerably more visible than in earlier years of the medium' (Gray 2010, p. 108).

The notion of authorship in the new *Doctor Who* universe is therefore tied up with the current marketplace, the reach of a global transmedia brand, the reputation of the BBC and, inevitably, the status and personae of those seen to be in creative control of a given series. TV authorship now consists of a constructed ideal or, as Jonathan Gray terms it, 'the author function as a discursive entity' which is 'used by the industry to communicate messages about these texts to audiences' as well as 'by the creative personnel often conflated into the image of the author(s) to communicate their own messages both to each other and to the industry' (2010, p. 113). This can be seen across a range of personnel associated with *Doctor Who*, *Torchwood* and *The Sarah Jane Adventures*, and the 'author function as discursive entity' will firstly be examined in relation to the highly visible showrunners of *Doctor Who*. Russell T. Davies' connection to all three shows will be analysed, looking at his strategies for attracting a mainstream audience beyond existing *Doctor Who* fans, as well as his involvement in *Torchwood* and *The Sarah Jane Adventures*. Steven Moffat has increasingly been criticised for not doing more to include women writers and directors during his tenure as showrunner. The role of female writers, directors, producers and executives is also explored here, especially in comparison with the preponderance of male writers, directors and showrunners working on *Doctor Who* and its spin-offs to date. Although there are other prime-time BBC series that do employ greater numbers of women, various industry reports and studies indicate low numbers of female directors in British television generally, making *Doctor Who* a high-profile example that is indicative of a much larger picture.

Matt Hills has criticised scholarly accounts that 'typically read TV's "author functions" in relation to credited creatives/show-runners [...] rather than exploring the roles played by flesh-and-blood writers who may not even make it into official credits and official promotion' (2013c, p. 201). Hills notes: 'By starting from TV credits, work on authorship all too often accepts industrial power relationships rather than questioning who has been credited and why, and considering who goes uncredited as well as whose work doesn't even make it to the screen' (p. 201). The aim in this chapter, and indeed in the book, is to acknowledge the industrial power relationships at work in the *Doctor Who* stable of TV series, not by actively seeking to 'reinstate' or unpick the complexities of collaborative writing and the equally thorny issue of credits, but by looking at TV authorship in the context of an industry that is seemingly resistant to becoming more inclusive. 'Authorship,' Kompare argues, 'is a connection, as well as a claim; it functions both as a relationship between producer and user, *and* a proprietary discourse, with particular cultural, legal, and social attributes' (2010, p. 97). It therefore has very particular gendered attributes, examined here through the construction and self-presentation of the two post-2005 *Doctor Who* showrunners, as well as through the small numbers of female writers and directors on the 'main' series, and the two spin-offs. As Paul Booth points out, even using the showrunner to periodise the series 'puts an emphasis on dividing *Doctor Who* into eras based entirely around white, male hierarchies (with the notable exception of first producer Verity Lambert)', and 'examining the series from a production standpoint emphasises and reinforces this privilege' (2014, p. 200). In this case, therefore, I attempt to engage in an analysis that takes account of such 'white, male hierarchies'.

RUSSELL T. DAVIES: CULT AUTEUR?

The position of screenwriter may, as Conor argues, be ranked lower than other roles within TV and film production:

> It is generally framed, for example, as much less powerful than other adjacent roles such as producing and directing. Even other forms of writing are seen as placing the writer in a much more central and visible creative role. [...] Screenwriters are often much less visible, are openly barred from film sets or other screen production processes, are framed as 'hired hands' or replaceable cogs in the capitalist-intensive entertainment industries (2014, p. 2).

In British television production historically the writer has had more significance than in film production. *Doctor Who's* two high-profile showrunners are both screenwriters and the role of head writer has relatively recently, as Hills points out, been applied to the British TV context, making the position and 'creativity' of Davies and Moffat in relation to the show more visible than it might have been in the past. Given the success of the reboot and the continuing flagship status of the series for the BBC, both have inevitably become key 'voices' speaking about and on behalf of *Doctor Who*.

In addition, *Doctor Who's* status as cult science fiction programme as well as mainstream family show brings with it another way of talking about and framing authorship – the cult auteur. 'The figure of the cult "auteur", i.e., the attributed creator of the cult object,' observes Kompare, 'is important within most media fandoms, providing a nexus of critical fan activity, and [...] anchoring the claim in traditional constructions of the author as Romantic genius' (2010, p. 99). The long history of *Doctor Who* means that the series is generally understood to be a collaborative production, but it is notable that in comparison to other long-running science fiction series like *Star Trek*, it lacks 'a major fixture of cult television fandom' whereby 'certain creative personnel (most often show-runners) [are] identified by fans as the originating intelligence(s) behind the object of their fandom' (Kompare 2010, p. 100). While Gene Roddenberry and his 'vision' is often alluded to in relation to *Star Trek*, there is no such genius or originating intelligence associated with pre-2005 *Doctor Who*. Perhaps this is because it would mean referring to the series as Verity Lambert's *Doctor Who*. Yet at the same time, the rebooted series is often seen as 'created by', or at least sustained and driven by, Davies and subsequently Moffat. Davies is certainly often credited with persuading the BBC that a reboot was worthwhile, and with managing to make it a major success.

While producer Julie Gardner also played an active and significant role in supporting and sustaining the reboot (see below), it is Davies who has come to stand – and speak – for the new incarnation and its spin-offs. This is partly down to his willingness to do so, as well as his established profile as a writer of other successful TV productions, and his self-confessed *Doctor Who* fandom, something he shares with many of those involved in the post-2005 series. Conor argues that screenwriters often enact or perform 'a number of diverse laboring identities – pioneer, maverick, egoist, masochist, geek' (2014, p. 12), and certainly traces of all these models are apparent in Davies' self-presentation in interviews, commentaries and his own accounts of his creative labour across two volumes of *The Writer's Tale* (a published e-mail 'conversation' between Davies and journalist Benjamin Cook about writing, script-editing and showrunning *Doctor Who*). Davies' roles as writer and showrunner, as well as advocate for *Doctor Who*, make up a fairly complex picture of him as 'author' that is clearly constructed but based on other identifiable models now associated with contemporary television: the successful showrunner, the creative visionary and the fanboy-producer.

Catherine Johnson suggests that positioning Davies as 'author' of the rebooted *Doctor Who* allows it to be seen, and sold, as 'a quality text created by a "visionary" that could appeal to the fan and non-fan audience' (2013, p. 101). Open admission of his own fandom does not appear to affect Davies' desire to make the series a popular mainstream product ('very, very Saturday night' – Davies, quoted in Hills 2010, p. 117), avoiding the 'fanwank' that is one explanation for its decline and eventual cancellation in 1989. (Fanwank is described by Hadas and Shifman as 'a strongly derogatory term: basically meaning fiction that only fans could understand and derive pleasure from, obtuse to outsiders and thus of little if any value'; 2013, p. 280.) Rather, Davies is seen to draw on critically acclaimed models from American network TV like *Buffy the Vampire Slayer* to restructure and repackage the *Doctor Who* 'brand' for a twenty-first-century audience. There are various accounts, including Davies' own, of how this was achieved, including adopting longer episode runtimes in line with current practice, but also incorporating season arcs, or threads of continuing serial narrative; positioning the companion not just as an everywoman who allows us to enter the world of the Doctor but also as a more fully developed character, evolving through experiencing travel with the Time Lord; and, perhaps more contentious, introducing the possibility of romance between the Doctor and his companions. These have been examined and debated earlier in this book, and elsewhere, and will not be reiterated here.

Davies attracted media attention for his TV creations prior to *Doctor Who*, most notably with *Queer as Folk*, a groundbreaking series in terms of representing homosexuality, yet he is now indelibly associated with the 2005 reboot of this successful series and its spin-offs, which have made him a household name. 'The show-runner offers a model of a more empowered writer-producer who exerts creative control in the screenwriting labor market and strong (usually, though not exclusively, male) personalities such as David Chase [...], David Simon [...] and Matthew Weiner [...] are now oft-cited' (Conor 2014, p. 31) in relation to 'quality' TV series, as Johnson also suggests. Davies emerged early on as exactly this kind of figure. In his discussion of the cult auteur, Kompare recalls Caldwell's argument that '"outward-directed" discourses like podcasts and similar publicity [...] are far from transparent or monolithic' (2010, p. 102) and Davies (as well as Moffat) has been criticised by fans for upholding the corporate line in some respects (especially on leaked information about future storylines). In a sense, such criticism more firmly establishes Davies' role as 'author' or creative controller of the series: he could be more relaxed about spoilers, if he wanted to be, the logic suggests. Davies discusses, trails, promotes and teases the series like other cult auteurs who 'increasingly participate in virtual real time, at the pace of the television season, rather than after the fact' (Kompare 2010, p. 102) and is thus presented as an authority on, as well as an author of, *Doctor Who*. Christine Cornea identifies Davies' 'role as interpretative anchor' in bolt-ons like *Doctor Who Confidential* and *Torchwood Declassified* (2009, p. 116), another role that bolsters his authority.

Discussing changes to *Doctor Who* in the 1980s, Miles Booy expresses surprise that the series' new writers are 'revealed [at conventions] to be young men in jeans and T-shirts, media-hip and wielding smart-alec senses of humour. Fans could look at them, and [...] see themselves in a few years time' (2012, p. 135). Eventually, of course, writers like these came to work for the rebooted series, and its first season was populated, as Booy observes, by (generally male) writers 'drawn from *Who* fandom and spin-off novels' (2012, p. 189), though its directors were typically already established and experienced in working with the BBC. In this sense, *Doctor Who* exemplifies how TV writing fits 'a model of contact-based and network-centered writing dominated by the writer's room and the show-runner' (Conor 2014, p. 31). Yet the 'fanboy' element, however controlled by Davies and the official BBC line in promoting the series, adds a further, gendered dimension to how the show's authorship is perceived and presented. One of the models for screenwriters that Conor identifies is the 'geek', and in terms of Davies this combines with the fanboy-producer or fanboy-auteur noted as a significant persona for contemporary TV 'creators' (as skilfully constructed by Joss Whedon or J. J. Abrams). This model enables the 'author' to present themselves as an authority because they are creating new stories and new characters with new motivations, but also because they have a fan's detailed and obsessive knowledge of the fictional universe of the series.[16] It further allows, as Johnson implies, the figure of the 'author' to bridge any perceived gap between a successful commercial media product marketed and branded according to corporate policy, and fans who see themselves as discerning, invested and critical consumers. Kompare analyses specific cult auteurs and notes that someone like Ronald D. Moore, screenwriter and producer of the reimagined *Battlestar Galactica* (2004–9) and *Outlander* (2014–), 'is a television author who performs authorship in a way that attempts to align more with fannish engagement than with the usual discourses of Hollywood publicity' (2010, p. 107): Davies' persona, in contrast, is more formal despite still 'insuring that his personality represents the show on a regular basis' (Kompare 2010, p. 109).

Discussing *Lost* podcasts, Kompare notes how showrunners Carlton Cuse and Damon Lindelof's 'self-presentation shifts between being all-knowing authors, eager fans, and lowbrow Internet entertainers' (p. 103), and it is interesting to note that Davies engages primarily with official (authorised) paratexts and channels of communication around *Doctor Who*, rather than using more informal types of communication. Thus, although as a self-confessed fan he does at times engage with what Kompare describes as 'the more informal and jokey modes of fannish interaction' (p. 104), he rarely outright 'mock[s] the idea of the all-knowing serious author' (p. 104) and continually maintains his position as 'author'. This is especially obvious in *The Writer's Tale*, where Davies frequently notes how much work he does on scripts written by other writers, as well as explaining how grateful they are for his help in making their work not just 'better' but 'more *Doctor Who*'.

Hills sees this as particularly significant in relation to *Torchwood*, noting:

> The key issue […] is the extent to which *Torchwood* is positioned as 'belonging' to Russell T. Davies, hence aligning it with his work on the 'mothership' of *Doctor Who*, as well as thematically linking it back to *Queer as Folk*. […] Interviewed within the promotion of Torchwood series four, Davies himself exaggerated and played up this lineage' (2013c, p. 203).

This results in *Torchwood* 'becom[ing] powerfully articulated with discourses of Davies as an auteur […] thereby marginalizing the input (and empirical, flesh-and-blood) writing of other creatives such as Chris Chibnall' (Hills 2013c, p. 201), and Hills argues that 'Chibnall is recurrently rendered invisible, whilst Davies' creative role is stressed' (p. 204). The first two seasons of *Torchwood* are, according to Hills, 'marked both by Davies' (strategic) conceptualization *and* by Chibnall's (tactical) working-out and working-through of this – which in turn informs series three and four' (2013c, p. 207; emphasis in original), though Hills also acknowledges the reason for this particular assigning of authorship to Davies.[17] It clearly makes sense from a branding point of view, given that Davies is the household name and part of the brand able to sell this spin-off at home and abroad as a less mainstream product that derives from 'Davies' vision' because 'its representations of fluid sexuality are aligned with the cultural politics of his earlier work' (Hills 2013c, p. 207). Notably, at least one reviewer of *Torchwood*'s debut rather harshly comments that, '*Torchwood* by someone else would have sunk without trace' (George 2007, p. 6), implying that only Davies' name brought the series backing. Likewise, when the second spin-off, *The Sarah Jane Adventures*, launched, the show was 'almost guaranteed a substantial adult following' (Richardson 2007, p. 30), with the implication that both its ties to the parent show and Davies' association with it guarantee this.

Davies thus straddles the commercial/creative divide and the fan/producer divide in the way he negotiates his authorship of *Doctor Who* and *Torchwood*, balancing the demands of industry promotion with a fan's desire to maintain, perpetuate and develop the *Who* universe. His refusal to engage with informal modes of communication like social media may be a protective measure designed to keep him safe from trolling (see Hills 2013c, p. 201).

Naturally, this has not spared Davies his share of criticism. While he worked hard to include and develop 'real' female characters and attract a wider audience for the reboot in 2005, and might even be credited with mounting a serious challenge to male-dominated *Who* fandom in the UK, the ways in which this was achieved have not been popular with everyone. 'The focus on romance and relationships, associated with female fan fiction writers,' argue Leora Hadas and Limor Shifman, 'is pegged by doctorwho members *as Davies's own special brand of fanwank*' (2013, p. 286; emphasis in original). In their analysis of fan–producer relations, they summarise responses from the doctorwho community about Davies thus: 'He may not write as the continuity-obsessed male fan that makes fandom dread a return to cult days, but he writes as a fan nonetheless – a feminized unruly fan who refused containment, to the disapproval and distress of doctorwho posters' (p. 286).

Davies, then, and his self-representation as *Doctor Who* universe author, is self-consciously 'characterized by isolation and collaboration, industrial awareness and entrepreneurialism, egotism and insecurity, inequality and hierarchization' (Conor 2014, p. 1). As one reviewer concludes after reading *The Writer's Tale*, 'He's a moody, complex old bugger, often ruthless and bloody-minded and the grinning, camp version is just simply a media construction, a way to deal with the circus' (Collins 2008). Moreover, though Davies might emphasise his own sexuality, his work in representing male homosexuality, and highlight his efforts to maximise female audiences, many aspects of his author persona maintain what Conor terms the '*ideal* subjectivity for a contemporary screenwriter of film and/or television' (2014, p. 84); that is, one defined by traditionally white, middle-class and masculine perspectives and behaviours. This 'bias' in *Doctor Who*'s 'vision' was compounded by the appointment of the white, middle-class, heterosexual Steven Moffat as Davies' successor. Both Davies and Moffat could be counted among

> a small number of 'writer-producers' or well-known, consecrated writers [who] function, survive and flourish at the top end (the 'show-runners' of television, for example, and usually male). They are generally able to secure ongoing and rewarding work, are well remunerated, critically recognized, are able to resist attempts to rewrite or change their work and are concerned about 'property rights' such as residuals payments (Conor 2014, p. 42; 'residuals' in television generally refers to payments for reruns and repeat broadcasts).

STEVEN MOFFAT AND THE 'BOYS' CLUB'

In recounting her work on *Doctor Who* in earlier decades, Elisabeth Sladen gives several examples of 'the casual sexism on the show at the time', admitting that '*Doctor Who* in those days could be a bit of a boys' club, I think it's fair to say' (Sladen and Hudson 2012, p. 100). Moffat's tenure has attracted similar comment, and he has been increasingly criticised for the series not employing female writers and directors, with no women screenwriters between 2008 and 2015. Gavia Baker-Whitelaw is one of many who challenged this situation, which has regularly made headlines in UK newspapers as well as in the more niche or 'cult' spaces of the blogosphere and social media:

> Back in the 1960s, at a time when vanishingly few women were working in television at all, the show's first seasons were shaped

by Verity Lambert. For the next 40 years, *Doctor Who* had its ups and downs, but it always pressed forward towards the future, with Russell T. Davies' 21st century reboot introducing a far more racially diverse cast than ever before, as well as LGBT characters including Captain Jack Harkness.

For a show whose success was built on a rebellious attitude towards the sci-fi establishment, why go back to hiring exclusively from the Boys' Club? (2014)

Arguably, Moffat could have done more, sooner to address the situation – and season 9 includes female writers and directors – but the gender inequalities apparent in production of the Moffat 'era' are certainly indicative of the bigger industrial picture.

Like other industries, television production relies on social capital, or in simpler terms, networking. It is fairly obvious that social networks tend to consist of the same kind of people, hence the preponderance of white, well-educated men with high-profile showrunner jobs in television. 'The discovery that success in the labour market varies by gender, race and class is both a depressing and a familiar finding,' note Irena Grugulis and Dimitrinka Stoyanova at the conclusion of an article about social networking in TV production (2012, p. 1322). *Doctor Who* is by no means the only series to function on homophilic social capital – the 'Boys' Club' – but it is an example that attracts public attention and consequently public scrutiny. This is only exacerbated by the BBC's position as a public service broadcaster with a commitment to diversity and 'fair' representation.

A report by Directors UK about low numbers of female directors notes that:

Both broadcasters and independent production companies expressed shock at the findings. All companies approached have equal opportunities statements and strategies in place, yet these results are in direct contradiction to a corporate ethic

uniformly expressed on company websites and in mission statements, which promote equality of opportunity for all (Directors
UK 2014, p. 21).

Such responses indicate the way 'tradition' and the 'common sense'
of social networking skew the picture. In an article published two
years earlier, Vicky Ball observes:

> [A]lthough women now represent 48 per cent of the terrestrial
> television workforce (Skillset 2010, p. 7), research by feminist
> academics (Brunsdon 2000; Julia Hallam 2007; Lizzie Thynne
> 2000), but also reports from the British Film Institute (BFI)
> (1999) and Sector Skills Council for the UK (Skillset 2008, 2009,
> 2010), suggest that this figure betrays the extent to which gen-
> dered hierarchies continue to structure broadcasting industries
> (2012, p. 251).

This gendered hierarchy and structuring is certainly apparent in
the recruitment of writers and directors for *Doctor Who* under
Moffat, which bears out 'anecdotal evidence' from Directors UK
'that both hiring practices and cultural assumptions are having a
negative impact on the hiring of women (Directors UK 2014, p. 21).
Cultural assumptions might be – as Moffat has suggested himself
(to some derision) – that women don't want to work on *Doctor Who*
or on science fiction more generally. Hiring practices contribute
to a lack of or decline in diversity because directors or writers are
employed on the basis of their successes, but if they are not given
the opportunities they cannot build up a list of such successes. It
is also likely that on a flagship series like *Doctor Who*, fewer risks
will be taken on new or unproven talent.

It is somewhat ironic that one of the influences in the apparent
change of direction for season 9, in terms of the recruitment and
announcement of female directors and writers, seems to have been
the public statements of writer Neil Gaiman. Gaiman himself has

benefited from the Boys' Club, writing 'The Doctor's Wife' (6.4; see Brooker 2013 for an analysis of this episode in terms of the author function and co-creation of a TV text). Many female figures had called out the inequalities on *Doctor Who*'s production team, but Gaiman attracted much publicity for doing so, particularly perhaps because of his 'cult' credentials. His initial observation was notably couched in what Sam Maggs for The Mary Sue calls 'sarcasm' (2014a), and was followed by more detailed comments about how the production team are trying to hire more women (Maggs 2014b).

Moffat, as 'author', showrunner and 'voice' of the series, has taken the blame for these inequalities, though they are endemic in the industry. All the discourses surrounding screenwriting (and indeed the cult auteur in television) as well as what Conor calls '"ideal", performative screenwriting subjects' in interviews, press releases, fictional representations and other paratexts 'work repeatedly to gender screenwriting work but also to deny inequalities and exclusions in this field' (2014, p. 119). It may well be true, as Moffat has stated in response to criticism, that women turned down the opportunity to work on *Doctor Who* (and the weight of cultural assumption may be significant as a disincentive), but this kind of justification denies the ways access to such job openings is not equal. The UK television industry has evolved to produce an organisation of the market that 'builds stereotyping and discrimination into everyday working practices' (Bielby in Conor 2014, p. 107) and thus reproduces an industry model that is 'masculine, fraternalist and homophilic in orientation' (Conor 2014, p. 107). Moffat's author persona in relation to *Doctor Who* has somewhat ineffectively countered criticisms about race, gender and sexuality behind and in front of the camera. It is worth remembering, though, that 'not all screenwriters are sexist or are cultural dupes who perpetuate gendered norms' (Conor 2014, p. 113), and whatever Moffat's gender politics or attitude to inequalities in television production may be, the series is working within a constrained field.

'[T]he broader discursive landscape in which […] work is circum-scribed and determined is regularly and consistently premised on and shaped by gendered notions of screenwriting and creative work' (Conor 2014, p. 113). This applies to directing as well as to writing.

DOING IT FOR THEMSELVES?

The social capital, working practices and cultural assumptions that structure and characterise the television industry in the UK mean that it does not offer equal access to women or minority workers. Women are employed in the TV sector, but tend to be found in particular types of work and at particular levels within the hierarchy. Ball notes:

> Although figures by occupational groupings collected by Skillset's 2009 Census cover the entire audio-visual industries (rather than just television), they nevertheless demonstrate how men are far more likely to be company owners (78 per cent) and to fill managerial and executive producer roles (61 per cent) despite a greater proportion of women being graduates and receiving more training than their male counterparts (2012, p. 251).

It is also the case that men and women tend to be employed in gendered areas:

> [W]omen [have] the highest representation in traditional 'femi-nine' areas such as costume and wardrobe (68 per cent), makeup and hairdressing (52 per cent) and the lowest representation in more 'masculine' areas such as camera work (12 per cent) and lighting (10 per cent) (Skillset 2009, p. 17) (Ball 2012, p. 251).

In terms of the new *Doctor Who* universe, bolt-on, behind-the-scenes programmes like *Doctor Who Confidential* and *Torchwood*

Declassified certainly demonstrate that the areas identified by Ball as 'feminine' are in this case occupied by women – though notably special-effects make-up might be done by men – and more technical positions are filled by men. However, the story of rebooting *Doctor Who* and its universe for the twenty-first century also involves several women in what might well be called 'top' TV jobs using their influence and their position to help get the series back on the air and maintain its position as a flagship series and significant export for the BBC: Julie Gardner's contribution is discussed below.

The 2014 Directors UK report suggests that the visibility of women in management roles is one of the reasons why the inequalities demonstrated by the low numbers of female directors across TV in the UK was greeted with such surprise by production companies and employers:

> There are significant numbers of women working in senior staff positions in film and television production offices. The relatively healthy proportion of senior women producers and women in media management has given these companies the impression that all is well in gender equality. This has unfortunately masked the truth of how different the situation is in the production environment (p. 21).

Of course, the mere presence of women (or 'minorities') in television management, at whatever level, does not guarantee improvements in the representation of women in the programming produced. The persistence of stereotyped representations of gender and sexuality cannot simply be attributed to low numbers of women in key roles that determine representation of gender, sexuality or other subjectivities. Men can strive to challenge stereotypes as much as women. In terms of the industry and employer statements about equality and diversity, however, the low numbers of women are certainly problematic.

Moreover, essentialist assumptions about the effect that more women working in the industry has or might have are circulated in and by the press. Ball's account of the 'feminisation' of television focuses on the perception that women taking more senior positions and female audiences becoming more vocal and more of a priority has led to a decline in 'standards' and 'quality' of programming (2012, p. 249). She cites one instance of a senior female executive countering these assumptions:

> Responding to Chris Dunkley's exasperation at the 'feminization of television' on *Woman's Hour* in March 2003 [...] Hilary Bell, a Senior Commissioning editor for Channel Four, claimed that the gender of the commissioner/programme-maker is not a significant factor in the types of programme that are commissioned: 'we are employed to spot trends. We are employed to gauge the temperature of the times and to provide programming that reflects that' (2012, p. 252).

This speaks back to the notion that gender discrimination is deeply rooted in the working practices of TV production, especially in conjunction with another of Ball's points:

> [T]here has been a shift to producing dramas such as Doctor Who (2005–) and Spooks (2002–), whose qualities 'transcend the local and make [them] universal: humanity, character', and 'character in adversity' (Caughie 1996, p. 216), but which omit, given their difficulty to sell on overseas markets, the social and political conditions which produce the adversity (Caughie 1996, p. 216) (Ball 2012, p. 258).

As already discussed in earlier chapters, on the surface *Doctor Who* valorises 'universal' values and ideals – yet these values are ingrained with (possibly unconscious) white, middle-class, male privilege that goes generally unremarked because of its pervasiveness in UK television. Caughie's comment was published in 1996, but little has changed 20 years on. Women may now be filling significant roles that determine the direction of TV programming, but they do so within the limitations of this admittedly 'masculine, fraternalist and homophilic' (Conor 2014, p. 107) industry. It is a Catch-22 situation. As Conor notes in her study of screenwriting, 'studies of creative labor have only just begun to interrogate the exclusionary dynamics of particular creative sectors, the ways in which inequalities are reinforced, even deepened, and often denied' (p. 6).

If Russell T. Davies was the voice, and face, of the *Doctor Who* reboot, Julie Gardner is the woman in the background. In the introduction to a Den of Geek interview with her, Simon Brew describes Gardner as 'the unsung hero of the likes of *Doctor Who* and *Torchwood*'. He observes that she 'has been the engine room of *Doctor Who* in the Russell T. Davies era of the show, and in her role at BBC Worldwide has been instrumental in the return of *Torchwood [Miracle Day]* to our screens' (2011). Given that Starburst's David Richardson describes her as 'without any doubt, one of the most influential creative figures in television today', citing 'her key role on *Doctor Who* and its spin-offs' as well as other executive producer credits, and her roles as Head of Drama at BBC Wales and Controller of Drama Commissioning as evidence (2006, p. 46), it is hard to see how Gardner has become an 'unsung hero'. The BBC Worldwide press room announces that 'she was responsible for spearheading the revival of *Doctor Who*, as well as the successful series, *Torchwood* and *The Sarah Jane Adventures*', attributes an 'unparalleled string of hit dramas' to her, noting that 'she received a multitude of awards' for these, and finishes by triumphantly citing her MBE for services to television and the media industry in Wales (BBC n.d. b). At the time she was working on *Doctor Who* and its spin-offs, Gardner gave many interviews and was regularly included in bolt-on programmes, yet she has, to an extent, been written out of the new *Doctor Who* universe's history, sidelined while enthusiastic fanboy auteurs take the spotlight. She may well be known to fans, and to those familiar with the TV industry, but her name is unlikely to have the instant recognition that Russell T. Davies and Steven Moffat have achieved, largely because of the way television authorship is attributed and constructed.

Given the factors working against women in the industry, Gardner's rise is indeed remarkable, and one article calls it a 'Cinderella tale' of career advancement (Bashford 2005, p. 25). While Davies is generally credited with making the 2005 *Doctor Who* reboot a success, 'It was Gardner who was given the job of pitching *Doctor Who* to Davies,' according to Richardson (2005, p. 101). Remembering this story during interviews, Gardner tends to describe Davies as the right man for the job, shifting credit from herself. (Likewise, when asked to identify what *Torchwood* is to her, the first of three things she lists is 'I think it's, obviously, Russell T. Davies. Having him as a lead writer and full time exec on the show, that defines it. With that, it's that tone, very light hearted, then spinning that into real tragedy and real consequence'; in Brew 2011.) In joint and sole interviews, each namechecks the other regularly as an important part of the creative collaboration.

One possible reason for Gardner not being in the frame as 'author' of *Doctor Who*, *Torchwood* or *The Sarah Jane Adventures* is that she is not classed as 'creative' in the sense that a writer or director might be. Another, perhaps with more weight given the nature of the production history around the reboot, is that she clearly does not fit the model of fanboy producer. Thus, Richardson notes, 'Gardner's passion for DW is evident', but adds the rather backhanded rider: 'she could certainly never classify herself as a long-time fan but she has learned to love the show from the inside looking out' (2005, p. 103). Similarly in the *Doctor Who Confidential* episode 'Do You Remember the First Time?' where David Tennant 'interviews' the many people responsible for rebooting the series, most of them male fans, he questions Gardner and Jane Tranter on their knowledge of previous Doctors. While this might be interpreted as a rather tongue-in-cheek scene constructed for entertainment purposes, it does position Gardner and Tranter as different to the other, male, fanboys involved in producing the series – Davies, Moffat, and writer and actor Mark Gatiss – that Tennant speaks to in this episode. Tennant, another self-confessed *Who* fan, takes up a position of authority in quizzing the two women, who – of course – fail the 'test' by getting the sequence of actors who played the Doctor wrong. In this way the women are positioned as invested in the show's success as part of their job but as not caring about continuity or having detailed knowledge of cast and crew in the way that 'real' fans might. They do gently poke fun at Tennant by pretending to forget who played the Tenth Doctor, but the little vignette nevertheless undermines their authority and contribution, and fails to fully acknowledge Tranter's and Gardner's key roles in getting *Doctor Who* back on TV.

The BBC is clearly aware to some degree of the mismatch between its commitment to diversity of representation and equality, and public criticism of *Doctor Who* and its low numbers of women. On International Women's Day 2015 a 'special picture' of female cast and crew from the yet-to-be-aired season 9 standing in the TARDIS was released on Twitter, followed by a number of images celebrating women in production (from Lambert to Gardner) as well as some post-2005 female companions and other characters. This may go some way to reinstating 'unsung heroes' like Gardner, but it is a small step in addressing the major inequalities still apparent in production of the series: most of the women featured from the production side were involved in the 'classic' series.

Much criticism has been directed at the lack of women writers on the post-2005 series, with articles and social media greeting the news of a new female writer appointed with headlines like 'Doctor Who Hires First Female Writer Since 2008' (Cox 2014 – the writer mentioned was Catherine Tregenna). Conor readily acknowledges that there are 'difficulties in drawing direct causal links between the lack of women writers for example, and the lack of female protagonists in prime-time television or in top-grossing films', yet she goes on to observe that 'plenty of tacit industrial knowledge circulates that explains away or justifies these continued inequalities, making explicit links between professional practices on-screen and off' (2014, p. 105). Moreover, she points out: 'Screenwriters are directly involved in representational processes, in producing views on and of the world, images and narratives for others to consume' (2014, p. 104). It may seem essentialist, but it is undeniable that women have a different perspective on living in a patriarchal society because their experience informs that perspective, just as lived experience is affected by race and ethnicity (as noted in Chapter 3). Certainly, looking at some of the episodes written by women, the perspective is often slightly different. Helen Raynor expressed a desire to write a Toshiko-centred episode of *Torchwood* for season 2, for example, resulting in 'The Last Man'. 'I'd really like to do a story for Toshiko. There's such a real unique spiritual quality about her, and I'd love to write a hero story for her,' Raynor explained, implying that no other writer had yet explored the character's heroic qualities (2006, p. 32).

FEMALE WRITERS

Raynor's introduction to writing for *Doctor Who* was the two-parter 'Daleks in Manhattan'/'Evolution of the Daleks' (3.4 and 3.5). Here, too, subtle differences in Raynor's approach to the material can be detected, for instance, in relation to the romance plot and also to systemic issues of inequality within the society depicted. Tallulah, a showgirl with ambition, does not care when her lover, Lazlo, is transformed into a pig slave, and in her conversations with Martha, Tallulah emerges as a strong and determined character. Likewise, Solomon, the black leader of the disenfranchised Hooverville population, is clearly heroic, working for the good of all, and his sense of self-worth leads him to challenge the Doctor's patronising attitude several times. Yet the episodes attracted some highly critical responses.

Davies, in *The Writer's Tale*, recounts Raynor's reaction to reading critical posts on Outpost Gallifrey about her story:

> She said that she was, literally, shaking afterwards. Like she'd been physically assaulted. I'm not exaggerating. She said it was like being in a pub when a fight breaks out next to you. I had to spend two hours on the phone to her, talking her out of it, convincing her that of course she can write, that we do need her and want her. That bastard internet voice gets into writers' heads and destabilizes them massively (Davies and Cook 2010, p. 104).

Booy cites this in *Love and Monsters* as indicative of Davies' attitude to fans and his approach of keeping fandom 'at arm's length' (2012, p. 185), but it is also revealing in gender terms. Davies presents himself here as supportive of Raynor yet also as a figure of authority with his own battle scars who has developed the appropriate thick skin to succeed in this environment. Additionally, this passage makes use of what Conor categorises as 'combat metaphors' (2014, p. 117) for writers' experiences, using violent, traditionally masculine imagery. Davies' description 'like she'd been physically assaulted' has particular resonance when applied to a female writer and Booy does not quote these phrases, eliding them from his discussion.

One notion that recurs in denial of inequalities in appointing female writers and directors is that women are not, unlike the fanboys of Moffat's Boys' Club, big enough fans to want to work on the series. Certainly Catherine Tregenna, writer of Hugo-nominated *Torchwood* episode 'Captain Jack Harkness' (1.12), admits that she is not particularly knowledgeable about science fiction, with the caveat that this neither prevents her from understanding how it works nor from writing it. 'I'm not a massive sci-fi buff, though I do appreciate the dramatic possibilities of the genre' (2009). She describes this particular episode as 'a love story' and points out that it 'was written in less than a fortnight due to production pressures'. Elsewhere she discusses how she handled Jack's development and role in this story: 'by now our Captain Jack was slightly different, not so much of a Time travelling tart [...], this takes him back to a very disturbing encounter and you see him go through the emotional mill' (2007, p. 43). Tregenna acknowledges that the episode is strongly written and that it received positive feedback from people in the gay community for its portrayal of 'two men in uniform in the Second World War dancing and kissing in public'. Yet, at the same time, on the subject of the Hugo nomination, she says, 'Everyone told me Steven Moffat would win and he did too, most deservedly,' apparently demonstrating the weight of cultural assumptions (women can't write science fiction as well as male fanboys).

In contrast, when it was announced that Sarah Dollard would be one of two female writers working on season 9 of *Doctor Who*, she went on record saying, 'Getting to play in the Doctor Who toy box is a dream come true. It's a total honour to contribute to a show that has brought me such joy as a fan' (in Jusino 2015), echoing the sentiments of the many male fans-turned-writers who have worked on the series since 2005. Writing for The Mary Sue, Teresa Jusino concludes an article about the (at the time) upcoming female writers and directors, by pointing out 'the next test' of the series' attempt to address gender inequalities: 'Will the same female writer ever come back and write a second episode the way Toby Whithouse, or Peter Harness, or Mark Gatiss continually contribute multiple episodes?' (2015).

Notably, the episode Tregenna wrote for *Doctor Who*, 'The Woman Who Lived' (9.6), was the second part of a two-part story, with the first part written by Moffat and Jamie Mathieson. These episodes are largely promoted as guest-starring Maisie Williams (known to many viewers from *Game of Thrones*) as Ashildr, a Viking who becomes first 'The Girl Who Died' (9.5) and then 'The

Woman Who Lived'. After dying in the first episode she is saved by the Doctor, and he admits to Clara that Ashildr may now be unable to die. In the second part of the story, this is proved at least partly true, and Ashildr, now calling herself Me, has lived long enough to rival Jack, if not the Doctor. Both Tregenna's writing and Williams' performance make Ashildr/Me a compelling character, yet her story arc is constrained by the existing dynamics of the series. She is able to challenge the Doctor, to talk back to him and resist his paternalism, yet it is revealed that she has acquired a male protector and sponsor (a male leonine alien, admittedly, but still a male) and then that he has duped her about his motives for their alliance. Leandro told her that they can open a portal and escape to the stars when he actually intends to open the portal to allow his people to invade Earth. In addition, the portal requires a death to open it, and Me is willing to sacrifice someone to do so, implying that centuries of existence have eroded her humanity. Eventually, as seems inevitable given how the series operates, Me realises Leandro's duplicity, admits that the Doctor is right and she is wrong, and helps prevent the invasion. As the Doctor leaves, Me swears to follow his example and help people.

Me's third appearance a few episodes later in 'Face the Raven' (9.10) is also written by a woman, Sarah Dollard. Here, Me is in another position of power, mayor of a group of refugee aliens, but through her strict management of this safe haven Clara dies and the Doctor blames Ashildr. Ashildr also appears in the season 9 finale, 'Hell Bent' (9.12), written by Moffat, which ends with her and Clara flying off in a(nother) stolen TARDIS, en route, presumably, to their own time-space adventures. The shifts of tone and the evolving story around this new female character imply that the series still cannot accommodate an autonomous woman with the experience and assurance to challenge, and match, the Doctor. Yet her inclusion in so many episodes suggests a conscious strategy to counter accusations of inequalities and poorly executed female characterisation.

Conor observes that 'there are now many visible and successful women and ethnic minority show-runners and "named" screenwriters of all kinds' (2014, p. 125), and one example of the *Who* series using such visible 'names' is contracting writer and producer Jane Espenson to write for *Torchwood: Miracle Day*. Julie Gardner recounts, 'We started with Jane Espenson. We have such a shared viewership with Jane. We love all the work that she's done, and she's watched *Torchwood* in previous years' (in Radish 2010). Here Espenson's cult credentials are highlighted as attractions for the production team and for the audience, since her name is likely to be familiar to them given her work on *Buffy the Vampire Slayer*, *Once Upon a Time* and *Game of Thrones*, among others. The other writers Gardner goes on to list all have similar cult or quality TV credentials (like Doris Egan and John Shiban), but Espenson is the real draw. Notably, her 'author' persona is little different to that of the fanboy-producers discussed above, and Lynette Porter notes how Espenson's tweets 'became a friendly bonus directed to UK viewers' (2012, p. 134) during *Miracle Day*'s run, showing her dedication to the fans and audience of the series. Conor also notes that Espenson shares tips for writers through her own personal blog (2014, p. 126), and in this way she establishes herself as a professional with expertise and experience worth passing on to others who might just be starting out.

FEMALE DIRECTORS

The Directors UK report from 2014 outlines why low employment of female directors is significant and has ongoing effects for the industry:

> There are a large number of programme series showing zero employment rates of women directors. Many of the most popular series on British television, and many high-profile programmes

which represent the pinnacle of ambition for television directors, have never been directed by a woman (p. 5).

Arguably, *Doctor Who* is just such a high-profile programme and it certainly, according to many interviews with cast and crew, 'represents a pinnacle of ambition' for people who work on it. Cultural assumptions around genre mean that numbers of female directors in science fiction and fantasy are very low, at 4 per cent compared with 96 per cent male (Directors UK 2014, p. 13), though notably *The Sarah Jane Adventures* has a better record on this than *Doctor Who* (Directors UK 2014, p. 11). This may be because a children's science fiction series is not as 'hard core' as a prime-time science fiction series, or possibly just because it is not as high profile and therefore can afford to take more risks, as suggested above. However, the report also notes:

> There have been some worryingly low numbers recently in genre-led (e.g. sci-fi and adventure) children's drama in the period covered by this report: there were no women directors on *M.I. High* [...] and the numbers [...] have dwindled to 0 per cent on *The Sarah Jane Adventures* in 2011 and 2012 (Directors UK 2014, p. 14).

As with the writers, in 2014–15, criticism of the small numbers of female directors was addressed by publicity surrounding the appointment of several for seasons 8 and 9: 'Female directors are suddenly in *Doctor Who*'s spotlight, with Sheree Folkson helming "In the Forest of the Night" and Rachel Talalay overseeing the upcoming Series 8 finale episodes' (Boynton 2014). This appears as a 'sudden' change because not only have there been so few female directors in the history of the reboot, but also, as Jusino (2015) pointed out about female writers, few have returned even after highly successful episodes, like Hettie MacDonald, who helmed 'Blink'. MacDonald returned for season 9, but given that

'Blink' is often cited as one of the best episodes of the new *Doctor Who* (see, for example, Mulkern 2015) the gap of seven or eight years seems inexplicable in comparison with the number of other returning directors, even allowing for clashes of schedules and other commitments. It is also notable that while 'Blink' is a frequently praised episode, its 'authorship' is generally attributed to Moffat, the writer, and not to the director. David Hill is not alone in pointing out that 'counting MacDonald, there have been all of three female directors in Steven Moffat's tenure as showrunner' and that this has attracted 'continual criticism', which now 'he certainly seems to be attempting to make up for' (2015). While these developments are generally welcomed, then, there is a certain amount of scepticism about the reasons for appointing more women directors and writers, as well as whether this will signal long-term change.

If nothing else, though, the promotion of these female names as an attraction for the series' audience starts to repair some of the gaps or erasures in the history and mythology of the series. Ancillary materials surrounding *Doctor Who* and *Torchwood* frequently elide female crew, or seem to privilege other, male, voices as more important or more authoritative. For example, 'news' from July 2014 on the BBC *Doctor Who* website about the season 8 episode 'In the Forest of the Night' focuses on writer Frank Cottrell Boyce ('I was flabbergasted to be asked to write an episode'), and concludes with Moffat's endorsement, '*Doctor Who* is born anew in the mind of a genius,' with the final comment, 'The episode will be directed by Sheree Folkson and produced by Paul Frift,' apparently included as an afterthought (BBC 2014). Likewise, the episode information on the website in the 'Factfile' highlights Cottrell Boyce but does not mention Folkson's direction, and although during the accompanying *Doctor Who Extra* 'episode' Folkson's voice is heard off-camera (saying 'action' or 'cut there'), she does not make an appearance to speak about the episode. This is rather ironic, given that reviews of the episodes tended to criticise the story while its aesthetics and direction, if mentioned, were praised (see, for example, DoctorWhoTV 2014c).

Similarly, Rachel Talalay's direction of the season 8 finale is not exactly ignored, but is certainly not emphasised on the official series website. This is in contrast to other articles that highlight Talalay's impressive credits, especially on genre films and TV shows, and emphasise her own fandom as informing her work on the series. One even quotes her noting how long she has aspired to direct on *Doctor Who*: 'I would say on *Doctor Who*, from the second of the reboot, that's what made me want to do it. That was eight seasons ago!' (in Brew 2014). This interview with Simon Brew for Den of Geek sees Talalay adopting many of the ways of talking about her work that have been identified by Conor as recurring tropes for screenwriters. Like Davies, she notes that she is aware of the weight of fan responses and the potential negative impact this can have, and she too mentions strategies she uses to 'protect' herself from this kind of criticism ('we all know there's no such thing as opinion on the internet. It's just "you're an idiot, and that's a fact!"'; in Brew 2014). And like other creatives, she discusses her professional input and what she, as director, contributes to an episode of *Doctor Who*: 'It was just expected that you embrace and bring one's own vision to it' (Talalay in Brew 2014), even saying that she prefers to work in the UK because 'you are absolutely treated like the director' and 'respected' as such.

In this context, then, Talalay is presented as 'right' for *Doctor Who* and is treated with 'respect' by the interviewer and the final article, in which she talks about her own work using the same language of creative labour and with the same authority as male creatives (and why not?). The contrast with the 'official' *Doctor Who* sources for these episodes is rather glaring. Here again, Talalay's name is seen on clapperboards but she is not included in the first of the *Extra* episodes, and the second, extended episode (15 rather than 10 minutes) features actors Michelle Gomez (Missy), Ingrid Oliver (Osgood) and Jemma Redgrave (Kate Stewart, inevitably cited frequently as 'the Brigadier's Daughter'), as well as behind-the-camera crew such as writer Moffat, the FX crew, and wardrobe – but not Talalay.

Talalay's work on season 9 was well received by audiences. After the broadcast of 'Heaven Sent' (9.11), she tweets, 'Hibernated for 24 hours, came back to this overwhelming tweet-explosion. THANK YOU ALL. I don't have words. #DoctorWho forever' (Talalay 2015). Some of the tweets she refers to mention that Talalay is 'the only director to have successfully shown a billion years in one hour. It is the next level' (JoshZ in Talalay 2015), while others invoke the series' continuing fandom being safe in her hands: 'possibly the defining moment of my children's childhood' (Jenny Colgan in Talalay 2015).

Admittedly, this emphasis in ancillary materials that help define and develop the series' and the fictional universe's history may simply depend on who is available for comment while filming *Confidential* or *Extra*, or *Torchwood Declassified*. Moreover, the DVD releases include 'cutdowns' of *Confidential* and *Declassified* (about half the length of the originally broadcast episode) and therefore provide only a selection of the available footage. However, these selections go on to establish the record, privileging male creators and sidelining the few women who are employed on the series.

Notably this is addressed in part at least on the official BBC website page for 'Heaven Sent', where short video clips include 'The Return of Rachel Talalay' as well as two where Talalay talks through some of her 'sketches' that became storyboards for the episode. 'The Return of Rachel Talalay' actually features less of Talalay and more of others talking about her – 'we love Rachel,' Moffat says, 'she's amazing.' Moffat is also at pains to put on record that he and the *Doctor Who* team have been trying to get Talalay back 'for ages' but schedules have never allowed it. The collaborative process between writer, director and actor in bringing the episode to life is discussed by Peter Capaldi ('She has ideas about what was going on'), and Moffat praises Talalay's work, observing: 'she can just decide what kind of movie we're going to make today' (BBC 2015b). Given the effort put into publicising the appointment of female writers and directors, this suggests that the overall approach to addressing inequalities in the series is not consistent, possibly justifying the cynicism apparent in some responses to the press releases. The press and promotion of the series is the subject of the next chapter, which also examines how some viewers have taken their own steps to rectify inequalities in the series – by writing their own stories.

6

RECEPTION

Squeeing, Trolling, Transforming

rom fanzines, to cosplay (a contraction of costume play, cosplay is costumed role playing of particular characters), to rewriting the stories of female companions, female fans have always been engaged with *Doctor Who*. Yet there is still an assumption that such fans are fanboys, and Leslie McMurtry points out that *Doctor Who Magazine*'s 'survey respondents are still 71 per cent male' (2013, p. 91). Academic work on fandom suggests a disruption of the male-dominance of *Doctor Who* fandom in the UK by new *Who*'s address to, and reception by, female viewers. Thus, this final chapter surveys and explores promotional materials, press coverage, audience response, fan response, and fan production related to the franchise. *Doctor Who*, as already made clear in the preceding chapters, is notable for being such a long-running series, for being a successful reboot, and for being a flagship BBC production and global export. All of these things make it both newsworthy and controversial, especially perhaps, for long-term fans. *Torchwood* and *The Sarah Jane Adventures* may receive less scrutiny, simply because they are new spin-offs and do not have the established lineage and storyworld of *Doctor Who* to negotiate. Certainly *The Sarah Jane Adventures* has attracted much less attention from the press, from audiences and from commentators, academic and otherwise, presumably because it is children's drama and therefore below the radar, and also because it was not exported internationally, and thus really only attracted a UK audience. *Torchwood*, on the other hand, seemed to court controversy from its debut and, as Hills puts it, acquired a fandom as soon as it was announced and well before any episodes were actually available to view (2013b, p. 69). However, the position of both spin-offs on minor or niche channels (for *Torchwood*'s first two seasons at least) opened up space for them to attempt something different, for different audiences, expanding the fictional world of *Doctor Who* and its commercial franchise in ways suited to contemporary television.

Changes in how television operates – as a platform, as a form, and as an industry – between 'classic' *Doctor Who* being taken off the air, and the 2005 reboot relaunching it with such success, also contribute to the attention paid to all three series. As Hadas and Shifman observe:

> The blurring of the borders between consumers and producers, as well as growing awareness of the added value of fan labor (Ross, 2008; Baym & Burnett, 2009), have led to a perception of unprecedented power held by audiences over production companies (2013, p. 275).

Terms like 'on demand' and the growing number of VOD (Video on Demand) and streaming services suggest that viewers are in control of when they watch television and what they watch it on, with more choice than ever before. However this might ignore other views of consumerist and commercial logics, there is certainly more lip service paid to the notion of interactive communication, and even of 'dialogue' between producers and consumers. The previous chapter discussed how showrunner Russell T. Davies and other 'authors' of *Who* productions might control such dialogue and avoid particular fan responses. This chapter analyses to what extent the franchise adopts certain strategies in relation to its audience and its fandoms, including what Matt Hills calls 'fanagement' (2014a).

Audiences and fans might choose to engage with or resist and critique commercial strategies in various ways. 'Digital technologies [turn] every form of text and media into a single, easy-to-work-with code that makes the widespread sharing and manipulation of existing content easier than ever,' note Hadas and Shifman, and thus 'almost appear to have been tailor-made to facilitate fannish involvement (Booth, 2010; Gray, Sandvoss, and Harrington, 2007)' (2013, p. 277). Chapter 4 discussed the imperative for major popular franchises to be transmedia, and *Doctor Who* has always had a catalogue of paratexts that expand its universe across other media than television, aiming to engage its audiences across various platforms and allowing viewers to consume or interact with the 'brand' by providing new content on multiple screens, not just on TV.

Press coverage and 'official' promotion is part of this strategy, and social media means that audiences and fans can keep up to date with the latest news – on productions, web content, celebrity or crew, and events – as it breaks (or leaks). Yet the way *Doctor Who* in particular is both mainstream and cult, and all the TV series in the franchise range across children's to adult viewing, inflects the press the franchise receives, as well as the official and unofficial news about it. The address of each of the three series to different and apparently distinct audiences has been touched on in previous chapters and is examined at more length in the first part of this chapter. The untimely death of Elisabeth Sladen brought an end to *The Sarah Jane Adventures*, and also elicited a number of tributes, official and 'unofficial', examined here in the context of perceived continuity from *Doctor Who* to *The Sarah Jane Adventures*.

The second major focus is the (gendered) nature of fan practice. 'One could argue,' Lincoln Geraghty observes, 'that the history of fandom is very much a history of gendered discourse around production, consumption, participation and celebration' (2014, p. 55). The 50th anniversary of *Doctor Who* serves as one case study here, given how it necessarily had to engage audiences of 'classic' and 'new' *Who*. This was done by releasing a range of anniversary 'specials' from the mainstream, event episode, 'The Day of the Doctor', to the historical celebration *An Adventure in Space and Time*, to the more niche and fannish 'The Night of the Doctor' minisode and *The Five(ish) Doctors Reboot*. Debates around the notion of an 'official' female Doctor and the season 8 'Missygate' controversy (when recurring female character Missy was revealed to be the Doctor's arch-nemesis and fellow Time Lord, the Master, now regenerated as female) are further examples of contested gender territory. Missy has been mentioned in the Introduction as a controversial – though possibly innovative – move for the main(stream) series in terms of representation; here the character is examined as an example of the kind of scrutiny *Doctor Who* attracts and incites, and the ways audiences, bloggers and fans discuss gender and gender politics in the series. The chapter concludes with a more lengthy analysis of female fandom and female-centred fan productions and activities, such as fan fictions rewriting Old Amy from 'The Girl Who Waited' (*Doctor Who* 6.10), to cosplay at fan conventions.

PROMOTION AND PRESS

As already noted, *Doctor Who*'s position as a flagship series for the BBC and the BBC's position as a public service broadcaster in the UK mean that it attracts commentary, not just from fans or even viewers, but from the mainstream press. As a result of this and of the success of the 2005 series reboot, careful handling of the two spin-off series was required, as mentioned in previous chapters. *Torchwood* in particular risked attracting children who had watched *Doctor Who* and enjoyed Captain Jack's appearances in it, despite its 'adult content'. This was the subject of discussion at the time of *Torchwood*'s launch, and Ross P. Garner (2013b) examines what he describes as the 'intertextual barricade' erected between the two by BBC promotion of the new series, minimising references to *Doctor Who* in *Torchwood*, especially in the first season, with the logic that this would minimise the 'risk' of children watching 'dark, wild and sexy' (Davies in Garner 2013b, p. 20) content in the BBC Three series. The clear water between the two series was emphasised in interviews with Julie Gardner and Davies. 'It's a way for Russell T. Davies to write Sci-Fi in a very different way to how he tackles it in *Doctor Who*,' says Gardner, 'a kind of British *X-Files* meets *This Life*' (2006, p. 44), and by referencing two series definitely aimed at adult audiences, the implication is that *Torchwood* will attract the same type of 'quality TV' viewers (see also Garner 2013b). While *Doctor Who* hybridises science fiction, action adventure and, at times, period drama and gothic horror, *Torchwood* is presented by Gardner as offering a different kind of hybridity, a combination more suited to an older audience. 'It's adult crime drama, and it plays very differently' to *Doctor Who*, she maintains, adding that children watching *Doctor Who* are 'not going to want to watch it' (p. 45). Davies himself dismissed the 'risk' in one interview, stating, 'I think we worry too much because the audience is not confused by this, they know what a nine o'clock show is' (in Richardson 2006, pp. 35–6). By scheduling the series on BBC Three, a niche channel aimed at a young adult audience, and at 9pm – the time designated in the UK as the 'watershed' distinguishing programming suitable for children from programming that might be considered inappropriate for them – *Torchwood*, the pre-release publicity suggests, targets its 'correct' audience and is thus able to revel in its 'very different' approach to science fiction and the *Doctor Who* universe.

In some senses, then, the rhetoric surrounding *The Sarah Jane Adventures*, produced for children's channel CBBC, is somewhat contradictory. The director of the pilot episode, Colin Teague, noted:

Russell was quite adamant that he wanted this to be full-blooded. By that we were saying that was definitely not going to be considered, or shot, as a children's show. This is a drama, as with any of the other shows we do in Cardiff (2007, p. 26).

As demonstrated by previous chapters, *The Sarah Jane Adventures* certainly covers 'dark' and 'wild' material, if it avoids the 'sexy', with several stories revolving around death or abandonment. And while it does not wholeheartedly maintain the kind of 'intertextual barricade' Garner ascribes to *Torchwood*, it features only occasional crossovers with *Doctor Who* itself, allowing it, too, to forge a 'very different' path as an Earth-bound series. In fact, although Garner notes that *The Sarah Jane Adventures* 'continually borrows or recodes' *Who* 'monsters' (2013b, p. 23) in ways that *Torchwood* does not, he never elaborates on the distinction between borrowing and recoding. These monsters are sometimes presented rather differently, overturning expectations of what a spin-off does and what a children's drama might do: 'Surprisingly – given this is a show for Children's BBC – the Slitheen are much scarier in their latest story' (Richardson 2007, p. 51), full of genuine menace rather than simply providing comic flatulence. In this way, despite *The Sarah Jane Adventures* being the third spin-off, it aligns itself with the BBC's ongoing production of children's drama that can tackle serious issues like parental separation, loss or homelessness; it is perhaps less concerned with 'commercial' requirements than with those of 'public service', something Garner also discusses in relation to *Torchwood*. In her autobiography, Elisabeth Sladen confesses that she initially thought the series might be sidelined, given it 'was pitched squarely at the children's strand. I had a nasty feeling that it might get overlooked again. [...] But then I saw the TV schedules. [...] After more than thirty years, I finally felt appreciated by the BBC' (Sladen and Hudson 2012, p. 319).

Arguably neither spin-off seeks to simply cash in on the success of the rebooted *Doctor Who* – this may well be a consideration, but it is not the whole story. Both develop their own style, themes and mode according to their target audience. (*The Sarah Jane*

Adventures is bright and optimistic despite dealing with serious issues and mixes action-adventure with emotional melodrama; *Torchwood* cultivates 'wild and sexy' with some self-conscious camp.) *The Sarah Jane Adventures* has not been exported internationally in the way the other two series have, either because (as Porter suggests) it is too localised, too enmeshed in British middle-class life, or because the other two series have been sold to international audiences as adult drama rather than family entertainment. When Gardner retrospectively comments that '[i]t was about doing three different forms of sci-fi that would appeal across a wide spectrum of age range' (in Brew 2011) this hints at the BBC's remit to provide programming for the whole population, not simply for the mainstream.

However, the very success of the post-2005 *Doctor Who* has highlighted possible tension between exploiting a popular product that is exported through a commercial arm of the BBC, and this public service remit. Some exhibits and events, as well as toy ranges and other merchandising, have attracted criticism (see Hills 2014a and 2014b). The BBC does not carry commercial advertising, yet some point out excessive advertising of its own productions, *Doctor Who* among them (Hills 2014b, p. 163), and others even complain about its pervasiveness in the everyday sphere, with viewers remarking, 'Dr. Who isn't real! So he shouldn't really be featured on the news' (quoted in Hills 2014b, p. 163). Hills uses the 50th-anniversary celebration as a means of analysing the BBC's changing position on public service and cultural value as it seeks to keep up with commercial rivals and an ever-expanding TV and media market. Marking a half-century of *Doctor Who* might seem somewhat frivolous, yet Hills notes that the BBC coverage puts stress 'firmly on historical value: public service is equated with remembering cultural history' (2014b, p. 163). The (record-breaking) global simulcast of the anniversary special 'The Day of the Doctor'[18] is then situated as part of a public service that 'provides a shared past of "creative and cultural value", binding generations together in collective memory' (Hills 2014b, p. 165), acting as 'social glue' and uniting the nation (along with participating international territories) 'in simultaneous experience', whether audiences were watching via a television set, a mobile device or a cinema screen. In 'The Day of the Doctor' publicity, social media was used extensively – for the first time, as noted in the previous chapter (see also Hills 2014b, p. 166). This widespread campaign reached out to the mainstream audience new *Who* was designed for, and Moffat was certainly aware that the simulcast episode had to 'speak to the generation who are watching it now' (in Hills 2014a, p. 108) so emphasis was on recent series history rather than all 50 years of the series.

While 'The Day of the Doctor', episode and 'event' alike, were deemed successful, the same cannot be said for Moffat's tenure as showrunner. As noted in the previous chapter, the way he has responded to criticisms of gender inequalities in the series has at times made for awkward moments. This has in turn elicited critiques of his defence for not having more women writers and directors ('There are fewer […] it's a statistical fact – it's shameful but it's true'; in Polo 2014), with bloggers and journalists responding confidently:

> How strange it is to hear showrunners/producers in high places express helplessness over the fact that there are few female directors and female writers with credits under their belts to equal their male counterparts. It's those showrunners and producers who are in the positions of power to change that gender gap (Polo 2014).

This echoes official reports produced by Creative Skillset and Directors UK and cited in Chapter 5, as well as many other industry reports from a range of countries that come to the same conclusions. Viewers have access to this information more readily because of digital communication technologies, and social media ensures that such statistics are circulated among those who are interested.

The recent wave of criticism about inequalities in the production team is not the first Moffat has had to field. The announcement that Matt Smith was leaving the series set off the usual speculation that a non-white, non-male actor might be cast as the Doctor. Admittedly, this had happened before, but this time more attention seemed to be paid to comments about gender and race, and the 'story' of casting the new Doctor ran for months, generating countless press articles, blog posts and social media debates (see also Jowett 2014). A poll in UK tabloid newspaper the *Mirror* had more votes for the 'first black Doctor' than the first female Doctor (see Leigh 2013), and both possibilities were much discussed. Dame Helen Mirren was one of the suggestions, and a bookmaker reportedly offered 25–1 odds on the possibility. 'Oh, please – I would put much longer odds on it than that,' she responded (in Lawless 2013), and many pointed out that the BBC could probably not afford to cast an actor of her calibre in a regular role. Mirren, despite her dismissiveness of even being asked, could not resist commenting on the situation, however: 'I think it's absolutely time for a female Doctor Who. I'm so sick of that man with his girl sidekick. I could name at least 10 wonderful British actresses who would absolutely kill in that role' (in Lawless 2013). Likewise, US writer and producer Jane Espenson, who wrote for *Torchwood: Miracle Day* and has a track record of being involved in productions that challenge traditional norms of gender and sexuality (*Buffy the Vampire Slayer*, *Battlestar Galactica*, *Husbands*, *Once Upon a Time*), expressed the view that it was time for a female Doctor (Just Cos 2013). Writer Neil Gaiman's contribution has already been mentioned, and many more weighed in, including author Stella Duffy, who posted about it on her blog (2013), while Moffat tried to defend or deflect criticism.

Following the announcement that the Twelfth Doctor would be Peter Capaldi, another white male, UK newspaper the *Telegraph* ran an article by an 11-year-old girl, Jessica Ebner-Statt, who expressed her disappointment with the news, making a case for a female Doctor:

> Nowadays, girls have few female role models to look up to. The most famous women I know of are pop or movie stars who are packaged and branded as hot sex idols. Despite the fact that these women look and sound incredible, many of them make girls become self-conscious about their looks, and dress inappropriately – something that is becoming more and more frequent (Ebner-Statt 2013).

Ebner-Statt, admittedly, is the daughter of a journalist (Sarah Ebner) and blogs with her mother and alone, about various topics, so she was not a random 11-year-old. All the same, her article was shared on social media more than two thousand times and attracted many comments, some dismissive or aggressive enough to prompt 'Grant Cruickshank' to comment 'Wow, so this is where all the misogynists hang out' (2013). Notably Ebner-Statt's article appeared in the 'Women's Life' section of the *Telegraph* website, while other articles on the casting announcement appeared in the 'Culture: TV and Radio' section. In addition, the author information pointed out that she was 'a computer-obsessed, chocolate-loving feminist' (Ebner-Statt 2013), allowing, perhaps, for dismissal of her opinion as biased.

This issue of casting the Doctor shows no signs of receding: the following year a reader of the *Financial Times* wrote in on the subject, his letter published under the headline 'Viewers are ready for a Time Lady – so how about it, BBC?' (Trybulski 2014). Stan Trybulski says very little about the series, but places its 50-year history in the context of the progress made by women in the public sphere, naming female presidents of various countries, and noting that in contrast 'Doctor Who has remained, if not quite misogynistic, abominably Victorian.' Since Trybulski gives his address as Connecticut, USA, he is presumably not a British television licence-fee payer directly supporting the BBC, but his comments are squarely addressed, perhaps with due irony and self-consciousness, to the 'chaps' at the BBC who would be able to effect such a change. Arguably, the BBC might even feel some responsibility to do so as one of its public purposes, set out in its Charter, is 'Representing the UK, its nations, regions and communities' by 'reflect[ing] the many communities that live in the UK' (BBC n.d. a). This wording may deliberately sidestep issues of gender and/or sexuality, but representing the UK would logically seem to include representing the half of its population identifying as female as something other than 'girl sidekicks', to return to Mirren's description of the series' formula.

Certainly the gender-swapping of the Doctor's long-term Time Lord antagonist, the Master, transformed into Missy during season 8, set off a new round of speculation about the Doctor and gender. Mathilda Gregory's blog for the *Guardian* had the (possibly rather optimistic) subheading 'Now that the Master has become the Mistress, it can't be long before we see a woman playing the Doctor. Who would you cast?' (2014). Missygate is examined at more length below, and reactions to this gender-swap varied widely. Some, however, were not convinced that one such transformation necessarily paved the way for another. As promotion for season 9 got underway, Sylvester McCoy, who played the Seventh Doctor, told the *Mirror*:

> I'm a feminist and recognise there are still glass ceilings in place for many women, but where would we draw the line? A Mr Marple instead of Miss Marple? A Tarzanette? [...] Doctor Who is a male character, just like James Bond. If they changed it to be politically correct then it would ruin the dynamics between the doctor and the assistant, which is a popular part of the show.
>
> I support feminism, but I'm not convinced by the cultural need of a female Doctor Who (in Hope 2015).

Published under the rather inflammatory headline 'Doctor Who legend Sylvester McCoy says only a MAN can play the Time Lord', this story was picked up by other UK newspapers. In the *Independent* Daisy Wyatt described McCoy as a 'former "feminist" Time Lord', and also pointed out Tilda Swinton's casting as the Ancient One in Marvel's *Doctor Strange* movie (2015) as just one example of how major franchises are taking steps towards more inclusive casting, regardless of a character's initial gender or race. Both the *Mirror* and the *Independent* included a reader poll. The story also featured in online news such as IGN, Screenrant and Digital Spy, as well as on more specialised websites like The Mary Sue (where it ran with the subheading 'Here's Why He's Wrong'; Lachenal 2015) and Legion of Leia, which also took issue with McCoy's stance (Busch 2015). One blogger even suggested that the whole of season 8 'repeatedly reflected – or perhaps satirised – the growing clamour that the Doctor be played by a woman' (Nicol 2015).

Partly this issue is divisive because, as with the James Bond or the Marvel and DC franchises, any long-running storyworld or character attracts a following who become invested in particular aspects of that world or characters. The need to adapt to cultural and social changes produces an inevitable tension between consistency or continuity and dynamic development appropriate for the current era and for new audiences. Of course, the voices that dominate such debates are not necessarily representative of all consumers: an extreme view makes a much better story for any news outlet.

Given the widely differing responses to Missy, it is interesting to compare the affection for a female character like Sarah Jane Smith, who not only aged with parts of the audience for the *Doctor Who* universe stories, but also remained relatively consistent. When news of Elisabeth Sladen's death broke in 2011 there was a public outpouring of grief. Porter notes how the montage in the final episode of *The Sarah Jane Adventures* was designed to imply that the character lived on (2012, p. 119), yet she also records what some viewers saw as a lack of respect when the tribute to Sladen/Sarah Jane was not broadcast in the US and fans sought it out online (p. 24). Sladen herself, in her autobiography, almost completed when she died, admitted that she was somewhat mystified by her popularity: 'My character, Sarah Jane Smith, seemed to have lived on in the memories and hearts of so many fans. I don't know why she was so popular' (Sladen and Hudson 2012, p. 2). This is perhaps all the more remarkable, or possibly a strong accolade to Sladen's warmth and personality, when she reveals that while a new companion like Freema Agyeman was 'given a course at the BBC on how to handle the media' as soon as her casting was announced, Sladen herself 'had no such training' (Sladen and Hudson 2012, p. 108).

Sarah Jane's lasting popularity with viewers seems to rest on her continuity, aged but still basically the same person, which seems rather paradoxical since Sarah Jane was introduced to shake things up in terms of how the classic series represented women. Audiences, male and female alike, were obviously ready for this kind of independent female figure, especially when paired with Tom Baker's eccentric Fourth Doctor. Yet attitudes to Sarah Jane as a character, consciously or otherwise, are somewhat proprietary, with countless tributes following Sladen's death hinging on her being 'my Sarah Jane'. David Tennant's foreword to her autobiography takes the same tone, and he admits that as a fan himself, working alongside Sladen when she reappeared on television screens as Sarah Jane in 'School Reunion' served as 'the realisation of a childhood fantasy I never imagined I would entertain' (in Sladen and Hudson 2012, p. xi). 'It could only have been with Elisabeth,' he continues, 'It was always the Doctor and Sarah […] It wouldn't have been the same if my TARDIS hadn't been graced by the lady who lit up my childhood and helped me fall in love with it all in the first place' (p. xi). That this description is firmly anchored to the 'classic' version of Sarah Jane is never commented on, and very few Sarah Jane tribute videos include more than cursory footage from the rebooted *Who*, and even less from *The Sarah Jane Adventures*. Perhaps, after all, Sladen's role as an older, wiser, Doctor-less Sarah Jane might present too much disruption of her as the ideal, the ultimate companion.

FANBOYS?

In one sense, reception has been complicated with *Doctor Who* because of the hiatus in its broadcast history, with no canonical TV series produced between 1989 and 2005. The failure of the 1996 TV movie, starring Paul McGann as the Eighth Doctor, only seemed to seal its fate. Rebecca Williams suggests 'that we can view such periods as "interim fandom" when fans assume that their fan object is dormant' (2013b). During the period of *Doctor Who's* long hiatus, the television text may have been suspended but fan production and consumption were still active with, as mentioned in Chapter 4, audio dramas and novels filling the gap and creating new stories. Such a period may be fertile in some ways – blogger and writer Philip Sandifer argues that in these 'wilderness years [...] Doctor Who gets its first ever feminist writers: Paul Cornell and Kate Orman' (2013), and the creation of Bernice Summerfield certainly seems to contribute to some of the female characters in the 2005 reboot, as already noted. Yet such paratexts can easily be dismissed as 'non-canon', allowing their developments to be sidestepped when the series is revived. Inevitably, a reboot or return after a production gap means change and reinvention for a new generation, and long-term fans, notes Williams, 'must readjust or negotiate this when the object becomes active again' (2013b). Williams is discussing *Torchwood*, and responses to the changes that occurred over its production history as it shifted channels and countries; fan response to the *Doctor Who* reboot has also been discussed, for example in Booth (2013b). One thing is clear: post-2005 *Doctor Who* did attract a new audience, or at least made segments of the audience more visible, and this disrupted assumptions about the gender of its viewers.

It is not surprising, then, that studies of fan communities around the series have emerged, especially given the new 'legitimacy' of television studies and fandom studies. Williams and Hills, among others, have discussed the potential division between fans of 'old' and 'new' *Who*, and Hadas and Shifman draw attention to the hiatus and its impact on fan communities in their analysis of the doctorwho online forum. They argue that it is an appropriate

> site for the study of the changing face of fandom, being both the place where fans had gathered before the airing of the new series, and where new fans take their first steps in fandom. Its entirely inclusive nature means that fans of many tastes, affiliations, and creative bents are represented and heard (2013, p. 282).

This is contrasted with *Doctor Who* fan sites such as GallifreyBase, by the authors and – as they demonstrate – by the fans themselves, especially in terms of views on gender and other issues of representation. Thus, *Doctor Who*'s 'post-2005 reincarnation has allowed for a reinvigoration of analyses and understandings of the programme, in both its classic and its contemporary forms' (Williams 2013c) by fans who may align themselves with one or other, or with both versions of the series. The apparent divide between the classic and contemporary series is also associated with gendered audiences, and with particular forms of fandom. Certainly female fans have become more visible in relation to the post-2005 series.

Hadas and Shifman paraphrase Hills' characterisation of 'post-television Doctor Who' as 'quintessential cult, cherished by a small and devoted group of those in the know' (2013, p. 280), which does nothing to undermine the stereotype of the British *Who* fan as an obsessive male geek. Despite Miles Booy's statement that there are 'more girls represented [in *Doctor Who Weekly*] than later stereotypes would suggest' (2012, p. 27), the 'stereotype' he refers to remains dominant. Some female fans from other countries express surprise when they discover how male-dominated *Doctor Who* fandom is and was in the UK (see, for example, Sullivan 2010, p. 129). This may be to do with cultural assumptions about genre, though logic suggests that if this were the case, then it should apply to other national science fiction fandoms too. As noted in the previous chapter, the male-dominated UK fandom of *Who* translated into its reboot, with many fans becoming professionals working on the post-2005 series. 'Certain now-influential figures have made the transition from hobbyist to paid expert,' notes Piers Britton. 'This inevitably complicates the definition of what it means to be a fan' (2011, p. 58). It does not necessarily, however, complicate fan identity in terms of gender, and fanboy-producers dominate the new *Who*.

The fandom of those involved in bringing *Doctor Who* back to television informed its approach in key ways, as signalled in the previous chapter: these fanboy-producers (with emphasis on the 'boy') knew the material and might therefore be 'trusted' with the storyworld and characters fans held dear, but they also attempted to avoid previous mistakes in producing material to please the fan audience at the expense of others:

> All involved knew that the test of the series would be in its ability to convert cult into mainstream: to turn an infamously clunky, campy, and continuity-rich science fiction classic into a leading family show, and relaunch the treasure of the few as the pleasure of the many (Hadas and Shifman 2013, p. 280).

This entailed the fanboy-producers distancing themselves from fandom's perceived overinvestment, as shown in the last chapter, yet simultaneously using their own fandom as a form of cultural or subcultural capital that validates their position. Hadas and Shifman, Hills, and others have examined the ways in which showrunners Davies and Moffat handle this, as well as the range of fan responses to their often aggressive and pathologising statements about fans who are overly critical or seek advance information, leaking spoilers.

Fanwank and its association with the 'wilderness years' of hiatus and fan production needed to be avoided in the transition from cult to mainstream and from appealing to a niche audience of fans to a mainstream 'very, very Saturday night' series able to attract a much wider audience. Noticeably, some criticisms of the Moffat 'era' focused on the return to fan-service, with accusations of overly complex storytelling and obscure references 'losing' the audience and only pleasing fans. Debates about the 'different' audiences for the series and about fan communities complicate as well as reinforce such distinctions, and analysis of them sometimes implies but does not articulate the ways in which such groupings are gendered. Views about whether fandom is 'broken' are being exchanged on the blogosphere and social media, analysing contemporary fans' attitude of 'entitlement' to the object of their fandom (see Faraci 2016 and Television FTW 2016 for differing views). Hadas and Shifman note that such pathologisation has been employed by fans for their own ends, most obviously to make similar distinctions between 'good' and 'bad' fans:

> The 'moaning minnies' are not 'us', but fans of a different sort who truly are as unpleasant and destructive to the show as Davies paints them. These other fans supposedly populate other sites, most often the forums at http://gallifreybase.com/forum/ (formerly The Doctor Who Forum (DWF) and before that Outpost Gallifrey). The pinning of the moaning minny image on this forum is not coincidental: to doctorwho, the DWF is the home of the 'anoraks', the old-school fanboys – again distinctly male – who, according to fan folk wisdom, really do resent any and all changes to their show and prefer it in its cult form (Hadas and Shifman 2013, p. 285).

In this way, certain groups of fans and certain fan sites consider themselves as inclusive and as embracing change and diversity, while 'old-school fanboys' perpetuate stereotypes of both fandom and gender. Notably, Hadas and Shifman do not examine specifically feminist sites for discussion of *Who* (such as Whovian Feminism) or of popular culture more generally (The Mary Sue, Legion of Leia), several of which have already been quoted in previous chapters.

The positions taken in the debate also emerge in some posts and blogs about the work of female writers on the series, such as Helen Raynor, whose first episodes ('Daleks in Manhattan' 3.4 and 'Evolution of the Daleks' 3.5) received harsh criticism from some fans and led Davies to 'defend' her, as outlined in the previous chapter. In this instance, 'real' fans bolster their authority by emphasising how open-minded they are, thus distancing themselves from the reactionary views of 'anoraks' as in the following, posted to behindthesofa.org:

> Whilst I have to admit that I haven't enjoyed much of Helen Raynor's contributions to the show, I haven't descended to mud-slinging. The trouble is that most forums are prone to minorities delivering inarticulate bile with no redeeming or constructive features to their credit. Many are full of monosyllabic grunting and, frighteningly, many hormonally challenged male fans who still haven't got over the fact that a person called Verity actually produced one of the greatest television shows on Earth. After all, Verity was a *woman*, for heaven's sake! Helen dared to write about Daleks and Pig Men. She's a girl and what do girls know about *Doctor Who*!? Well, the ones I've met know plenty (Collins 2008).

Several interesting features mark this 'defence' of Raynor. The writer notes that while not particularly enjoying Raynor's episodes, he has not 'descended' to 'mud-slinging', both descriptions suggesting

backwards or regressive views and aggressive, hostile (thus masculine?) behaviour, emphasised later by the words 'inarticulate' and
'monosyllabic grunting'. Collins certainly upholds the notion that
some fans see themselves as keeping the series and its characters
'safe' from those who cannot be trusted (viewers and creatives)
because they are not knowledgeable and authoritative fanboys with
vast amounts of subcultural capital. Pointing out that the object of
their fandom was produced by a woman, Verity Lambert, Collins
suggests that women creating *Doctor Who* is hardly new, in fact it
is extremely 'old school' – omitting mention of the lack of female
writers and directors since Lambert, or even Lambert's own position as the first female producer for the BBC. He also undermines
somewhat the apparent intention of his piece by concluding with
the 'some of my best friends are female' defence (yes, I've met some
women and they were even fans of *Doctor Who*).

Less unconscious in its position of male privilege, but just as
interesting, is a post calling for Raynor's return:

> There's a certain uniqueness to Raynor's writing that has defi-
> nitely been lacking in the last few series, a charisma and energy
> that comes across in her episodes. This is the main motivation
> that leads to Helen Raynor being the name on my mind and on
> my lips during my silent prayers to Lord Moffat God of Trolls
> every night. Helen Raynor needs to return! And here are 5 rea-
> sons why… (Johnston, 2014)

While presumably inspired by complaints about the lack of female
writers, this contributor actually avoids talking about gender altogether, focusing on the quality of Raynor's work and thus positioning her as a gender-neutral professional. This works to present the
writer of the post as both open-minded and as basing their opinion
on evidence of prior work – the possibility of 'uniqueness', 'cha-
risma and energy' is all that should be required to appoint writers
on *Doctor Who*, irrespective of gender. This therefore echoes the

'defence' Moffat has reiterated in several interviews: that casting, or appointing writers and directors, is not about gender, it's about the 'right person for the job'. Neither Moffat nor Johnston acknowledge, much less challenge, the institutional frameworks that lead to smaller numbers of women writers and directors working in top-level television productions and to envisaging particular roles as only for (white) men. Thus, as with those in charge of producing the post-2005 series, fans also take up positions that might seem to be 'liberal' and inclusive but that limit perception of how and why gender inequalities persist and the way creative and fan labour and discourses help structure them as highly gendered.

Given the debates about Capaldi's casting and about the lack of women writing and directing *Doctor Who*, it is hardly surprising that the transformation of the Master into Missy (played by Michelle Gomez) elicited similar commentary. If anything, the extremity of the views aired in public through the mainstream press and via social media and the internet was exacerbated by the fact that this was not speculation, it was accomplished story, entering the canon of the television series. Some comments carped:

> Why does everyone keep saying Moffat proved a Time Lord can change genders? Fucking Neil Gaimen [*sic*] did that ages ago (jemthecrystalgem 2014).

> It's also been part of the books and audio adventures since, like the 1990s (Cornah 2014).

Many others made the point that putting Missy in the television series established what had before been hinted at or achieved only in paratexts. As already noted, Gregory in the *Guardian* took this positively, assuming that it was now only a matter of time before a female Doctor graced TV screens. Others, acting out the fan identities described above, responded differently. Kasterborous published a 'how our team reacted' article (Cawley 2014). This ranged from the 'old-school fanboy' type, wanting to keep the toys strictly for the boys:

> What is the reason for it? None I can see. It doesn't serve the story at all. Just another shock revelation for the sake of a shock revelation. Moffat knew he'd never get away with turning the Doctor into a woman, so he did so to the Master. Wasn't clever, or interesting, and serves no purpose within the realms of the fictional world of *Who* (Andy Frankham in Cawley 2014).

> I'm pretty appalled. When I saw the rumour, I thought, 'it'll never be that. That's ridiculous.' The episode was good but the 'revelation', and its implications, has spoiled the character for me. I love Moffat, but I now want this era over – and that's something I never thought I'd say (Philip Bates in Cawley 2014).

To the slightly more insightful:

> Any feeling of 'meh...' I have is not so much at the thought of a female Master but more because we've been presented with yet another forty-something female character portrayed in that knowing, arch way so beloved of this era of the show (Jonathan Appleton in Cawley 2014).

All opinions are presented without comment by Cawley, leaving the reader to align themselves with whichever appeals most.

What was not in doubt, apparently, was the need for commentators, fans and fan sites to respond. Jon Cooper in the *Mirror* described it as 'the biggest *Doctor Who* fan foofaraw since Matt Smith mispronounced "Metebelis" in episode 12 of season 7 (for the record, Matty, it's 'met-a-BEE-lis', not 'met-A-bo-lis')' (2014). This opener established Cooper's own fanboy credentials from the start, if in a slightly tongue-in-cheek and self-satirising fashion designed, perhaps, not to put off readers without such subcultural capital. Cooper positions himself in the centre ground, adamant that both the fanboys and the feminists are wrong: 'Accusations of misogyny and transphobia were intercut with arguments over established canon and the quoting of arcane trivia. And it's all just missing the point, a bit. Because Michelle Gomez makes for one amazing villain' (2014). Like the defence of Raynor's writing above, Cooper argues that Gomez is simply 'the right person for the job' and evaluates Missy on Gomez' performance, rather than on gender. He too fails to acknowledge certain ingrained aspects of the industry, offering a rather naive argument: 'Character should ultimately come before ingrained and reactionary sexual politics, chiefly because it's a piece of TV entertainment, and should be viewed accordingly' (2014). Cooper then realises that his position is rather contradictory. 'Doctor Who has always been a piece of TV entertainment. Nothing more, nothing less. In the course of its fifty-oneish years, though, a core principle has been the idea of acceptance and change, but not necessarily in that order' (2014). This conclusion raises more issues than it resolves, neatly articulating the highly contradictory impulses and tensions within the series and its reception.

Feminist bloggers and sites also provided their own versions of the 'our response to' post, with Nathaniel Tapley on UsVsTh3m gleefully selecting some of the most extreme 'old school fanboy responses' and holding them up to ridicule (2014). Reading his selections can be an entertaining experience, but also a frightening one, and recalls the comment, 'So this is where all the misogynists hang out,' quoted above. WhovianFeminism offered more than one blog post on Missy, the first expressing disappointment: 'I wanted *the Doctor* to be portrayed by a woman, and given the timing, I can't help feeling like Missy is a consolation prize' (2014a). This writer demonstrates her subcultural capital in a second post citing Moffat's previous work in the pre-2005 era, when he wrote the parody discussed in Chapter 4 featuring Joanna Lumley as one in a line of regenerations of the Doctor (2014b), as well as connecting what she sees as the poor execution of the character with Moffat's back catalogue of female characters for the series. 'Moffat did just about everything I feared he would with Missy/The Master. I was particularly annoyed that Missy [...] was falling all over herself to make out with the Doctor and describe how in love she was with him' (2014a). The second post on Missy elaborates this evaluation of it all being a rather simplistic view of sex and gender:

> It's not just that the Master, while portrayed by a woman, willingly gave up her position of authority and control to the Doctor. Missy also did it with the horrible flirtation that's so common it's become a cliche of Moffat's female characters (2014b).

It is apparent, then, that male or female, 'old school' or liberal commentators all pick out the same features of post-2005 *Doctor Who* in order to make arguments about gender representation. While some are more insightful and convincing than others, none of this commentary changes anything. According to Hills, this might be because of stringent measures in fanagement, or means of managing fan expectations and responses, appearing to cater to them while not disrupting the mainstream popularity of a flagship BBC production.

FANAGEMENT

Hills' concept of fanagement aligns itself with what Jonathan Gray sees as one of the functions of paratexts, which 'can domesticate texts to specific communities [...], offering the prospect for those communities to construct a more intimate relationship to what may otherwise seem a "mass" text' (2010, p. 161). The 50th anniversary *Doctor Who* productions exemplify this: 'The Day of the Doctor' was the mainstream text, positioned as an international 'event', bringing audiences together in space where it was screened in cinemas, and in time by the global simulcast. Other specials catered for different audiences. BBC Two aired the drama documentary *An Adventure in Time and Space*, Mark Gatiss' affectionate look at the early history of the series, focusing on actor William Hartnell but also showcasing the contributions of producer Verity Lambert and director Waris Hussein. Lambert and Hussein are shown bonding over their outsider status, and it is clear that not only is Lambert given the series because it seems unlikely to succeed, but also that it only does so because of the support of Sydney Newman, depicted as Lambert's mentor. Paradoxically, for those familiar with both the classic and rebooted series, this only draws attention to the current domination of the post-2005 series by white fanboy professionals like Gatiss himself. 'An Adventure in Time and Space' and its position on BBC Two seemed intended to attract an audience familiar with the origins of the show (and thus probably much older than its current audience), or perhaps those who wanted to know more about these origins. Audiences might also be engaged by the human interest relationships it involved as well as by the 'high production values in its HD recreation of *Doctor Who*'s 1960s imagery' (Hills 2014b, p. 168), the latter contributing to its positioning as 'a prestigious TV production' (Hills 2015, p. 43).

Two other anniversary specials, minisode 'The Night of the Doctor' and online feature *The Five(ish) Doctors Reboot*, seemed definitively aimed at fans who knew the timeline of the series' characters ('Night') and had a fairly detailed knowledge of its cast and crew over the years (*Five(ish)*). 'The Night of the Doctor' was an online minisode just under seven minutes long, showing the Eighth Doctor regenerating into the War Doctor, and featured Paul McGann reprising his role, as discussed in Chapter 4. *The Five(ish) Doctors Reboot*, written and directed by Peter Davison (who played the Fifth Doctor and who had also written the 2007 Children in Need special, 'Time Crash'), was released on the BBC's Red Button service and online following 'The Day of the Doctor'. According to Davison:

[*The Five(ish) Doctors Reboot*] started off almost by accident. [...] I was asked a question at a convention – 'Will you be in the 50th?' – and I said if I wasn't, I would damn well make my own!

As a germ of an idea came into my head, the passion for it grew and so it got to a point where it was a real quest to complete it (in Jeffery 2013).

Moffat recalls:

I bumped into Peter at a party and was asked to be in it. [...] I said I'd give him a budget and a camera crew and some time and why don't you make it for real, make it for us? (in Jeffery 2013)

And Hills notes that the production received 'official support' from BBC Wales (2015, p. 50). It seems unlikely that this would happen for just any 'little fan video' (Moffat, in Jeffery), requiring Davison's connections to the *Who* production community to attract such backing, and therefore succeeding partly through social capital.

Described variously as a 'comedy spoof and homage' to *Doctor Who* (Wikipedia), as a 'madcap little self-deprecating celebratory half-hour' (Lloyd 2013), or even as 'something that affectionately sent up the anticipation' and hype surrounding the anniversary, while remaining 'a sweet, often funny, homage' to the series (Lawrence 2013), *Five(ish)* adopts a behind-the-scenes style and follows actors who played previous Doctors from the classic series trying to crash the anniversary special, which they have not been invited to appear in. It featured a plethora of actors, crew and *Who*-related creatives of all kinds (Dalek operators as well as 'Doctors'), from the classic and the contemporary series. As Robert Lloyd notes, one of its 'great pleasures [...] is seeing who shows up and how' and this, of course, relies on detailed fan knowledge. 'From a Peter Cushing reference to a "Dalek Operators' Gazette" it has been made as a treat for the fans,' Lloyd concludes (2013),[19] though his examples are perhaps chosen so that a more mainstream audience 'get' them without tedious fannish explanation. Given that *Five(ish)* incorporated and celebrated the classic as well as the rebooted series, it offset the official anniversary episode's focus on the contemporary series' history, which made almost no reference to the classic series barring Tom Baker's appearance in the conclusion and the complete line-up of every Doctor. In addition, *Five(ish)*, by including production team members, novel writers and other 'minor' contributors to the series, as well as former (McCoy, Colin Baker, Tennant) and current stars (Matt Smith, Jenna Coleman) and showrunners (Moffat and Davies both feature), manages to celebrate and salute the collective efforts of many people who have made the series such a long-lasting, affectionately held cultural artefact, rather than just the series' inception (as in *An Adventure in Space and Time*) or current incarnation.

For these reasons, Hills argues that *Five(ish)* 'amounts to a form of "fanagement"', responding directly and dialogically to fannish interests in seeing older Doctors on-screen again, but only in a niche format outside the primary text of the anniversary special' (2014a, p. 108). Engaging its audience through a different kind of nostalgia than that evoked by *An Adventure in Space and Time*, *Five(ish)*, like 'Night', was interpreted within fandom as 'fan-centric rather than media-centric' (Hills 2014b, p. 169): it 'had really been made for us fans', as *SFX* magazine put it (quoted in Hills 2014b, p. 169). Having the more famous faces of *Doctor Who* play 'themselves in a more or less parodic manner' (Wikipedia n.d.) offsets their 'media-centric' celebrity and makes the inclusion of less well-known figures much more 'fan-centric', both in terms of its homage to them and in terms of the effort and knowledge required to 'spot' them. The more you know about *Doctor Who*, the more jokes and guest appearances you can enjoy.[20]

Fan pleasures and subcultural capital aside, *Five(ish)*, while gently poking fun at the actors' (fictionalised) obsession with reliving the glory days of their classic Doctors, and taking care to include many guest appearances by women (actors and crew), cannot avoid presenting the series' production history as male-dominated – because it is. Hills notes that other 'specials' 'reinforced the status of BBC Wales' *Doctor Who* as a "fanbrand" – one run by professionalised fans' (2014a, p. 106), and these professionalised fans are mostly men. The majority of the women featured were actors who had played previous companions, while Georgia Moffett was included as David Tennant's wife, rather than as the Doctor's daughter, and the wife and daughters of Colin Baker personify the weary patience of non-fans with their husbands' and fathers' obsessive fanboy behaviour. Naturally, the majority of screen time was given to the Doctors. Of course, *Five(ish)* pays tribute to the actual history of *Doctor Who*, including the audio adventures that enabled fans to engage with the object of their fandom while it was not on television. But, like the foregrounding in *An Adventure in Time and Space* of Lambert and Hussein's roles in making the original series a success despite their marginal status at the BBC of the 1960s, this served ultimately to demonstrate how dominated by white men the series has been, and still is.

All of the anniversary specials, then, operate to reinforce, subtly or less so, the male-centred narratives and production of *Doctor Who*. This is perhaps not quite what Hills means when he notes that 'anniversary commemorations necessarily valorize longer-term arcs of meaning' (2015, p. 4) but all three productions demonstrate that one longer-term arc of meaning in the series is its privileging of a white male perspective. When it comes to fan production, however, things really can change.

FANGIRLS?

The 2005 reboot of *Doctor Who* brought it to new audiences and, as Deborah Stanish notes, the make-up of these new audiences bucked some of the stereotypes: 'Producer Russell T. Davies had brought *Doctor Who* back to life with a new sensibility that firmly embraced

female viewing tastes' (2010, p. 34). Despite problematic assumptions about what 'female viewing tastes' might be (Hadas and
Shifman cite 'an emphasis on emotional storytelling' as one attraction; 2013, p. 281), the burgeoning female audience encouraged
the formation of 'space for intensely feminine fandom that some
male-dominated, masculine fandom groups look down on' (Cherry
2013, p. 108). The supposed status quo was disrupted: 'Segments of
die-hard (i.e. male) *Doctor Who* fans had been grumbling online
about the droves of new female fans that were coming into their
clubhouse with their "squee" and fan fiction' (O'Shea 2010, p. 9).
Some accounts and comments suggested that female fans of the
series were something new, and this was certainly not the case.
However, awareness of the gendering of fan activity, fan discourse
and fan spaces (such as conventions) brought new perspectives to
bear. Rebecca Williams notes that fangirls had persistently been
devalued 'in society and within fandom' (2011, p. 169) because they
embody a threat to conventional male fandom via 'their hysteria,
their frenzy, their emotionality and desire; all traits which imply
an unruly body that cannot be contained' (2011, pp. 169–70).
Here Williams identifies the ways fangirls are characterised (or
stereotyped) in gendered terms that construct femininity (and
female fandom) as negative. Fans were also being gendered by the
activities that constituted their fandom. Geraghty points out that

> recent fan scholarship has focused on the differences between
> gendered conceptions of the fanboy and fangirl, with the former
> perceived as being more affirmational and celebratory of media
> texts while the latter is more likely to transform them and
> reconstitute them for the needs of the wider fan community'
> (2014, p. 54).

While this may also seem to be a generalisation, some of the female-
authored 'transformations' of *Doctor Who* speak directly to inequalities in 'official' representations and will be considered below.

Adding to apparent divisions within *Who* fandom, some female fans had no interest in the 'classic' series (Williams 2011, p. 170) and had been attracted to the rebooted series by Tennant's 'geek chic' (p. 169). As Alyssa Franke points out, 'Fangirls everywhere face a common frustration. [...] In any fandom based on visual media, fangirls are attacked because of the way the female gaze is misunderstood and misrepresented' (2015). She goes on to recount how, when Peter Capaldi was cast as the Twelfth Doctor, 'some fans became to wonder if an older Doctor would "drive away" female fangirls' because he would not appeal to the (heterosexual) 'female gaze':

> To these [male] fans, young female fans were interlopers in the *Doctor Who* fandom. They weren't real or serious fans that were dedicated to the show or its history. They were just silly little fangirls sucked into watching the latest Doctors because the actors playing them were young and cute (2015).

Even the term 'fangirl' continues to be debated given its pejorative overtones, though more recently it has, perhaps, been reclaimed. Williams offers the interesting suggestion that 'fangirling' might even be adopted as a response to 'the hostility of many male fans', positioning female fan behaviours 'as overt performances of female-ness, [...] exaggerated displays of appropriate hegemonic feminin-ity' (2011, p. 171) designed to highlight difference, since female fans are unlikely to be accepted on the same terms as fanboys.

Previous eras had, of course, engaged female viewers. Sladen mentions being invited to an LA convention organised by women, commenting, 'and people say there are no female *Doctor Who* fans!' (Sladen and Hudson 2012, p. 246). Sophie Aldred, who played the Eighth Doctor's companion Ace, talks about the let-ters she received 'from young girls who were so relieved to see a realistic, strong female character on British TV' (2010, p. 71) and female companions had been, and still were, evaluated as good or bad representations for audiences. Thus, Shoshana Magnet and Robert Smith? argue that Sarah Jane Smith 'in her spin-off show for children' is 'a better role model today than any new-series companion' (2010, p. 161). Others point out that 'there are more ways for a girl *Who* fan to identify than with the simple feminized companion/Doctor dichotomy' (McMurtry 2013, p. 86) and state 'I never wanted to be a companion. I wanted to be the Doctor' (Bear 2010, p. 16).

Outside of the canon, and perhaps especially in the particular space of the fan convention, gender tensions become apparent in ways that might be considered both positive and negative. It is largely acknowledged that convention spaces are often venues for predatory or abusive male behaviour towards female fans (see Chandler 2015, and Chines 2013, for example). Fans cosplaying female characters, and therefore often wearing skimpy outfits indicative of male-driven production, attract adverse comments heavily inflected by cultural assumptions and normative gender models. Finding an alternative mode thus requires some creativity. Brigid Cherry has written about *Doctor Who* Fem!Doctor cosplay or 'crossplay' where female fans dress as their favourite Doctor, but in 'female' clothing, enacting 'a form of cross-gender identification and cross-dressing' (2013, p. 109). The many examples of this type of costume show immense inventiveness and stand as evidence, as Cherry notes, of how 'these female fans are not (or not only) identifying with the main female characters, the companions, but identify as strongly as male fans with the Doctor' (2013, p. 110). In other words, these female fans not only resist their assigned role (identifying with the companions rather than the hero); by dressing as the Doctor – but female – they also clearly signal that they do not want 'to be men' or necessarily adopt a masculine role. They want to be female Doctors, and the series has, so far, denied them this on screen.

According to some, the rebooted *Doctor Who* has continued to cater for its female fans by offering 'positive' messages through its female characters. Philip Sandifer, defending Moffat against criticisms on the basis of gender equality, argues vehemently:

> This is a show that's repeatedly telling girls that they can be as cool as the boys, that the boys don't always know better than them, and that love and independence don't have to be antagonistic qualities for women. It's a show that tells rape survivors that it's OK to not be defined by the terrible things that happen to them. It's a show that says that women aren't done being sexy once they get a grey hair and their first wrinkle, and that tells the Doctor off for thinking otherwise (2013).

Sandifer, here, never engages with the critiques of Moffat's female characters written by the many female fans who take issue with them, and some counterarguments, or more complex discussion, of these characters has already been provided in Chapters 1–3.[21] Some female fans have turned to their own imaginations to rewrite the fate of characters they feel have been severely undercut or mistreated by the canonical television narrative. As Gray notes, 'Fan creativity can work as a powerful in media res paratext, grabbing a story or text in midstream and directing its path elsewhere, or forcing the text to fork outward in multiple directions' (2010, p. 146). Many 'fix-it' fan fiction stories rely heavily on the established narrative to start with and then proceed to offer an alternative version, 'directing its path elsewhere' and 'fixing' the problems the fanwriters identify in the official story. Bethan Jones' paper on fix-it fanfic derived from 'The Girl Who Waited' 'make[s] the case for fans actively seeking out weaknesses and points of contention within texts, and addressing these in their own works' while 'repeating words and phrases used in the episode to lend their stories an air of authenticity' (2013).

Taking controversial companion Amy as an example, the 'problem' for many female fans is not necessarily who she is but more that the writers 'cannot seem to come up with anything for [her] to do that doesn't involve being a sexual or romantic object, a damsel in distress, or – more recently – a uterus in a box' (Lindsay Miller, in Jones 2013). It is hardly surprising, then, that 'The Girl Who Waited', a story featuring an old, embittered version of Amy, should attract the attention of female fans looking for more depth in this particular companion. Jones analyses several fics, establishing that 'fan reaction draws attention to that which we don't see in the episode,' in this case 'the 36 years Amy spends on Apalpucia developing her fighting skills and surviving' (2013). In much the same way, Sherry Ginn has noted that we never see the interim years Sarah Jane Smith spent waiting for the Doctor before she finally meets him again and then decides to start her life afresh (2013).

One of the key things that Jones notes about most of the fanfics she examines is a 'changing attitude to the Doctor' (2013), as stories offer resistant readings of the canonical text from a female perspective. While such stories might not make up the majority of *Doctor Who* fanfic, it is certainly a strong thread, with many fix-it stories focused on companions and other female characters (such as Mercy Hartigan from 'The Next Doctor' 4.14). 'Five Things No One is Allowed to Say to the Doctor' by Jude provides an alternative ending for every female companion of the rebooted series up to the time of writing, starting with Martha and ending with River (who is not even generally acknowledged as a companion) because: 'One of these things actually happened. Perhaps the other four should have happened too.' The one that 'actually happened' is Martha leaving the TARDIS and the Doctor, and Jude's story incorporates dialogue from the TV episode but accompanies it with Martha's point of view. In Jude's version of the story, as Martha walks away she knows she is 'walking back to a life where she was loved and felt that she was doing more than cleaning up for someone who never noticed or said thank you'. In the next four brief rewritings Rose rejects being fobbed off with a 'filthy stunt double' Doctor and walks off along the beach with her mother; DoctorDonna dumps the Tenth Doctor on Earth and takes the TARDIS for herself; Old Amy, the 'Woman Who'd Survived', talks Rory round and prepares to kill the Eleventh Doctor; and Melody Pond refuses to become River Song. Jude grounds her alternate endings in familiar situations and reactions, signalled by the way several of the section titles allude to the everyday sexism women face (the second is called 'No, I will not smile for you,' the third 'Actually, I'm a Doctor'). Yet the author's note that precedes the story anticipates that not all readers will derive satisfaction from 'fixing' the endings of these characters' arcs: 'Warning: This might upset people who don't think the Companions get a bum deal.' The overall title also suggests that the author is aware that her story is something that canon text would not 'allow', or not more than once.

Perhaps the only thing that is clear within the promotional material used to advertise and record each series in the *Who* universe, as well as the press coverage surrounding it, and the recurrent criticism and often resistant readings coming from the audiences who watch them, is that there are many contradictions and complexities regarding gender and how it is represented.

AFTERWORD

'The twenty-first century is when everything changes.'
Torchwood season 1 introduction

There is undoubtedly more to be said about gender and its representation with the *Doctor Who* franchise, particularly as it continues to develop and add new characters. As I began writing and researching for this book, I realised just how large this topic was, and how it impinged on almost every area of this long-running story. None of the things I uncovered are, perhaps, surprising: as I said in the Introduction, *Doctor Who* and its spin-offs, paratexts and so on operate in much the same ways as other popular media brands. This, coupled with the valorisation of freedom and free will in all three series, make it an ideal case study for an examination of gender, sexuality, race and ethnicity and any form of television studies. *Torchwood* and *The Sarah Jane Adventures* may indeed demonstrate that in the twenty-first century things are changing, yet *Doctor Who*, the series that carries on ten years after the reboot that few thought could make it, seems to be a victim of its own success in some respects. The possibility of Time Lord regeneration across genders has now been firmly established within the television episodes (see also 'Hell Bent' 9.12, where Gallifrey's Time Lord president Rassilon regenerates into a woman), but audiences have yet to see *Doctor Who* changing its lead character into anything other than a white, educated, nominally heterosexual male.

As debates continue to rage about representations of gender, sexuality, race and ethnicity in other major and established franchises such as Marvel, DC and *Star Wars*, it seems that those producing new media stories and experiences will have to listen to their audiences or lose out in the marketplace. Nostalgic affection and 'tradition' work against this to a certain extent – fans will go to see a movie or watch a television series out of loyalty, rather than necessarily because they think it is 'good' – but the television market is now so vast, apparently offering so much choice, that this loyalty cannot be relied on to retain wider audiences. And more mainstream or casual viewers are not likely to feel any loyalty at all, and can just switch off when the series stops entertaining them, as fluctuating audience figures for *Doctor Who* in the UK seem to demonstrate. The *Guardian* reports that around 4.6 million people watched the season 9 premiere, 'the lowest viewing figure for a season premiere since *Doctor Who* returned a decade ago' (Johnston 2015). Chris Johnston observes in the same article that Peter Capaldi has complained falling audience numbers can be put down to the BBC using *Doctor Who* as 'a pawn' in the Saturday-night ratings war waged with its commercial rival ITV, moving *Who* around the schedule to run directly opposite *The X Factor*. It doesn't seem a coincidence that this article carries the headline '*Doctor Who* writer Steven Moffat denies he has made the show more misogynist' (Johnston 2015), as though this were the primary reason for falling ratings. This kind of discussion points, more than ever, to the combination of factors at work in maintaining a television audience for a mainstream, family programme.

Torchwood asserted, in the opening sequence of its first two seasons, that 'the twenty-first century is when everything changes.' But both *Torchwood*'s and *The Sarah Jane Adventures*' distinctive takes on the universe of *Doctor Who* are now defunct, and only the most mainstream series is left. Unfortunately, headlines like the one quoted above imply that twenty-first-century *Doctor Who* is moving backwards rather than forwards in terms of its representation of gender, and that this directly affects the series' popularity. In the finale of season 9, the Twelfth Doctor asserts,

'I am answerable to no one' ('Hell Bent'), and although this episode saw the Doctor looking a little vulnerable, by its conclusion he appeared to be returning to his old self and was last seen spinning through the time-space vortex in the TARDIS. For all kinds of reasons, the team responsible for *Doctor Who* need to be answerable, to the British public who fund its continuing production, and to its audiences across the world, who have criticised its take on representation as much as they have praised it.

A recent interview with Rachel Talalay, one of the female directors who has worked on *Doctor Who* (as discussed in Chapter 5), highlights some of the issues raised in the preceding chapters. Talking to Whovian Feminism, Talalay is fairly open about the limitations that women work under in what is still a male-dominated industry. In response to an initial question about the reactions to the announcement that she will direct the season 9 finale, Talalay reveals:

> People have been asking if I got this job because I'm a woman, if I got this job because Steven Moffat is just turning things around because there has been so much pressure against him. Did he finally hire a woman writer for Series 9 because of the pressure, and does that diminish who we are? (2014)

This perception of the appointment of female writers and directors is also damaging and neither Talalay nor the interviewer can resolve the situation, which seems another catch-22. The discussion highlights how women working in the media industry may actually be more constrained by their highly visible status as women, becoming reluctant to jeopardise opportunities by questioning something that might seem 'off' in terms of gender representation. When asked if she has any message or query for the fans, Talalay asks, 'Is it more important to be able to get the jobs and keep the jobs and do good things as a woman director, or is it more important to be seen as the squeaky wheel?' (2014). This is indeed a pressing question, and answering it is very tricky. The whole interview – between one of the few female directors on *Doctor Who* and a blog dedicated to providing 'feminist commentary' on the franchise – demonstrates what this book has argued: different facets of the industry and how it works impact on representation; consumers now seem to be more vocal and – possibly – more influential; and increasing calls for 'better' representation in media behind and in front of the camera result in further problematic negotiations of gendered identity.

As the author of this book, publicly putting my name to such criticism, I am acutely aware that I may well be deemed answerable – and trollable – for what the book has to say. I continue to believe, however, that these things need to be said, not just about *Doctor Who* but about all kinds of popular stories that permeate our culture. The Doctor may be able to move on in his TARDIS but, as Ashildr points out in 'The Woman Who Lived' (9.6), the rest of us have to 'live in the world [he] leaves behind'. Working on this book, I have been forcibly reminded of the conclusion to Joanna Russ' fiercely polemical feminist science fiction novel *The Female Man*, a work completed at least four years before it managed to see publication in 1975. The closing sentences of the novel admonish the 'little book' not to become sad, angry or irritated when it is no longer relevant or understood, 'for on that day, we will be free' (Russ 2010, p. 207). Thirty years after the publication of Russ' novel, it would be satisfying to think that the day when analysing gender inequality meets with outright incomprehension is close. Closer now, perhaps, but still not close enough.

*

'It's still not finished. It's like […] the pattern's not complete. The strands are still drawing together. But heading for what?' ('Journey's End' 4.13).

NOTES

1 The casting of James Marsters, who played the popular vampire character Spike in *Buffy the Vampire Slayer* and *Angel*, added intertextual subcultural capital to John's character.

2 This is even more remarkable given 'the casual sexism on the show at the time' (Sladen and Hudson 2012, p. 100).

3 In her autobiography, Elisabeth Sladen makes several references to costume in relation to playing Sarah Jane across the years, introducing the topic initially with the rather tongue-in-cheek, 'Now the most important question: what would she wear?' (Sladen and Hudson 2012, p. 83). She does note that once she had established the character, she felt more freedom to make changes to the character's appearance, observing, 'I didn't need to keep the suits on anymore to be seen as a "serious" woman' (Sladen and Hudson 2012, p. 196). While Sarah Jane in her own series does not wear suits, it is notable that her clothes still seem designed to present her as a 'serious' woman, one who can fulfil the roles of action hero, investigator and adoptive mother equally effectively.

4 Capaldi refers here to a popular series of advertisements for the Renault Clio that aired in the UK in the 1990s. The adverts depicted a series of unexpected meetings between 'Papa' and daughter 'Nicole'.

5 In Rory's father, Brian, who appears first in 'Dinosaurs on a Spaceship' (7.2), a glimpse is offered of what has shaped Rory, and what he might become. Brian is 'a conservative 50-year-old with a limited world view', according to Loborik, Gibson and Laing (2013, p. 28), and his never-ending supply of tools and gadgets suggests a practical, if cautious and over-prepared, approach to life. 'Brian's horizons are massively broadened by his space adventure,' Loborik, Gibson and Laing assert (2013, p. 28), presumably drawing this inference from the sight of Brian sitting in the doorway of the TARDIS enjoying a cuppa and sandwich while looking at the stars (7.2).

6 Rory is also physically as well as emotionally 'vulnerable' as a feminised companion: he 'dies' several times in the television narrative.

7 Alec Charles describes the multitude of meanings tied up in the gangers, as trope and as name: 'at once economic subjects who perform hazardous industrial tasks for the colonial masters (workgangers), uncanny doubles of those masters (doppelgangers), criminal outsiders (gangsters) and members of an ethnic underclass (gangstas)' (2013, p. 168).

8 Though some interpret this as an allusion to Mickey's parallel universe counterpart, Ricky, suggesting that the Doctor already knows what will happen to both Ricky and Mickey.

9   Thanks to Bronwen Calvert for illuminating discussion of this connection.

10 The British tradition of social realism, especially in soap opera, offers many more examples of such matriarchs, from Annie Walker in *Coronation Street* to Peggy Mitchell in *EastEnders*.

11 In the same way the recent legislation affording 'same-sex' couples the right to marry provoked debates about whether 'gay marriage' was an inappropriate term.

12 Certainly, 'the thin, fat, gay Anglican marines' (6.7) seem to be extreme tokenism passed off as parody. Accusations of queerbaiting might be levelled particularly at episodes like 'Closing Time' (6.12), where the Eleventh Doctor, Craig and baby Stormageddon are frequently taken as a family. The Doctor's response to a question about his 'partner' elicits the rather confused response, 'Partner? Yes, I like it. Is it better than companion?' which, given the emphasis on romance and sexual attraction between the Doctor and his companions in the post-2005 series, does little to clarify anything.

13 These characters include Spitfire pilot 'Danny Boy' ('Victory of the Daleks' 5.3), trader Dorium ('The Pandorica Opens' 5.12), and Henry and Toby Avery ('The Curse of the Black Spot' 6.3).

14 In 'The Curse of Clyde Langer', Clyde strikes up a friendship with homeless Ellie and eventually they share a kiss, but Ellie disappears at the end of the story. Hints of romance between Rani and Clyde are never developed beyond the occasional glance.

15 Bernice Summerfield, introduced as a companion to the Doctor in the novels, eventually has her own series, telling of her adventures without the Doctor and thus becoming a precursor to *The Sarah Jane Adventures* as well as to River Song.

16 'Part of the reason for the success of *Doctor Who* is that it is made by people who are passionate about the show. RTD, Phil Collinson, David Tennant, Mark Gatiss, Steven Moffat, Paul Cornell... they are all long-time fans, people who are fluent in its rich history.' 'He might not be able to reel off story titles, but John Barrowman admits he has always loved the series' (Richardson 2006, p. 42; ellipsis in original).

17 It will be interesting to see if this changes when Chibnall takes over as *Doctor Who*'s next showrunner, succeeding Steven Moffat.

18 Hills notes in a later publication that the 'Guinness World Record feels like meta-hype' (2015, p. 52), observing that it was soon beaten by a *CSI* simulcast.

19 Cushing played the Doctor in two films: *Dr. Who and the Daleks* (1965) and *Daleks – Invasion Earth: 2150 A.D.* (1966).

20 Indeed, some fans demonstrated their knowledge by sharing *Five(ish)* in annotated YouTube versions that identified the many cast and crew featured.

21 Bethan Jones quotes from a selection of other responses: Jane Clare Jones writes that Moffat's 'tendency to write women plucked straight from a box marked "tired old tropes" has seriously affected the show's dramatic power', while Foz Meadows argues that Moffat has 'a habit of depowering [*sic*]' his female characters to make his 'male protagonists look stronger' (2013).

WORK CITED

All URLs active as of 15 September 2016.

Abbott, Stacey (2013). 'Walking Corpses, Regenerating Dead and Alien Bodies: Monstrous Embodiment in *Torchwood*'. In Rebecca Williams (ed.), *Torchwood Declassified: Investigating Mainstream Cult Television*. London: I.B.Tauris, pp. 120–34.

Aldred, Sophie (2010). 'An Interview with Sophie Aldred'. In Lynne M. Thomas and Tara O'Shea (eds), *Chicks Dig Time Lords: A Celebration of Doctor Who by the Women Who Love It*. Des Moines: Mad Norwegian Press, pp. 68–73.

Anghelides, Peter (2008). *The Sarah Jane Adventures: The Time Capsule*. Audio CD. AudioGo.

Asher-Perrin, Emily (2013). 'No room for old-fashioned cats: Davies era *Who* and interracial romance'. In Lindy Orthia (ed.), *Doctor Who and Race*. Bristol: Intellect, pp. 65–6.

Baker-Whitelaw, Gavia (2014). 'Guess how many female writers are joining "Doctor Who" this season?' Daily Dot. 1 May. http://www.dailydot.com/parsec/doctor-who-season-8-male-writers/.

Ball, Vicky (2012). 'The "Feminization" of British Television and the Re-Traditionalization of Gender'. *Feminist Media Studies*, 12:2, pp. 248–64.

Barron, Lee (2010). 'Out in Space: Masculinity, Sexuality and the Science Fiction Heroics of Captain Jack'. In Andrew Ireland (ed.), *Illuminating Torchwood: Essays on Narrative, Character and Sexuality in the BBC Series*. Jefferson, North Carolina: McFarland, pp. 213–25.

Bashford, Suzy (2005). 'The Drama Doctor'. Interview by Julie Gardner. *Broadcast*. 11 March, p. 25.

BBC (n.d. a). 'Public Purposes'. Inside the BBC: Who We Are. Website. http://www.bbc.co.uk/corporate2/insidethebbc/whoweare/publicpurposes.

—— (n.d. b). 'Julie Gardner'. BBC Worldwide press room biography. http://www.bbcwpressroom.com/bbc-worldwide-productions/bios/julie-gardner/.

—— (n.d. c). CBBC Extra web page. http://www.bbc.co.uk/programmes/b04xg63t.

—— (2009). 'Tonight's the Night offers viewers chance to win incredible Doctor Who experience'. Press release. 25 March. http://www.bbc.co.uk/pressoffice/pressreleases/stories/2009/03_march/25/night.shtml.

—— (2014). 'Award-winning children's novelist and screenwriter Frank Cottrell Boyce confirmed as Doctor Who writer'. *Doctor Who* BBC website. 4 July. http://www.bbc.co.uk/blogs/doctorwho/entries/ff184f5f-16e9-3ec1-96b2-c6b7ef2075fd.

—— (2015a). 'BBC Worldwide announces record returns to the BBC'. BBC Worldwide press release. 14 July. http://www.bbc.co.uk/mediacentre/worldwide/2015/bbc-worldwide-annual-review-2015.

—— (2015b). 'The Return of Rachel Talalay'. Video. *Doctor Who* BBC website. 29 November. http://www.bbc.co.uk/programmes/p03987rn.

Bear, Elizabeth (2010). 'We'll Make Great Pets'. In Lynne M. Thomas and Tara O'Shea (eds), *Chicks Dig Time Lords: A Celebration of Doctor Who by the Women Who Love It*. Des Moines: Mad Norwegian Press, pp. 12–17.

Berger, Richard (2010). 'Screwing Aliens and Screwing with Aliens: *Torchwood* Slashes the Doctor'. In Andrew Ireland (ed.), *Illuminating Torchwood: Essays on Narrative, Character and Sexuality in the BBC Series*. Jefferson, North Carolina: McFarland, pp. 66–75.

Big Finish (n.d.). *UNIT – Extinction*. Product/plot description. https://www.bigfinish.com/releases/v/unit---extinction-1208.

—— (2015). *UNIT – Extinction*. Press release. 9 February. http://www.bigfinish.com/news/v/unit---extinction.

Booth, Paul (2013a). 'Reifying the Fan: Inspector Spacetime as Fan Practice'. *Popular Communication: The International Journal of Media and Culture*, 11:2, pp. 146–59.

——, ed. (2013b). *Fan Phenomena: Doctor Who*. Bristol: Intellect.

—— (2014). 'Periodising *Doctor Who*'. *Science Fiction Film and Television*, 7:2, pp. 195–215.

Booy, Miles (2012). *Love and Monsters: The Doctor Who Experience 1979 to the Present*. London: I.B.Tauris.

Bouch, Matthew (2007). 'Let the Adventures Begin'. Interview by David Richardson. *Starburst* 354, pp. 26–32.

Bowell, T. (2011). 'Feminist Standpoint Theory'. In James Fieser and Bradley Dowden (eds), *The Internet Encyclopedia of Philosophy*. http://www.iep.utm.edu/.

Boynton, Drew (2014). 'Fiona Cumming Talks Doctor Who Credentials'. Kasterborous. 27 October. http://www.kasterborous.com/2014/10/fiona-cumming-talks-doctor-credentials/.

Bradford, K. Tempest (2012). 'The Women We Don't See'. In Deborah Stanish and L. M. Myles (eds), *Chicks Unravel Time: Women Journey Through Every Season on Doctor Who*. Des Moines: Mad Norwegian Press, pp. 103–10.

Brew, Simon (2011). 'Julie Gardner interview: Torchwood, Doctor Who, Miracle Day and Russell T. Davies'. Den of Geek. 14 July. http://www.denofgeek.com/tv/doctor-who/20887/julie-gardner-interview-torchwood-doctor-who-miracle-day-and-russell-t-davies#ixzz3du1YavT2.

—— (2014). 'Rachel Talalay interview: directing Doctor Who series 8's finale'. DenofGeek. 30 October. http://www.denofgeek.com/tv/doctor-who/32726/rachel-talalay-interview-directing-doctor-who-series-8s-finale.

Britton, Piers D. (2011). TARDIS*bound: Navigating the Universes of Doctor Who*. London: I.B.Tauris.

Brooker, Will (2013). 'Talking to the TARDIS: *Doctor Who*, Neil Gaiman and Cultural Mythology'. In Matt Hills (ed.), *New Dimensions of Doctor Who: Adventures in Space, Time and Television*. London: I.B.Tauris, pp. 71–91.

Busch, Jenna (2015). 'Doctor Who's Sylvester McCoy Says Only a Man Should Play the Doctor'. Legion of Leia. 24 July. http://legionofleia.com/2015/07/doctor-whos-sylvester-mccoy-says-only-a-man-should-play-the-doctor/.

Butler, David (2013). 'A Good Score Goes to War: Multiculturalism, Monsters and Music in New *Doctor Who*'. In Matt Hills (ed.), *New Dimensions of Doctor Who: Adventures in Space, Time and Television*. London: I.B.Tauris, pp. 19–38.

Caron, Nathalie (2015). 'Big Finish announces the Brigadier's Daughter, Kate Stewart, will headline her own Doctor Who adventures'. blastr. 9 February. http://www.blastr.com/2015-2-9/big-finish-announces-brigadiers-daughter-kate-stewart-will-headline-her-own-doctor-who.

Cawley, Christian (2014). 'How Our Team Reacted to the Missy Master Reveal'. Kasterborous. 2 November. http://www.kasterborous.com/2014/11/team-reacted-missy-master-reveal/.

Chandler, Abigail (2015). 'Dear Comic-Con attendees, grabbing the lycra-clad backside of a cosplayer is not ok'. Metro. 9 July. http://metro.co.uk/2015/07/09/is-sexual-harassment-ruining-comic-con-for-cosplayers-5286543/#ixzz3v4J0Zny7.

Chapman, James (2006). *Inside the TARDIS: The Worlds of Doctor Who*. London: I.B.Tauris.

—— (2013). *Inside the TARDIS: The Worlds of Doctor Who*. 2nd edition. London: I.B.Tauris.

Charles, Alec (2013). 'The allegory of allegory: Race, racism and the summer of 2011'. In Lindy Orthia (ed.), *Doctor Who and Race*. Bristol: Intellect, pp. 61–177.

Cherry, Brigid (2013). 'Extermini…Knit!: Female Fans and Feminine Handicrafting'. In Paul Booth (ed.), *Fan Phenomena: Doctor Who*. Bristol: Intellect, pp. 106–15.

Cheyne, Ria (2010). 'Touching the Other: Alien Contact and Transgressive Touch'. In Andrew Ireland (ed.), *Illuminating Torchwood: Essays on Narrative, Character and Sexuality in the BBC Series*. Jefferson, North Carolina: McFarland, pp. 43–52.

Chines, Jim (2013). 'Nicole Stark's Survey of Harassment Policies at Fan Conventions'. Blog post. 11 December. http://www.jimchines.com/2013/12/stark-survey-of-harassment-policies/.

Cole, Stephen (2008). *The Sarah Jane Adventures: The Ghost House*. Audio CD. AudioGo.

Collins, Frank (2008). 'Moody Blues'. Book review. Behind the Sofa. 28 September. http://www.behindthesofa.org.uk/2008/09/moody-blues.html.

Conor, Bridget (2014). *Screenwriting: Creative Labor and Professional Practice*. Abingdon: Routledge.

Cooper, Jon (2014). 'Doctor Who's Missy is The Master: Why some Whovians are Missy-ing the point with the latest Time Lord reveal'. *Mirror*. 7 November. http://www.mirror.co.uk/tv/tv-news/doctor-whos-missy-master-whovians-4588354.

Cornah, J. K. (2014). Tumblr post. November 2014. http://thedinosaurprince.tumblr.com/post/102602790961/whovian-feminism-reviews-dark-water-and-death.

Cornea, Christine (2009). 'Showrunning the *Doctor Who* Franchise: A Response to Denise Mann'. In Vicki Mayer (ed.), *Production Studies: Cultural Studies of Media Industries*. London: Routledge, pp. 115–22.

Cox, Carolyn (2014). 'Baby Steps, Yay! *Doctor Who* Hires First Female Writer Since 2008'. The Mary Sue. 24 November. http://www.themarysue.com/doctor-who-female-writer/.

'Cruickshank, Grant' (2013). 'Wow, so this is where all the misogynists hang out?' Comment. 8 August. http://www.telegraph.co.uk/women/womens-life/10225006/Doctor-Who-I-was-really-hoping-for-a-new-female-hero-an-11-year-olds-take-on-Peter-Capaldi.html.

Davies, Russell. T. and Benjamin Cook (2010). *A Writer's Tale: The Final Chapter*. London: BBC Books.

—— (2013). Audio commentary for *The Green Death: Special Edition* (DVD). BBC.

Directors UK (2014). 'Women Directors – Who's Calling the Shots? Women Directors in British Television Production'. Report. May 2014.

DoctorWhoTV (2014a). 'Moffat: It's time for the "kick-up-the-arse" Doctor'. 9 January. http://www.doctorwhotv.co.uk/moffat-its-time-for-the-kick-up-the-arse-doctor-57758.htm.

—— (2014b). 'The War Doctor Returns in "Engines of War"'. 9 May. http://www.doctorwhotv.co.uk/the-war-doctor-returns-in-engines-of-war-62958.htm.

—— (2014c). 'In The Forest of the Night Advance Review'. 22 October. http://www.doctorwhotv.co.uk/in-the-forest-of-the-night-advance-review-67799.htm.

Dodson, Linnea (2013). 'Conscious colour-blindness, unconscious racism in *Doctor Who*'s companions'. In Lindy Orthia (ed.), *Doctor Who and Race*. Bristol: Intellect, pp. 29–34.

Duffy, Stella (2013). 'Dr [*sic*] Who and the Missing Women'. *Not Writing but Blogging*. 26 March. http://stelladuffy.wordpress.com/2013/03/26/dr-who-and-the-missing-women/.

Duncan, Andrew (2011). 'Doctor Who: Alex Kingston Interviewed'. *Radio Times*. 27 August. http://www.radiotimes.com/blog/2011-08-27/doctor-who-alex-kingston-interviewed.

Dunn, Carrie (2010). 'The Alien Woman: Othering and the Oriental'. In Andrew Ireland (ed.), *Illuminating Torchwood: Essays on Narrative, Character and Sexuality in the BBC Series*. Jefferson, North Carolina: McFarland, pp.113–20.

Ebner-Statt, Jessica (2013). '"I was really hoping for a new female hero" – an 11-year-old's take on the male Doctor Who'. *Telegraph*. 6 August. http://www.telegraph.co.uk/women/womens-life/10225006/Doctor-Who-I-was-really-hoping-for-a-new-female-hero-an-11-year-olds-take-on-Peter-Capaldi.html.

El-Mohtar, Amal (2013). 'Sub Texts: The Doctor and the Master's Firsts and Lasts'. In Sigrid Ellis and Michael Damien Thomas (eds), *Queers Dig Time Lords: A Celebration of Doctor Who by the LBGTQ Fans Who Love It*. Des Moines: Mad Norwegian Press, pp. 61–9.

Ellis, Sigrid and Michael Damien Thomas, eds (2013). *Queers Dig Time Lords:*

A Celebration of Doctor Who by the LBGTQ Fans Who Love It. Des Moines: Mad Norwegian Press.

Evans, Elizabeth (2011). *Transmedia Television.* London: Routledge.

—— (2013). 'Learning with the Doctor: Pedagogic Strategies in Transmedia *Doctor Who*'. In Matt Hills (ed.), *New Dimensions of Doctor Who: Adventures in Space, Time and Television.* London: I.B.Tauris, pp. 134–53.

Faraci, Devin (2016). 'Fandom is Broken'. BirthsMoviesDeaths. 30 May. http://birthmoviesdeath.com/2016/05/30/fandom-is-broken.

Firefly (2013). 'The White Doctor'. In Lindy Orthia (ed.), *Doctor Who and Race.* Bristol: Intellect, pp. 15–20.

Franke, Alyssa (2015). 'The Capaldi Conundrum: How We Attack the Female Gaze'. BitchFlicks. 28 August. http://www.btchflcks.com/2015/08/the-capaldi-conundrum-how-we-attack-the-female-gaze.html#.Vnle5fnhDIX.

Frankham-Allen, Andy (2013). *Companions: Fifty Years of Doctor Who Assistants: An Unofficial Guide.* Cardiff: Candy Jar Books.

Freund, Katharina (2013). '"We're making our own happy ending!": The Doctor Who Fan Vidding Community'. In Paul Booth (ed.), *Fan Phenomena: Doctor Who.* Bristol: Intellect, pp. 96–105.

Gardner, Julie (2006). 'Lighting the Torchwood'. Interview by David Richardson. *Starburst* 343, pp. 42–7.

Garner, Ross P. (2010). '"Don't You Forget About Me": Intertextuality and Generic Anchoring in *The Sarah Jane Adventures*'. In Ross P. Garner, Melissa Beattie and Una McCormack (eds), *Impossible Worlds, Impossible Things: Cultural Perspectives on Doctor Who, Torchwood and The Sarah Jane Adventures.* Cambridge: Cambridge Scholars Publishing, pp. 161–81.

—— (2013a). 'Remembering Sarah Jane: Intradiegetic Allusions, Embodied Presence/Absence and Nostalgia'. In Matt Hills (ed.), *New Dimensions of Doctor Who: Adventures in Space, Time and Television.* London: I.B.Tauris, pp. 192–215.

—— (2013b). 'Access Denied? Negotiating Public Service and Commercial Tensions through *Torchwood*'s Intertextual Barricade'. In Rebecca Williams (ed.), *Torchwood Declassified: Investigating Mainstream Cult Television.* London: I.B.Tauris, pp. 13–32.

George, S. (2007). 'Feedback'. *Starburst* 347, p. 6.

Geraghty, Lincoln (2014). *Cult Collectors: Nostalgia, Fandom and Collecting Popular Culture.* Abingdon: Routledge.

Ginn, Sherry (2013). 'Spoiled for Another Life: Sarah Jane Smith's Adventures With and Without Doctor Who'. In Gillian I. Leitch (ed.), *Doctor Who in Time and Space: Essays on Theme, Character, History and Fandom, 1963–2012.* Jefferson, North Carolina: McFarland, pp. 242–52.

Goss, James (2013). *Doctor Who: Summer Falls and Other Stories.* London: BBC Books.

Gorton, Neill (2006). 'Under Your Skin'. Interview by David Richardson. *Starburst* 344, pp. 22–6.

Gray, Jonathan (2010). *Show Sold Separately: Promos, Spoilers and Other Media Paratexts.* New York, London: New York University Press.

Gray, Scott (2011). *The Sarah Jane Adventures: Judgement Day*. Audio CD. AudioGo.

Grugulis, Irena and Dimitrinka Stoyanova (2012). 'Social Capital and Networks in Film and TV: Jobs for the Boys?' *Organization Studies*, 33:10, pp. 1311–31.

Guerdan, Stephanie (2013). 'Baby steps: A modest solution to Asian under-representation in Doctor Who'. In Lindy Orthia (ed.), *Doctor Who and Race*. Bristol: Intellect, pp. 73–6.

Gupta, Amit (2013). 'Doctor Who and Race: Reflections on the Change of Britain's Status in the International System'. *The Round Table: The Commonwealth Journal of International Affairs*, 102:1, pp. 41–50.

Hadas, Leora and Limor Shifman (2013). 'Keeping the Elite Powerless: Fan-Producer Relations in the "Nu Who" (and New YOU) Era'. *Critical Studies in Media Communication*, 30:4, pp. 275–91.

Hamad, Hannah (2010). 'A Whoniverse of Runaway Brides'. Flow TV. 3 December. http://flowtv.org/2010/12/a-whoniverse-of-runaway-brides/2010.

—— (2011). 'A Tear for Sarah Jane – A Feminist Aca-Obit'. Flow TV. 6 May. https://www.flowjournal.org/2011/05/a-tear-for-sarah-jane/.

Haraway, Donna (1988). 'Situated Knowledges: The Science Question in Feminism and the Privilege of Partial Perspective'. *Feminist Studies*, 14:3, pp. 575–99.

Hay-Gibson, Naomi V. and Andrew K. Shenton (2009). 'The Enigma of the Television Tie-In'. *New Review of Children's Literature and Librarianship*, 15:1, pp. 21–41.

Hill, David (2015). 'Hettie McDonald Set to return to Doctor Who'. Doctor Who Watch. 13 February. http://doctorwhowatch.com/2015/02/13/hettie-macdonald-set-return-doctor/.

Hills, Matt (2010). *Triumph of a Time Lord: Regenerating Doctor Who in the Twenty-first Century*. London: I.B.Tauris.

——, ed. (2013a). *New Dimensions of Doctor Who: Adventures in Space, Time and Television*. London: I.B.Tauris.

—— (2013b). 'Transmedia Torchwood: Investigating a Television Spin-off's Tie-in Novels and Audio Adventures'. In Rebecca Williams (ed.), *Torchwood Declassified: Investigating Mainstream Cult Television*. London: I.B.Tauris, pp. 65–83.

—— (2013c). 'From Chris Chibnall to Fox: *Torchwood*'s Marginalized Authors and Counter-Discourses of TV Authorship'. In Jonathan Gray and Derek Johnson (eds), *A Companion to Media Authorship*. Chichester: Wiley-Blackwell, pp. 200–20.

—— (2014a). 'When Doctor Who Enters Its Own Timeline: The Database Aesthetics and Hyperdiegesis of Multi-Doctor Stories'. *Critical Studies in Television: The International Journal of Television Studies*, 9:1, pp. 95–113.

—— (2014b). 'The Year of the Doctor: celebrating the 50th, regenerating public value?' *Science Fiction Film and Television*, 7:2, pp. 159–78.

—— (2015). *Doctor Who: The Unfolding Event*. New York: Palgrave Pivot.

Hope, Hannah (2015). 'Doctor Who legend Sylvester McCoy says only a MAN can play the Time Lord'. *Mirror*. 22 July. http://www.mirror.co.uk/tv/tv-news/doctor-who-legend-sylvester-mccoy-6119330.

Ireland, Andrew, ed. (2010). *Illuminating Torchwood: Essays on Narrative, Character and Sexuality in the BBC Series*. Jefferson, North Carolina: McFarland.

Jaye, Victoria (2014). 'New iPlayer – Celebrating the Best of British Creativity'. BBC Blog. 11 March. http://www.bbc.co.uk/blogs/aboutthebbc/entries/f33478da-f004-3386-a14d-a7233c119468.

Jeffery, Morgan (2013). 'The Inside Story on the Fiveish Doctors Reboot'. Digital Spy. 26 November. http://www.digitalspy.co.uk/tv/s7/doctor-who/tubetalk/a533941/doctor-who-the-inside-story-on-the-fiveish-doctors-reboot. html#ixzz3gXBZH7fr.

jemthecrytsalgem (2014). Tumblr post. 13 November. http://jemthecrystalgem. tumblr.com/post/102588657075/whovian-feminism-reviews-dark-water-and-death.

Jenkins, Claire (2013). '"I'm saving the world, I need a decent shirt": Masculinity and sexuality in the new Doctor Who'. In Stella Bruzzi and Pamela Church (eds), *Fashion Cultures Revisited: Theories, Exploration and Analaysis*. London: Routledge, pp. 377–89.

Johnson, Catherine (2013). 'Doctor Who as Programme Brand'. In Matt Hills (ed.), *New Dimensions of Doctor Who: Adventures in Space, Time and Television*. London: I.B.Tauris, pp. 95–112.

—— (2014). 'Spinning the Doctor: New Cast, Old Characters in Doctor Who'. CST online. 27 November. http://cstonline.tv/spinning-the-doctor-new-cast-old-characters-in-doctor-who.

Johnston, Connor (2014). 'Bring Back… Helen Raynor'. DoctorWhoTV. 16 May. http://www.doctorwhotv.co.uk/bring-back-helen-raynor-63065.htm.

Johnston, Chris (2015). 'Doctor Who writer Steven Moffat denies he has made the show more misogynist'. *Guardian*. 28 November. http://www. theguardian.com/media/2015/nov/28/doctor-who-writer-steven-moffat-denies-misogynist-claims.

Jones, Bethan (2013). 'The Girl Who Waited/Survived: Fan rewritings of Amy Pond'. Paper presented at *Doctor Who: Walking in Eternity – An international interdisciplinary conference celebrating 50 years in time and space*. School of Creative Arts and School of Humanities, University of Hertfordshire. 4 September.

'Jones, Martha' (2007). aproperdoctor. MySpace. Archived at https://aproperdoctor. dreamwidth.org/53519.html.

Jowett, Lorna (2014). 'The Girls Who Waited? Female Companions and Gender in *Doctor Who*'. *Critical Studies in Television: The International Journal of Television Studies*, 9:1, pp. 77–94.

Jude (2014). 'Five Things No One is Allowed to Say to the Doctor'. 26 January. http://archiveofourown.org/works/1154629.

Jusino, Teresa (2015). 'Introducing Doctor Who's Newest Female Writer, Sarah Dollard!' The Mary Sue. 11 June. http://www.themarysue.com/doctor-who-female-writer-sarah-dollard/.

Just Cos (2013). 'Women of Doctor Who'. Video. YouTube. 17 April. http://www. youtube.com/watch?v=zqD-8uU7ViM.

Kang, Helen (2010). 'Adventures in Ocean-Crossing, Margin-skating and Feminist-

Engagement with *Doctor Who*'. In Lynne M. Thomas and Tara O'Shea (eds), *Chicks Dig Time Lords: A Celebration of Doctor Who by the Women Who Love It*. Des Moines: Mad Norwegian Press, pp. 38–45.

de Kauwe, Vanessa (2013). 'Through coloured eyes: An alternative viewing of postcolonial transition'. In Lindy Orthia (ed.), *Doctor Who and Race*. Bristol: Intellect, pp. 141–57.

Kavanagh-Sproull, Patrick (2014). 'George Mann on Writing the War Doctor'. Interview. DoctorWhoTV. 5 August. http://www.doctorwhotv.co.uk/george-mann-on-writing-the-war-doctor-65121.htm.

Kompare, Derek (2010). 'More "moments of television": Online cult television authorship'. In Michael Kackman et al. (eds), *Flow TV:Television in the Age of Media Convergence*. New York: Routledge, pp. 95–113.

Lachenal, Jessica (2015). '7th Doctor Sylvester McCoy Doesn't Want a Female Doctor for Doctor Who'. The Mary Sue. 25 July. http://www.themarysue.com/sylvester-mccoy-female-doctor/.

Lawless, Jill (2013). 'Helen Mirren talks Royalty and "Doctor Who"'. *Daily Star*. 10 June. http://www.dailystar.com.lb/Entertainment/Celebrities/2013/Jun-10/219935-helen-mirren-talks-royalty-and-doctor-who.ashx.

Lawrence, Ben (2013). 'The Five(ish) Doctors Reboot, Red Button'. *Telegraph*. 24 November. http://www.telegraph.co.uk/culture/tvandradio/tv-and-radio-reviews/10470797/The-Fiveish-Doctors-Reboot-BBC-Red-Button.html.

Leigh, Rob (2013). 'New Doctor Who IS a Man, photographer Rankin Reveals'. *Mirror*. 2 August. http://www.mirror.co.uk/tv/tv-news/new-doctor-who-male-rankin-2123869.

Lemish, Dafna and Varda Muhlbauer (2012). '"Can't Have it All": Representations of Older Women in Popular Culture'. *Women & Therapy*, 35: 3–4, pp. 165–80.

Lloyd, Robert (2013). 'Watch: "The Five(ish) Doctors Reboot", a Starry Doctor Who Comedy'. *LA Times*. 23 November. http://articles.latimes.com/2013/nov/23/entertainment/la-et-st-watch-the-fiveish-doctors-reboot-doctor-who-20131123.

Loborik, Jason, Annabel Gibson and Moray Laing (2013). *Doctor Who: Character Encyclopedia*. London: Dorling Kindersley.

McCormick, Joseph Patrick (2014). 'Ofcom will not investigate *Doctor Who* lesbian kiss following six complaints'. *PinkNews*. 28 August.

McMurtry, Leslie (2013). 'Do It Yourself: Women, Fanzines and *Doctor Who*'. In Paul Booth (ed.), *Fan Phenomena: Doctor Who*. Bristol: Intellect, pp.84–95.

Maggs, Sam (2014a). 'Neil Gaiman is not impressed with *Doctor Who*'s gender imbalance'. The Mary Sue. 8 October. http://www.themarysue.com/gaiman-women-writers-doctor-who/.

——— (2014b). 'Neil Gaiman talks about fixing the *Doctor Who* gender disparity'. The Mary Sue. 14 October. http://www.themarysue.com/gaiman-on-doctor-who-gender-disparity/.

Magnet, Shoshana and Robert Smith? (2010). 'Two Steps Forward, One Step Back: Have We Really Come That Far?' In Lynne M. Thomas and Tara O'Shea (eds), *Chicks Dig Time Lords: A Celebration of Doctor Who by the Women Who Love It*. Des Moines: Mad Norwegian Press, pp. 154–62.

Mann, Denise (2009). 'It's Not TV, It's Brand Management TV: The Collective Author(s) of the *Lost* Franchise'. In Vicki Mayer (ed.), *Production Studies: Cultural Studies of Media Industries*. London: Routledge, pp. 99–114.

Mann, George (2014). *Engines of War*. London: BBC Books.

Mellor, Louisa (2012). '9 things we learned from *Doctor Who*: Pond Life'. Den of Geek. 31 August. http://www.denofgeek.com/tv/doctor-who/22517/9-things-we-learned-from-doctor-who-pond-life.

Moore, Rebecca (2014). 'University Study on Sexism in BBC's *Doctor Who* (Infographic)'. 29 May. http://rebeccaamoore.com/tag/steven-moffat/.

Mulkern, Patrick (2015). '10 *Doctor Who* adventures you must watch before the show leaves Netflix'. *Radio Times*. 17 March. http://www.radiotimes.com/news/2015-03-17/doctor-whos-top-ten-episodes-of-nuwhos-first-ten-years-as-voted-by-you-6.

Myles, Eve (2007). Interview by Cindy White as part of *Torchwood* special. *Starburst* Special 85, pp. 21–2.

Newman, Kim (2005). *Doctor Who*. London: BFI Publishing.

Nicol, Danny (2015). 'Missy and the Doctor: isn't *Doctor Who* political?'. *Politics and Law of Doctor Who*. 3 January. http://politicsandlawofdoctorwho.blogspot.co.uk/2015/01/missy-and-doctor-isnt-doctor-who.html.

Nye, Jody Lynn (2010). 'Hopelessly Devoted to Who'. In Lynne M. Thomas and Tara O'Shea (eds), *Chicks Dig Time Lords: A Celebration of Doctor Who by the Women Who Love It*. Des Moines: Mad Norwegian Press, pp. 103–11.

Oró-Piqueras, Maricel (2014). 'Challenging stereotypes? The older woman in the TV series Brothers & Sisters'. *Journal of Aging Studies* 31, pp. 20–25.

Orthia, Lindy (2010). '"Sociopathetic Abscess" or "Yawning Chasm"? The Absent Postcolonial Transition in *Doctor Who*'. *Journal of Commonwealth Literature*, 45:2, pp. 207–25.

——, ed. (2013). *Doctor Who and Race*. Bristol: Intellect.

O'Shea, Tara (2010). 'The Tea Lady'. In Lynne M. Thomas and Tara O'Shea (eds), *Chicks Dig Time Lords: A Celebration of Doctor Who by the Women Who Love It*. Des Moines: Mad Norwegian Press, pp. 98–102.

Pinborough, Sarah (2011). *Long Time Dead*. London: BBC Books.

Polo, Susannah (2014). 'Steven Moffat Says Women Usually Just Don't Want to Write for *Doctor Who*'. The Mary Sue. 23 December. http://www.themarysue.com/steven-moffat-women-write-doctor-who/.

Porter, Lynette (2012). *The Doctor Who Franchise: American Influence, Fan Culture and the Spinoffs*. Jefferson, North Carolina: McFarland.

—— (2013). 'Chasing Amy: The Evolution of the Doctor's Female Companion in the New Who'. In Gillian I. Leitch (ed.), *Doctor Who in Time and Space: Essays on Themes, Character, History and Fandom, 1963–2012*. Jefferson, North Carolina: McFarland, pp. 253–67.

Radish, Christina (2010). 'Executive Producer's [*sic*] Russell T. Davies and Julie Gardner Exclusive Interview Torchwood: the New World'. Collider. 5 November. http://collider.com/russell-t-davies-julie-gardner-interview-torchwood-the-new-world/.

Raynor, Helen (2006). 'Writes of the Dead' Interview by David Richardson. *Starburst* 344, pp. 28–32.

Richards, Justin (2013a). 'The Angel's Kiss'. *Doctor Who: Summer Falls and Other Stories*. London: BBC Books.

—— (2013b). 'The Devil in the Smoke'. *Doctor Who: Summer Falls and Other Stories*. London: BBC Books.

Richardson, David (2005). Julie Gardner interview. *Starburst* Special 69, pp. 100–4.

—— (2006a). 'Introducing Torchwood' special. *Starburst* Yearbook (Special 78), pp. 28–36.

—— (2006b). 'Lighting the Torchwood'. Julie Gardner interview. *Starburst* 343, pp. 42–7.

—— (2007a). 'Going It Alone'. Elisabeth Sladen interview. *Starburst* 345, pp. 28–32.

—— (2007b). 'Alice in Wonderland'. Alice Troughton interview. *Starburst* 355, pp. 48–52.

Richie C. (2013). Comment on 'Doctor Who: watch The Night Of The Doctor mini-episode here'. Den of Geek. 14 November. http://disq.us/p/ikg0cw.

Robinson, Joanna (2015). 'How *Doctor Who* Finally Became Great Again'. *Vanity Fair*. 24 October. http://www.vanityfair.com/hollywood/2015/10/doctor-who-season-9-great-woman-who-lived-maisie-williams.

Rowe, Kathleen (1995). *The Unruly Woman: Gender and the Genres of Laughter*. Austin: University of Texas Press.

Rudd, Matt (2014). 'Peter Capaldi: BBC's new Doctor drops the bedside manner'. *Sunday Times*. 27 July. http://www.thesundaytimes.co.uk/sto/news/uk_news/article1439405.ece.

Russ, Joanna (2010). *The Female Man*. London: Gollancz.

Russell, Gary (2008). *Torchwood Archives*. London: BBC Books.

Sandifer, Philip (2012). 'The Definitive Moffat and Feminism Post'. http://www.eruditorumpress.com/blog/the-definitive-moffat-and-feminism-post/.

Sladen, Elisabeth (2007a). 'Going It Alone'. Interview by David Richardson. *Starburst* 345, pp. 28–32.

—— (2007b). 'Companion Pieces'. Interview by David Richardson. *Starburst* Yearbook (Special 84), pp. 28–34.

—— (2012). 'Elisabeth Sladen Interviews'. Season 1 Extras. *The Sarah Jane Adventures: The Complete Collection*. DVD. BBC Worldwide/2 Entertain.

Sladen, Elisabeth and Jeff Hudson (2012). *Elisabeth Sladen: The Autobiography*. London: Aurum Press.

Smith, Matt (2013). 'Dave and I sat back and listened to Johnny Hurt's funny stories'. Interview. *Big Issue*. 25 November. http://www.bigissue.com/mix/news/3239/matt-smith-interview-having-us-all-set-was-wonderful-thing.

Stanish, Deborah (2010). 'My Fandom Regenerates'. In Lynne M. Thomas and Tara O'Shea (eds), *Chicks Dig Time Lords: A Celebration of Doctor Who by the Women Who Love It*. Des Moines: Mad Norwegian Press, pp. 31–7.

Stanish, Deborah and L. M. Myles, eds (2010). *Chicks Unravel Time: Women Journey Through Every Season on Doctor Who*. Des Moines: Mad Norwegian Press.

Stewart, Malcolm (2014). 'Our reaction to the Missy reveal in "Doctor Who"'. CultBox. 1 November. http://www.cultbox.co.uk/features/opinion/our-reaction-to-the-missy-reveal-in-doctor-who.

Stoker, Courtney (2012). 'Maids and Masters: The Distribution of Power in *Doctor Who* Series Three'. In Deborah Stanish and L. M. Myles (eds), *Chicks Unravel Time: Women Journey Through Every Season on Doctor Who*. Des Moines: Mad Norwegian Press, pp. 121–8.

Sullivan, Kathryn (2010). 'The Fanzine Factor'. In Lynne M. Thomas and Tara O'Shea (eds), *Chicks Dig Time Lords: A Celebration of Doctor Who by the Women Who Love It*. Des Moines: Mad Norwegian Press, pp. 122–32.

Talalay, Rachel (2014). 'An Interview with Rachel Talalay'. Whovian Feminism. 16 December. http://whovianfeminism.tumblr.com/post/105397652672/an-interview-with-rachel-talalay.

—— (2015). 'Hibernated for 24 hours, came back to this overwhelming tweet-explosion. THANK YOU ALL. I don't have words. #DoctorWho forever'. Twitter. @rtalalay. 29 November. https://twitter.com/rtalalay/status/671025470918496257.

Tapley, Nathaniel (2014). '16 sexually confusing feelings that *Doctor Who* fans have had since The Mistress revealed her secret'. UsVsth3m. 4 November. http://usvsth3m.com/post/16-confusing-feelings-that-doctor-who-fans-have-had-about-the-latest-plot-twist.

Tardis Data Core (n.d.). 'The Curse of Fatal Death'. http://tardis.wikia.com/wiki/The_Curse_of_Fatal_Death_(TV_story).

Tasker, Yvonne (1993). *Spectacular Bodies: Gender, Genre and the Action Cinema*. London: Routledge.

Teague, Colin (2007). 'Director's Adventures'. Interview by David Richardson. *Starburst* 346, pp. 24–8.

Telegraph (2010). 'Viewers Think New Doctor Who is Too Sexy'. 5 April. http://www.telegraph.co.uk/culture/tvandradio/doctor-who/7554825/Viewers-think-new-Doctor-Who-is-too-sexy.html.

—— (2013). '*Doctor Who* "Thunderously Racist"'. 26 May. http://www.telegraph.co.uk/culture/tvandradio/10081580/Doctor-Who-thunderously-racist.html.

Television FTW (2016). 'There is a Difference'. 1 June. https://televisionftw.wordpress.com/.

Thomas, Lynne M. and Tara O'Shea, eds (2010). *Chicks Dig Time Lords: A Celebration of Doctor Who by the Women Who Love It*. Des Moines: Mad Norwegian Press.

Tregenna, Catherine (2007). 'Writing Takes Time'. Interview by David Richardson. *Starburst* 345, pp. 41–4.

—— (2009). BBC Writer's Room Blog. http://dev12.mh.bbc.co.uk/writersroom/insight/cath_tregenna.shtml.

Trybulski, Stan (2014). Letter to the Editor. *Financial Times*. 30 August.

Welch, Rosanne (2013). 'When white boys write black: Race and class in the Davies and Moffat eras'. In Lindy Orthia (ed.), *Doctor Who and Race*. Bristol: Intellect, pp. 67–71.

Whitbrook, James (2015). 'Doctor Who's Kate Lethbridge-Stewart Is Getting Her Own Audio Spin-off'. Io9. 10 February. http://io9.gizmodo.com/doctor-whos-kate-lethbridge-stewart-is-getting-her-own-1684925499.

Wikipedia (n.d.). The Five(ish) Doctors Reboot. https://en.wikipedia.org/wiki/The_Five(ish)_Doctors_Reboot.

Whovian Feminism (2014a). 'A Few Thoughts on Missy'. 8 November. http://whovianfeminism.tumblr.com/post/102107450712/a-few-thoughts-on-missy.

—— (2014b). 'Whovian Feminism Reviews "Dark Water" and "Death in Heaven"'. 14 November. http://whovianfeminism.tumblr.com/post/102580814837/whovian-feminism-reviews-dark-water-and-death.

Wilkes, Neil (2008). 'Chris Chibnall Talks Torchwood'. Digital Spy. 1 April. http://www.digitalspy.com/tv/torchwood/news/a92590/chris-chibnall-talks-torchwood-lo-london/.

Williams, Rebecca (2011). 'Desiring the Doctor: Identity, Gender and Genre in Online Fandom'. In Tobias Hochscherf and James Leggott (eds), British Science Fiction Film and Television. Jefferson, North Carolina: McFarland, pp.167–77.

—— (2013a). 'Tweeting the TARDIS: Interaction, Liveness and Social Media in Doctor Who Fandom'. In Matt Hills (ed.), New Dimensions of Doctor Who: Adventures in Space, Time and Television. London: I.B.Tauris, pp. 154–73.

—— (2013b). 'Tonight's the Night with… Captain Jack! Torchwood's John Barrowman as Celebrity/Subcultural Celebrity/Localebrity'. In Rebecca Williams (ed.), Torchwood Declassified: Investigating Mainstream Cult Television. London: I.B.Tauris, pp.154–71.

—— (2013c). 'Torchwood and its Interim Fandom'. Who Watching. 5 November. https://whowatching.wordpress.com/2013/11/05/torchwood-and-its-interim-fandom/.

Winstead, Antoinette F. (2013). 'Doctor Who's Women and His Little Blue Box: Time Travel as a Heroic Journey of Self-Discovery for Rose Tyler, Martha Jones and Donna Noble'. In Gillian I. Leitch (ed.), Doctor Who in Time and Space: Essays on Theme, Character, History and Fandom, 1963–2012. Jefferson, North Carolina: McFarland, pp. 227–41.

Wolverson, E. G. (2009). 'From Raxicoricofallipatorius with Love'. Television Review. 13 March. http://www.doctorwhoreviews.altervista.org/SJA%20 2.X.htm.

Wyatt, Daisy (2015). 'Doctor Who should never star a woman, says former "feminist" Time Lord Sylvester McCoy'. Independent. 23 July. http://www.independent.co.uk/arts-entertainment/tv/news/doctor-who-should-never-be-a-woman-says-former-feminist-time-lord-sylvester-mccoy-10409987.html.

Yeager, Iona (2013). 'Too brown for a fair praise: The depiction of racial prejudice as cultural heritage in Doctor Who'. In Lindy Orthia (ed.), Doctor Who and Race. Bristol: Intellect, pp. 21–7.

TV AND FILMOGRAPHY

TELEVISION

An Adventure in Space and Time (BBC Four, 2013)
Angel (WB, 1999–2004)
Battlestar Galactica (SciFi, 2004–9)
Brookside (Channel 4, 1984–2003)
Brothers and Sisters (ABC, 2006–11)
Buffy the Vampire Slayer (WB, 1997–2001; UPN, 2001–3)
Coronation Street (ITV, 1960–)
CSI: Crime Scene Investigation (CBS, 2000–15)
Dexter (Showtime, 2006–13)
Doctor Who (BBC, 1963–89, 2005–)
Doctor Who and The Curse of Fatal Death (BBC, 1999)
Doctor Who Confidential (BBC Three, 2005–11)
Doctor Who: The Infinite Quest (CBBC, 2007)
Doctor Who: Time Crash (BBC One, 2007)
EastEnders (BBC, 1985–)
The Five(ish) Doctors Reboot (BBC Red Button, 2013)
'From Raxacoricofallapatorius with Love' (BBC One, 2009)
Game of Thrones (HBO, 2011–)
Husbands (YouTube, 2011–)
Jackanory (BBC, 1965–96)
Lost (ABC 2004–10)
Merlin (BBC One, 2008–13)
Old Jack's Boat (CBeebies, 2013–)
Once Upon a Time (ABC, 2011–)
Outlander (Starz, 2014–)
Queer as Folk (Channel 4, 1999–2000)
Robin Hood (BBC One, 2006–9)
Sarah Jane Adventures, The (CBBC, 2007–11)
Sarah Jane's Alien Files (CBBC, 2010)
Shield, The (FX, 2002–8)
Star Trek: The Original Series (NBC, 1966–9)
Supernatural (WB, 2005–6; CW, 2006–)
This Life (BBC Two, 1996–7)
Tonight's the Night (BBC One, 2009–11)

Totally Doctor Who (BBC One, 2006–7)
Torchwood (BBC Three, 2006–7; BBC Two, 2007–8)
Torchwood: Children of Earth (BBC One, 2009)
Torchwood Declassified (2006–11)
Torchwood: Miracle Day (BBC One, 2011)
Wire, The (HBO, 2002–8)

FILM

Daleks: Invasion Earth 2150 A.D. (Gordon Flemyng, UK, 1966)
Doctor Strange (Scott Derrickson, US, 2016)
Doctor Who (Geoffrey Sax, UK/US/Canada, 1996)
Dr Who and the Daleks (Gordon Flemyng, UK, 1965)
Rogue One: A Star Wars Story (Gareth Edwards, US, 2016)
Star Wars: The Force Awakens (J. J. Abrams, US, 2015)

INDEX

WHO WATCHING

EXPLORING AND CELEBRATING THE WORLDS OF DOCTOR WHO

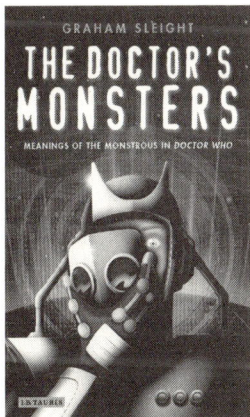

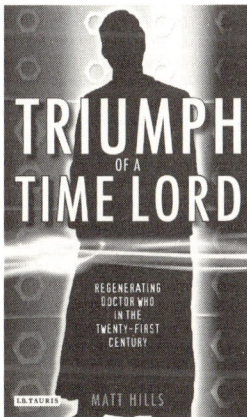

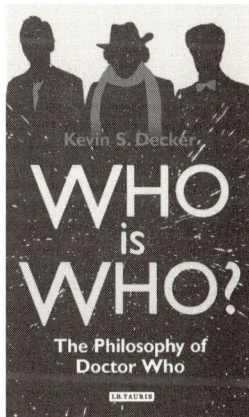

INSIDE THE **TARDIS**
THE WORLDS OF **DOCTOR WHO**

'The best overview of *Doctor Who* that I have ever read.'
DOREEN KAYE
DOCTOR WHO MAGAZINE

'Extremely good for anyone wishing to think seriously about *Doctor Who*.'
MATTHEW SWEET,
THE INDEPENDENT

James Chapman

I.B.TAURIS

Edited by **Andrew O'Day**

DOCTOR WHO
THE ELEVENTH HOUR

A CRITICAL CELEBRATION OF
THE MATT SMITH AND STEVEN MOFFAT ERA

I.B.TAURIS

PIERS D. BRITTON

TARDISbound

NAVIGATING THE
UNIVERSES OF
DOCTOR WHO

I.B.TAURIS

GRAHAM SLEIGHT

THE DOCTOR'S MONSTERS
MEANINGS OF THE MONSTROUS IN DOCTOR WHO

I.B.TAURIS

TRIUMPH
OF A
TIME LORD

REGENERATING
DOCTOR WHO
IN THE
TWENTY-FIRST
CENTURY

MATT HILLS

I.B.TAURIS

Kevin S. Decker

WHO
is
WHO?

The Philosophy of
Doctor Who

I.B.TAURIS

Ideas and submissions for Who Watching to Philippa Brewster: philippabrewster@gmail.com

www.whowatching.com